SIGUIRIYA

Cantora

SIGUIRIYA

A Novel

✢

Sylvia López-Medina

HarperCollins*Publishers*

HarperCollins books may be purchased for educational, business, or sales promotional use. For information please write: Special Markets Department, HarperCollins Publishers, Inc., 10 East 53rd Street, New York, NY 10022.

FIRST EDITION

Designed by Lynne Yeamans

Library of Congress Cataloging-in-Publication Data

López-Medina, Sylvia, 1942–
    Siguiriya : a novel / Sylvia López-Medina. — 1st ed.
      p. cm.
    Includes bibliographical references.
    ISBN 0-06-017271-1
    I. Title.
PS3562.0675S55   1997
813'.54—dc21   97-249

97 98 99 00 01 ❖/RRD 10 9 8 7 6 5 4 3 2 1

And most of all
for my father,
Antonio Cozar López

انتونيو كوزار لوبيز

1902–1981

. . . upon that day faces will be radiant

*Let the glory of God be extolled, and God's
great name be hallowed in the world whose
creation God willed. May God rule in our
own day, in our own lives, and in the life
of all Israel, and let us say: Amen.*

*Let God's great name be blessed for ever and ever.
Beyond all the praises, songs, and adorations
that we can utter is the Holy One, the Blessed
One, whom yet we glorify, honor, and exalt.
And let us say: Amen.*

*For us and for all Israel, may the blessing of
peace and the promise of life come true, and
let us say: Amen.*

*May the One who causes peace to reign in
the high heavens, cause peace to reign among us,
all Israel, and all the world, and let us say:
Amen.*

Mourner's Kaddish

＊

*Siguiriya: believed to be the genuine, perfect
prototype of deep song [cante jondo], the one
that most preserved its ancient oriental
origins. Siguiriyas are sung with a rising
emotional tension, interrupted by sudden
cries of anguish (the ay!) . . . The lyrics
express life's most tragic dramas, its intensest
moments. The Siguiriya represents the
existential character of the Andalusian soul
that the Andalusian people had traditionally
used to express their feelings. Influenced by
the Spanish church adopting the Byzantine
liturgical chant, [by] the Saracen invasion,
[and by] the arrival of the numerous bands
of Gypsies.*

—from the introduction by
Carlos Bauer of *Poema Del Cante Jondo*
by Federico Garcia Lorca

ACKNOWLEDGMENTS

Siguiriya is a work of fiction, based on the stories of our family that my father, Antonio Cozar López, told me when I was a child. He spoke often of the grandmother he left behind in Cadiz in order to come to America with his parents. His love for her was evident. Before he left at the age of twelve, my great-grandmother told him our history, and gave him a belief in angels. I know this belief is the most important legacy she has left to my children and me.

After my father died, a part of a manuscript that he had written about our history was found among his belongings. I realized then that he did not want our heritage lost, and so *Siguiriya* is written in his memory.

I wish to thank my sons, Paul Elliott and J. Nicholas—you are both my inspiration—and my friends, for their love and support during the writing of *Siguiriya*: Robert Roybal, the charming renegade; and Marie Clary, my research assistant. Marie's family—her husband, Mike Meuser, her son, Aran, and her daughter, Elan—have been most supportive, and so have Cameo Moore and Kasey Hicks, and their erudite daughter, Hannah.

Rabbi Robert A. Seigel, of Temple Beth Israel in central California, was most generous and responsive to my inquiries about Sephardic traditions that still exist today. To Rabbi Seigel, my gratitude.

To Robert and Marsha Guizar, and their children, Graham, Collin, beautiful Brianna, and little Cierra, for their love and nurturing friendship, my sons and I offer our love in return. I am grateful to Robert for making available to me his research material on the art of the bullfight. Olé, Roberto!

I also wish to acknowledge my friendships with Stewart and Diane Doolittle and their son, Blair; and Mike and Sue Mellana and their sons, Bobby and Judd. Also, my friends Art and Marilyn Teagarden, for offering a grandparent's love to my sons, and Melinda, Elisa, Gina, Shannon, and Sean, for keeping me in one piece during the writing of this novel.

To Gerda Baardman, my Dutch translator, and Dr. Francine Jageneau, of Amsterdam, The Netherlands; the University of Amsterdam and the Free (Protestant) University of Amsterdam, I am forever indebted for their contributions in the research of *Siguiriya.*

Without my agent, Bonnie Nadell, of the Frederick Hill Literary Agency, *Siguiriya* would never have been written. To her, I am most grateful.

Sylvia López-Medina
December 31, 1996

PART I

PROLOGUE

From the memoir of
Meschianza de Lucena Cozar-Velasquez
December 23, 1492
Lisbon

At a very young age, my grandfather began telling me the stories of our family. I sat quietly and listened, for I was not too small to realize that I was his only comfort. He was seventy-two when I was born, but he was alert and vigorous, and his memories vivid. He taught me the history of Andalusia, our home for many generations. It is there that our Moorish traditions are strongest. My grandfather called our region by its Moorish name, the Al-Andalus, and it was with great pride that he traced our Spanish roots back to the beginning of the twelfth century, the time of the Cid.

My grandfather's estate in Cadiz has been in our family's possession since 1095. The land was granted to an ancestor, a Moorish general who brought his armies to join in the struggle against the Cid. His mission was to foil the Spanish armies' efforts as they tried to drive the Moors out of Spain forever. My grandfather explained that the Moors first entered Spain from the south in the year A.D. 711, and ruled Spain until A.D. 732, when Charles Martel defeated them. This marked the slow but steady decline of Moslem rule. Our ancestor decided, like many of his Moorish contemporaries, to pledge his loyalties to Spain. The land we now call home was a reward for his change in allegiance. Over the centuries, the Spanish armies continued to slowly drive the Moors from Spain, confiscating many of the estates in Al-Andalus.

For generations, most of Andalusia was composed of three major cultures and religions: Moslems, Catholics, and Jews. Each had lived in peace during the Moslems' occupation of southern Spain, but when my grandfather retired from the Spanish military and returned to his childhood home, the climate was changing. It had been only fifty-seven years since the burning of the Jewish quarter in Seville, north of Cadiz. The persecutions spread throughout Castile, until there were piles of dead spanning seventy cities.

In fear for their survival, many members of the Jewish community throughout the southern provinces were converting to Catholicism despite their families' scorn. These converts were called Marranos, and they were not trusted by the Catholic Church. Their loyalties doubted, many were burned to death in the auto-da-fés.

My grandfather was a man filled with grief and loneliness, a man with an abiding faith in his God. He was strong, and his integrity filled my being. During his military years, he did many things of which he was not proud, and he carried his guilt as if it were a benediction that humbled him. His daily prayers reflected his gratitude for the gifts he was given during his life, and I know that he considered my Grandmother Bianca to be the evidence of God's forgiveness of the sins of his youth.

He was fifty years old when he retired from the military, yet he had no wife or children. He was ill-at-ease in his new role as a farmer. Certainly, he needed a wife, but how would he find one in the province? There were few Moslem families remaining in Cadiz since the armies had purged them. The families were either killed or sold into slavery. Their lands were devastated by lack of proper care, the horses and livestock either conscripted for the soldiers or eaten by them. The Cozar estate was one of few protected from the purge, because my grandfather and his brothers had served in the King's military, as had all the Cozars before them.

I tell our history with pride. I tell it for my unborn children. My name is Meschianza de Lucena Cozar-Velasquez. I am the surviving daughter of Efraim and Justina Cozar-Velasquez, and the sister of Jaime. My grandfather and grandmother were General Amahl Cozar and Bianca de Lucena Cozar, she the daughter of Naphtali and Rosalia de Lucena, and the general, the son of Atiq and Zoraya Cozar.

My Great-grandmother Zoraya descended from gypsies who came to southern Spain from Egypt, joining the great migrations to our peninsula. My Great-grandfather Atiq's descendants traveled from the city of Medina to join in the conquest of Spain, as well.

My Great-grandfather Naphtali de Lucena was a Jewish merchant whose family had lived in the province of Cadiz for many generations. The Sephardic people began to enter Spain in the year A.D. 117. Because of this history, my Grandfather Amahl always said that every Spaniard is part Jewish and part Moslem.

My family has been in Spain for eight hundred years. We have lived there and died there. We have fought for our King and supported (with our blood and our wealth) his many efforts to drive out the Moors! This is our history, a heritage I give to my children, so that they will know who they are. We are one people under Jehovah, one people under Allah, and all family under our Creator.

We are Andalusians.

✤

I

Autumn, 1448
Cadiz, Spain

Amahl Cozar's journey to the seaport of Tarifa, to his father's estate, required five weeks. There were few trees in the barren mountain ranges through which he traveled. The mountains did not run in one direction; rather, they circled like fortresses, walling off entire sections of the countryside, adding to his feelings of isolation. Each day, he waited for the sunsets and the reflections of lilac- and rose-colored shadows that brought peace to his weary spirit.

At night, he stopped at *hostals*, or if he could not locate one, he camped in the woods. He knew the roads were not safe, and since his packhorses carried the accumulation of years of raiding, he was especially attuned to his surroundings. He hid a leather pouch of jewels and gold coins on his person. He wanted to reach his land safely and bury the gold and silverplate he carried in his saddlebags. He traveled slowly, leading his tired packhorses. His only companion was a falcon tied to a leather guard on his wrist. On the final day of his journey, he was anxious to arrive at his destination, so he continued riding through the night and the following day until he came to the outskirts of Tarifa.

He rode through the village at sunset, and was approaching the outskirts, when he was distracted by a commotion taking place on a cobbled lane that branched off from the main road. He followed the sounds of distress and came upon a stalled carriage in the middle of the lane. A well-dressed man cowered behind the carriage, fending off the blows of two younger men. The driver was attempting to pull the men away from the injured one, but he was also suffering painful blows from a third man. When they saw Amahl ride toward them, the three ruffians ran to the side of the street and attempted to enter through a door in one of the tenements. Amahl rode over to them, placing his horse sideways against the men, pressing them to the wall. His horse, well-trained for battle, stood almost on top of the three men as Amahl dismounted. He knew the horse would remain until his return, and that the bullies could not move with the great stallion pushed against them.

He untied the falcon to free his right hand. As it flew above the tenement rooftops, he rushed to the old man and helped him up from the ground. The man trembled as Amahl attempted to brush the dirt from his clothes.

"Señor, we thank you for your aid."

Amahl let go of his arm and looked behind to see if there were more attackers, but, finding none, he returned his attention to the old man.

"What happened here? Are you all right? Did they hurt you?"

Bewildered by the kindness shown to him, the man answered Amahl.

"We were leaving the synagogue and returning to our estate when we were accosted by those men. I stepped out of the carriage—they threw rocks at my horses."

At the front of the enclosed carriage, Amahl saw the driver attempting to calm the distressed animals. He led the old man to the door of the conveyance and helped him in. As he closed the door, he caught sight of another passenger cowering behind a middle-aged women in the corner of the seat. Startled, Amahl forgot his manners and stared at her just long enough to see how beautiful she was. A typical Andalusian, her dark skin and green eyes reflecting her Moorish-Semitic heritage, Bianca de Lucena looked back at Amahl, affronted by his audacity, confused by her gratitude for her father's safety. Seated in the dark recesses of the carriage, his daughter's hand gripping his arm in relief, Naphtali de Lucena addressed Amahl, who continued to stare at Bianca.

"Señor, how can we show our gratitude? You have saved us from harm."

"I am happy to help you. You must not thank me. I am pleased that you are safe, Señor. I will take my leave of you now."

He turned to go as the man placed his hand on Amahl's shoulder. Amahl paused and turned around.

"You did not give us your name. Please tell us who you are."

Standing at attention before the man, Amahl announced himself formally.

"I am General Amahl Cozar."

He took Naphtali's offered hand, glancing again at the young lady.

"And I, General, am Naphtali de Lucena. This is my daughter, the Donzella Bianca, and seated next to her is her duenna, Señora Martinez."

He turned to his daughter, who nodded at Amahl, her stare direct and her pride evident as her father introduced her to the stranger. Amahl, afraid to touch her, did not reach for Bianca's hand. Instead, he nodded back.

"Donzella."

She looked away, embarrassed by his intense surveillance. The driver of the carriage called to the horses, and the conveyance resumed its journey as Naphtali waved and smiled his farewell.

Amahl stood in the middle of the narrow lane and watched the carriage proceed down the street and turn the corner onto the main road of Tarifa. He whistled for his falcon, and it returned swiftly to his wrist. The stallion still stood against the three men, but Amahl did not address them as he mounted his horse. He rode away, leaving them shaken and outraged as he led his pack animals out of the village.

During his last visit to his parents' home, his mother, Zoraya, had died. Then word of his father's death had reached him. This was his first return to the estate since his mother's death, and it saddened him to realize there would be no one to welcome him when he arrived.

His brothers had died when he was still quite young. All of Zoraya's sons had been conscripted into the Spanish army when they were twelve, taken from her by force. Amahl never forgot being carried away on a horse, his mother in the dirt before their house, cursing the soldiers as they took him.

In the darkening sky above, he watched the first seabirds. They glided in a graceful arc above him before alighting on the tree limbs. The smell of the sea drifted toward him, and, impatient now, he began galloping his horses. It was a few moments before he reached his destination.

He led the horses up a low hill and broke through a stand of old, gnarled trees upon a breathtaking vista of sloping meadows that unfolded to the sea below. To the left of the meadows, Amahl saw the orange groves he had played in as a child. The fruit was not harvested, and it lay on the ground in various stages of decay. Wild boars rooted at the bases of the trees, feasting on the oranges that were still edible. A small herd of deer picked their way past the boars.

Hungry, Amahl dismounted. He untied the falcon, removing

the bird's small black hood, watching as it soared above the trees, searching for prey. Taking his crossbow from the saddle, he ran upwind of the boars through the dry grasses of the meadow. The sun was almost below the horizon, but he believed there was still enough light for him to make a good kill. He was within five yards of the grove when he found his dinner. Taking careful aim, he dispatched an arrow that pierced the side of a small deer. As the animal fell with a grunt, the boars panicked and ran away across the meadow and into the trees.

Amahl returned to his horses, mounted, and led them to the downed animal. On the ground again, he inspected the kill and, satisfied, lifted the body of the deer onto the pommel of his saddle, leading the horses through the trees to his father's castle.

The massive iron gates were closed. Ivy and other climbing vines entwined their branches through the grillwork and over the surrounding stone walls of the castle's courtyard. Amahl attempted to open the gates so he could lead his animals through, but the wrought iron was rusted and held to the ground by months of neglect. He cut away the undergrowth with his sword and put his shoulder to the gate. Slowly, it gave way to the pressure, and he continued walking along the dark lane.

The castle looked undisturbed, but Amahl, a veteran of many raidings, knew that this could be deceiving. As he approached, he saw that the massive wooden door stood ajar. He pushed it open, then took a large candle from the table where his mother had kept them, lit one, and allowed the light to flood the entry. He cautiously stepped inside.

Moorish rugs covered the stone floors. Brilliantly colored tapestries hung on the cavernous walls. His mother had arranged enormous carved pieces of wooden furniture in groupings, and the wrought pieces of silver Zoraya had gathered over the years were displayed on the mahogany tables. A thick layer of dust covered everything, dulling the rich, jewel-like colors.

The candlelight illuminated the sweeping stone staircase, and the stairs, each at least five feet wide, floated against a circular wall and curved into the darkness above. There were no banisters or railings. The steps appeared suspended in the dusty air and opened onto a balcony that surrounded the entry on three sides. The balcony was protected by carved ivory railings that rose waist high and were inlaid with gold and silver. Amahl started walking up the stairs, puffs of dust billowing around his boots with each step.

There were fourteen rooms on the two top floors. Dirt was everywhere. All the rooms showed evidence of elegant grillwork similar to that on the balcony, and each contained its own fireplace, all of them full of ashes. The windows of his parents' bedchamber overlooked the sea at the back of the castle. Amahl opened the casements and breathed in clean air.

He heard the scurrying sounds of mice as he walked through the remaining upper floors. Satisfied that all was in order, he went down the stairs to the lower floor and exited the castle. As he removed the deer's carcass from his horse, he noticed that the darkness in the courtyard was complete. It was well past sunset. He carried the deer into the kitchen, dropping it onto the stone floor.

Outside, he surveyed the area behind the kitchen door, which was surrounded by a low stone wall. There were overgrown herbs in the garden, and some of the plants had bolted and flowered. The spicy scent of the tiny blooms was pungent and overpowered the smell of the sea below. Trailing roses covered many sections of the wall, choking the larger flowering vines that grew at the base of the stones. It appeared that an untidy hand had tossed the plants about the area, leaving them to secure themselves where they pleased.

He followed the path leading through the garden to an opening in the wall, and turned left to a promontory that overlooked the sea. The groundcover was low and mossy, and as he stood near the edge of the high cliff, he saw that the sun was below the horizon. Only a golden halo of light reflecting off the water remained. It was time for the evening *salat*.

Amahl walked to the front of the castle to unpack his clean clothes. He went to the well and, after pulling up the wooden bucket filled with water, performed only the minor ablutions required by his religion, rinsing his hands, mouth, nose, and forearms. He continued this ritual by cleaning his face, head, and ears. Finally, he removed his shoes and washed his feet. During his journey home, there were often evenings when he could not find water to perform his ablutions. At those times, he used a *tayammum*, or stone, to prepare himself, according to Islamic teachings.

When he finished bathing, he put on his clean clothes. Refreshed, he returned to the mossy promontory and placed his *sajjada* on the ground before him. He stood humbly on the prayer carpet as he faced the sea, waiting for the last disappearance of the light on the horizon.

Keeping his back straight, he bowed at the waist and stood up again. Immediately, he placed his knees, hands, and head on the *sajjada* before him. He remained prostrated for many seconds, then changed to a sitting position. He prostrated himself a second time, thus ending the first cycle of the *salat*. He returned to a standing position and began the second cycle, performing it exactly the same as the first. In a seated position again, he recited the *Shahadah*.

There is no god but God. There is no god but the Merciful. Muhammed is the messenger of God. Have I not seen how all that is in heaven or in earth, and the birds in flight, give praise to God? For God's is the Kingdom of the heavens and the earth, and unto God is the journeying.

With tears gathering in his eyes, he repeated this cycle of prayer three times, and in each standing part he recited the *Fatiha,* the first chapter of the Koran.

God sent down one hundred books and four books, and He placed the one hundred in the four, that is, the Torah, the Gospel, the Psalms, and the Koran. Then He placed all of them in the Koran, and He placed everything in the Koran in its long chapters, and He placed everything in the long chapters in the Fatiha.

His voice, a clear tenor, wavered gently over the water as he completed his evening prayers, his chant a dedication of gratitude. There was a tone of loss and nostalgia mingled in the *siguiriya* he sang as he prayed for his parents.

God is greater. God is greater. God is greater. God is greater. I bear witness that there is no god but God. I bear witness that there is no god but God. I bear witness that Muhammed is the messenger of God. I bear witness that Muhammed is the messenger of God. Hurry to the salat. Hurry to the salat. Hurry to salvation. Hurry to salvation. God is greater. God is greater. There is no god but God.

His hands together in prayer, Amahl Cozar knew he was home at last.

✦

From the memoir of
Meschianza de Lucena Cozar-Velasquez
January 10, 1493
Lisbon

The sky in Lisbon is not at all like the sky in Cadiz. Here, the sun cleaves the horizon, wounding itself as it bleeds onto the water, slowly transforming the day into night. It is not a gentle passing. In Cadiz, the sun is golden as it gives itself to the land. Tarifa humbly bows to the light as it surrenders the day.

I am homesick, and the ache of it tears my heart as I recall the orange and olive groves of my childhood. The great oak trees protected me beneath umbrella branches as I lay in the mist and fog, and dreamed.

Last month, my parents died in the most recent torment of the Jewish quarters. I know now that I will never return to Tarifa, or to my brother, Jaime. Everything I have known is lost to me. Pisa, my friend and sister, I will never see you again. You will not hold my children, and I will not know yours.

So much is lost now. Yesterday Raul and I learned that we may not be able to remain in Lisbon. The King will expel all the Jewish refugees soon, for the Inquisition continues here in its unholy work. I pray it is just a rumor. There are so many, and the story changes every day. Where can we go? Even now, Raul is at the docks searching for information. He says I should not be afraid, but my maidservant Ana and I are very frightened.

If my father were still alive, perhaps he would know where we should go. My father knew everything, as did my precious mother. We buried them in secret, for even the graves of my people are desecrated. Now my parents will remain in Lisbon for eternity.

My father's gold maravedis are secure on Raul's ship, and Ana and I will take the few things we were able to bring from the castle. I have my father's books and my mother's linens. I have my grandfather's *vihuela*, but I must have the delicate strings replaced. The lute is so fragile now, brought to Tarifa by my Great-grandmother Zoraya. She sang to her son, my Grandfather Amahl, the gypsy lullabies her mother taught her. Before we left Tarifa, he gave the *vihuela* to me, and told me the stories of how he would sing to me when I was a child. In the forgetfulness of his ninety-one years, he did not realize he had already taught me the songs.

I must go now. Raul will return soon, and then we will know his plans. We expect more persecutions, but we do not know when they will occur. There are never any warnings. The fear in our community is palpable. We live our fear; we breathe it daily. It numbs our senses, but it does not cause us to forget our love for one another.

2

⁜

In the early days after Amahl's return, his feelings of isolation often pervaded the castle. He felt as if a gray fog shrouded him, leaving him immobile in his chair, where he spent the chilly evenings before the fire in the great room. He did not remember ever being by himself. As a child, his parents and brothers had surrounded him with a shelter of love. Now his security was gone, and he was desolate.

For many days, he surveyed the estate, searching out the damage in the groves caused by neglect after his father's death. The workers who had populated the land for generations were gone, and now the orange and olive trees were overrun with weeds and rotting fruit. The wooden olive cisterns that were buried in rows between the olive trees were empty. Many of the tiles that lined the deep cisterns were cracked from dryness.

If he was to restore the land that had provided for the family, he must hire the workmen necessary to clean the groves and prepare them for the approaching winter.

It was several days before he visited the stables where his father had once bred some of the finest Andalusian horses in Cadiz. In his last letter to his son, Atiq Cozar had described his despair when his horses, including his finest breeding stock, were appropriated by the military. He could not object or his loyalty to the King would be suspect. Sadly, he had let the beautiful animals go. Now it was Amahl's intention to restock the stables and begin breeding Andalusians again.

As Amahl walked through the cavernous building, his steps echoed on the wooden floor. The lonely sound traveled throughout the fifty stone and wooden stalls standing empty in the western corridor. He entered the east wing through heavy wooden doors into a large indoor exercise paddock. The ceiling was vast, with a supportive ridge beam spanning the full length of the hall. The sawdust, musty with green mold, was soft under Amahl's shoes.

He walked to the center and recalled the winter mornings when he had helped his older brothers exercise the horses. In the stillness, he listened to his brothers' spectral voices shouting orders to him, instructing him in the proper way to hold the reins as the great stallions circled within the paddock.

He returned to the courtyard and led the pack animals and his stallion into three of the stalls, then fed and watered them. After closing the heavy oak doors at the entrance to the stables, he turned to see a man entering the courtyard.

Amahl waited in silence as the man approached him.

"Are you General Cozar?"

"Yes, I am."

"I am pleased to have found you, my Lord General. I searched the groves and came upon this path by accident. I did not know where it led."

Amahl did not reply, but looked with curiosity at the man.

"I am Khalid al-Hassan, and I am in the employ of his Grace, Señor de Lucena of the estate adjoining yours. I bring you a message from him, my Lord General."

He nodded to the servant.

"His Grace has asked me to tell you that he would be honored if you, my Lord General, would join him and the Donzella, his daughter, for their Sabbath dinner tomorrow evening."

With equal formality, Amahl replied, "Will you please convey my pleasure to your patron, Señor de Lucena, and tell him that I will be honored to join him and his daughter."

"He will be pleased to hear that you will come, my Lord General. I will go now and tell him."

Khalid bowed to Amahl, then turned and walked out of the courtyard toward the castle, where his horse awaited him. Amahl watched him go.

As he walked to the castle, purple shadows of twilight dotting the path before him, he wondered if the Donzella would find pleasure in his acceptance. He recalled her face, her evident resistance, and her pride as strong as Lucifer's. Somehow, he did not believe she would be anything but indifferent to his presence.

✤

3

⁜

Amahl rode along the shoreline toward the de Lucena estate, often guiding his mount through the rocks and tide pools that decorated the sandy coves. It was not difficult to recognize the road leading from the beach to the de Lucena property. A line of palm trees bordered both sides of the wide path, and as he rode between them to the entrance, the spicy scent of oleander blooms assaulted his nostrils. The large trees crowded between the palms, filling the spaces with pink, white, and red flowers. Beyond the palms and oleander, Amahl saw fields of sugarcane. Olive groves, well-tended and already harvested, blended with the other crop. Señor de Lucena was a prosperous man.

Amahl entered through stone pillars into a small courtyard and dismounted as a groom held the reins of his horse. He approached the door of the villa and searched for a bell, but all he saw was a *mezuzah* and a small, grilled aperture set into the door at eye level. As he peered inside, the tiny wooden door behind the grill opened and an old man looked out, surveying him with a distrustful eye.

"I have come to see Señor de Lucena."

"Who are you?"

"I am General Cozar."

The small door closed and Amahl heard the shuffling of the servant's bare feet, and then the sound died away. He was not certain if he should stay or leave, but he did not have long to wait, for soon the door of the villa opened and he was face to face with a very different man from the one he had met several days ago in

Tarifa. That man had been dressed according to the edicts of King Henry's reign, after the riots of Seville, which dictated that Jews could dress only in somber colors and plain fabrics. No silks or satins were allowed in the attire of Jewish men, women, or children.

Yet, in the privacy of his villa, Naphtali de Lucena was dressed in a sumptuous blue velvet robe. His lifelong love of finery displayed itself in a blouse of snow-white silk peeking out from beneath the robe's gold-braided collar. His cheeks were a robust shade of pink. His eyes, black and piercing, were as exuberant as his dress as he examined Amahl, quickly scanning his clothing before looking him in the eye.

Amahl was overwhelmed by Naphtali's enthusiasm as the old man reached out, grabbed him by the elbow, and pulled him into the entryway. When he closed the door, Amahl found himself in semidarkness. Candles glowed in a multitude of sconces set in the mahogany panels of the entry. As Amahl's eyes adjusted to the amber reflections of the flames on the wood, the man led him past the foyer and into the villa.

"Forgive me my foolish servant. He has no manners. I will attend to him soon. For now, I am so happy that you have agreed to join us. You honor my house."

Naphtali led Amahl into a dining room that was aglow with more candles. Amahl realized, as Naphtali pressed him into a large mahogany chair, that he was the only guest. He had not yet said a word, as Naphtali had not stopped talking.

"You are the son of the general. Am I correct?"

"Yes, Señor de Lucena. I am retired from the military."

They sat in silence for a few moments, then Naphtali resumed speaking.

"Tell me, how do you find your estate? Is all well with you?"

"Yes, all is in order, but I have much work to do before winter befalls us."

"And the men who worked for your father, they will continue to work for you?"

"I don't know. They are gone, and I must rehire many people if I'm to be ready before the rain season begins."

"I hope you will allow me to help you. You will need a manservant. I have people here. We will devise a plan. You must not despair. I wish to provide whatever assistance I can to make your homecoming a happy occasion. Is there anything else I can do?"

"Your offer is very kind, but there is time to hire servants. Today, I am here to buy horses, Señor de Lucena. I recall my father saying that you have the finest in the province."

"I am in despair when I tell you that I cannot sell my horses to you."

Taken aback, but undaunted, Amahl replied, "I will implore you to reconsider."

"You may implore all you wish, but it will do no good. The decision is not mine to make."

He poured marc, a distilled grape liquor, into a crystal goblet and offered it to Amahl. Uneasy, Amahl looked at the glass and hesitated.

"It is a fine liquor. I will see to it that you take several bottles home with you."

"You are too generous, Señor. I regret I cannot accept your kind gift."

"Why not?"

"My religion forbids me from placing spirits in my body."

"You are Moslem?"

"Yes."

"And you consider spirits to be sinful?"

"Yes, Señor."

"But do you not agree that sin is the product of our human condition?" Naphtali had a mischievous glint in his eyes.

"Yes, I do agree, but I also believe we are given our will to resist sin."

Naphtali studied his guest for several moments before he continued.

"I have vacillated all of my life between sensual impulse and moral restraint."

"Have you ever seriously considered the latter?"

"Never!"

The two men laughed together, then Naphtali continued.

"As a *mudejar*, are you safe here? A purge took place five years ago, and most of the Moslems were either killed or expelled from the province. Those who are left live in great danger."

"Yes, I am safe. I was a general in the armies of the King."

"I see." Naphtali was thoughtful as he studied his new neighbor.

"You must forgive me, General Cozar. Actually, I am bewildered."

"Señor de Lucena, my family has fought for the King for many generations. More than half of my life has been spent defending this country."

"So you do not consider yourself a traitor to your country, or your faith?"

Amahl was beginning to feel uncomfortable with Naphtali's questions, but he continued his explanation.

"My family's country has always been Spain, and our faith a part of our heritage. There has never been conflict for us in this. If we left Spain, where would we go? This has been our home since the first Cozar came here from the city of Valencia."

"I see, and I welcome you as my neighbor, but I cannot help but wonder, how will you practice your religion here? There are no mosques. They are all destroyed."

"I have been practicing my faith in the fields and meadows of Spain for over thirty years. I have lived the military life since I was conscripted at the age of twelve, and I have not been in a mosque since I was a child, but Allah is everywhere."

"Are you still active in the military, General?"

"No, now that I am retired, I will fight no more. I wish to be a farmer and to raise horses. I seek peace, Señor de Lucena, peace for myself and for my spirit."

"Yes, I understand."

"How is it, Señor, that you can live here on your estate, and not in the walled quarters of your community? I thought all land holdings of the Sephardim were confiscated since the horrors of Seville began."

"Yes, most holdings were taken by the King after the tragedy, but this land was granted to my grandfather in perpetuity, as long as we pay the taxes that are levied every year. Here, in the rural areas of Andalusia, the Inquisition has not fully reached us. What you witnessed in Tarifa last week is only the occasional harassment instigated by ruffians and the malcontents. As the Moors were driven from Spain, many of their estates were granted to Jews. My grandfather was one of the recipients, and now this farm produces revenues that are taxed in enormous sums. Though most of the people of my community live in the *aljama*, Jewish land ownership continues to grow as these estates are confiscated."

"I see." Amahl hesitated and then continued. "Why is it not your decision to sell your horses? Whose decision is it?"

"It is my daughter's decision."

"Your daughter's?"

Naphtali nodded, his fingers restless on the fabric at his wrists.

"I mean you no disrespect, but why is it a woman's decision to sell or not to sell horses?"

"If I sell them, my daughter will be very unhappy."

"How does it come about that a woman makes this decision for you?"

"It is a long story, and a sad story."

"Tell me, my friend."

"My children's mother died when Bianca was born. My son was three years old. He was such a beautiful child."

He looked at Amahl, barely containing the tears in his eyes.

"My son was tutored by one of the finest teachers in the province, but my daughter was a lonely child, so I allowed her to be tutored with her brother. She should have learned the womanly arts, but without her mother, how was she to be taught? I would not remarry. How could I? I loved my wife, but our Lord took her from me, blessed be His name."

Amahl nodded to Naphtali, silently encouraging him to continue his story.

"The stables were for my son, Benjamin. He loved the horses. After their lessons, he and Bianca ran to the stables. The horses were their lives."

He reached into a desk drawer and removed a large ledger.

"Here, you see? This book contains the records my son kept. All the champions are listed here, their births, the dams they come from. The bloodlines are here."

"Where is your son?"

"Dead." He sighed. "He is dead, trampled by one of his own stallions."

"When did this happen?"

"Four years ago. He was twenty-one years old. Bianca was eighteen. We were both devastated by his death. Bianca was inconsolable. I cannot mention his name to her, it hurts her so much. I wanted to destroy the horse, but Bianca wouldn't let me. Zilis was the favorite of Benjamin's stallions. Now I fear Bianca has buried herself along with her brother. The horses are her life. She seldom goes to temple since her brother died. It is a constant grief for me, her stubbornness. I will never see her married. I will die knowing she will have no one to take care of her. The matchmaker believes it is hopeless. Bianca told her that she will not marry. I have discussed this with Bianca many times, for this is not our tradition, but still Bianca insists."

Naphtali was silent. He appeared exhausted as he looked around the room. Finally, his glance settled on Amahl, who was looking at the ledger in Naphtali's hand.

"General, I no longer hold to her mother's wishes that I arrange a proper marriage for Bianca with a good Jewish man. I would agree to any marriage to a good man who loves her."

Amahl was pensive as he nodded at Naphtali.

"Where is your daughter, Señor?"

"She is at the stables." Naphtali began to chuckle. "You are most welcome to inspect my stock. Benjamin was dedicated to breeding superior horses, but his sister guards them and I cannot sway her. I fear, General, that I have raised a very stubborn young woman."

✠

4

⁜

The groom who had led Amahl's horse away upon his arrival now showed Amahl to the stables. Naphtali had business to discuss with some of his fellow merchants, who had arrived as he was telling Amahl about his children.

The stables were not as large as Amahl's. Grooms were hard at work, either feeding the horses or exercising them in the yard at the back. Amahl entered the building from the courtyard at the front and began examining the horses to the left of the entrance. Naphtali believed his daughter to be there, but Amahl spotted only stable boys walking about, caring for the animals.

One of the boys was cleaning droppings from an otherwise spotless stall. He was shorter than the others, although he appeared to be strong for his size. Amahl concluded he was one of the younger lads hired by Naphtali to clean the stables. He did not look old enough to be given any more responsibility than that. As he bent into his work, the shovel the boy wielded swung in an arc toward Amahl, its contents aimed at a wooden wheelbarrow that already showed evidence of his diligence.

Without looking behind him, the boy released the shovel's contents down the front of Amahl's robe. He turned and looked at Amahl in disgust, for the hem of the exquisite robe was covered with excrement from the knees down.

"Why are you standing there? Don't you know better? Can't you see that I am cleaning this stable?"

Amahl stepped back and tried to shake the mess off his robe.

The lad dropped the shovel and walked to a small enclosed shed. Hanging inside the door were some rags. He grabbed a handful and gave them to Amahl, "Forgive me, your Grace, for my impertinence." Then he returned to the stall and continued shoveling while Amahl wiped the hem as best he could.

He walked around again looking for Bianca, then returned to the stall, carefully avoiding the onslaught of the shovel.

"Would you tell me where I might find the Donzella?"

"Why?"

Amahl was taken aback by the young man's impertinence.

"I would like to speak to her."

The boy returned to his work but continued his conversation with his back to Amahl.

"And why do you want to speak to her?"

"The horses, of course."

The boy stopped his shoveling and turned to Amahl with a look of impatience. It was the first time Amahl was able to see his face from beneath his hat. He had hazel-colored eyes, and as he stared at Amahl, they turned a deep green. Amahl, fascinated, watched the eyes change.

"Your Grace, the horses are not for sale."

"I know that. I did not say I wanted to buy them."

"Then exactly what do you wish to do with them?"

"I am a neighbor of the de Lucenas. I am going to raise horses on my property. Do you know if any of these stallions are at stud?"

The boy returned to the cleaning, shovel in hand. With his back to Amahl, he replied, "Only one of them is presently at stud."

"Only one? Where is he? Can you show him to me?"

"If you took any notice, your Grace, you would see that I am busy with more important things. And you really should move to the side. You are in my way, sir."

Amahl stepped aside in time to avoid being showered with manure again. He was appalled by the boy's insolence. He turned away and continued his tour of the building, ignoring the lad as he studied the horses.

He was impressed by the excellent bloodlines represented in the stalls that lined the north side of the stables. He counted twenty-three horses—ten mares, seven foals, and six stallions. Two of the mares were pregnant. Later in the afternoon, the stable boys and groom brought another eight mares into the building. Amahl did not see the insolent boy among them, nor did he see Naphtali's daughter. They began feeding the mares, and Amahl, discouraged, walked back to the villa.

Naphtali was bidding farewell to the merchants as Amahl approached them.

"Were you able to find my daughter before she returned to the villa?"

"She is here?" Amahl looked about the room, expecting Bianca to emerge from the paneling.

"No. She is upstairs dressing for dinner. She will come down soon. What do you think of our stables?"

"There are some very fine horses there. The bloodlines are excellent."

"Bianca and Benjamin kept exact records, and she personally attends the birth of each new foal. Perhaps she will allow you to examine her books."

"I would like that very much."

"Of course, you know you may be preparing yourself for disappointment."

"There is always hope, isn't there, your Honor?"

Again, the merchant chuckled. "I suppose, but if I were you, I wouldn't rely on it."

A servant appeared at the library door and signaled to Naphtali.

"Come, my friend. We are to go into dinner now."

They entered the dining room. The Sabbath table was covered with a glistening white linen cloth. There were three places set with heavy, ornate silverware. Crystal goblets, for both water and wine, stood at each place setting. Two loaves of bread, beautifully braided, peeked out beneath a red velvet cloth that was embroidered with gold Hebrew lettering. An elegant silver goblet was filled to the brim with red wine. It was placed at the head of the table beside two Sabbath candles.

At last he was about to see Bianca again. They sat at the table, Naphtali at the head and Amahl on his left. A young woman dressed in a rose-pink gown walked sedately into the room and took her seat across from Amahl.

"Forgive me, Father. I am late again, but there was so much to do at the stables today."

She reached over and kissed her father on the cheek, and then she looked at Amahl. As Naphtali introduced Bianca again, Amahl could only stare at her. She was more beautiful than he remembered.

Her black hair was drawn to the back of her head in a gentle chignon secured at the nape of her neck. Her hair was thick and lustrous, and her features were delicate and familiar, but it was her eyes, dark green and mocking, that caused him to recognize the insolent stable boy. His face reddened deeply as he recalled their conversation on the breeding of horses. His embarrassment was such that he could not respond to the introduction.

Naphtali looked proudly at his beautiful child.

"Shabbat Shalom, daughter."

"Shabbat Shalom, Father."

Bianca stood and raised the shawl she wore about her shoulders. As she covered her black hair with it, Amahl found it difficult to reconcile this lovely young woman with the insolent boy he had met that afternoon. He continued to watch her in awe as she lit the Sabbath candles. Her countenance reflected the appearance of an angel, and her face, in its sudden, innocent sweetness, was directed toward the candles. As she took her father's place at the head of the table, the flame reflected and glistened on her pink silk gown. Bianca covered her eyes with one hand and lifted the silver wine goblet with the other. Amahl, enchanted by her presence, watched as she began the kiddush.

Blessed Art Thou, O Lord Our God, Ruler of the Universe, who has created the fruit of the vine.

Bianca drank from the goblet and passed it to Amahl. Offering it to him with both hands, she looked into his eyes. The calmness of a deep pool of water enveloped Amahl as he took the cup from her hands and drank from it. Spirits had never passed his lips until that moment, and he was briefly shocked. He could not know then that his action would be symbolic of his future capitulation to his awakening love for Bianca, for, never having been in love, he did not recognize the emotion. He turned and passed the goblet to Naphtali as a servant brought a silver tray that held a crystal bowl of water. She offered it to Bianca, who washed her hands according to ritual. The servant handed Bianca a white linen towel, and after she dried her hands, Bianca picked up the braided bread, the *challah*. The servant carried the water to

Amahl, and then to Naphtali. Each cleansed his hands as Bianca had done, and she closed her eyes again.

Blessed Art Thou, O Lord Our God, Ruler of the Universe, who bringest forth food from the earth.

She broke off pieces of the bread, and after dipping them in salt from a small silver bowl, she passed the pieces to Amahl and her father.

Naphtali, his eyes closed, continued the chant for his daughter. The room filled with the sound of his devotion until the prayer ended. Amahl stood transfixed as Bianca and her father sat down in their chairs.

"Please, Lord General, sit. We will eat now."

He clapped his hands at the servants, and they moved quickly around the table, serving Amahl, and then Bianca. Their plates were filled with the rich and pungent food. Naphtali poured wine, and added water from a crystal pitcher to Bianca's goblet.

It was several moments before Bianca looked at Amahl again.

✤

From the memoir of
Meschianza de Lucena Cozar-Velasquez
February 16, 1493
Lisbon

I have memories of seeing my grandfather standing by my bed and watching over me in the middle of the night. The light from his candle awakened me, and as I opened my eyes, he smiled at me and adjusted my covers. Then he sat in the chair by my bed and strummed his *vihuela.* He sang to me a lament of grief and joy mixed together in a rhythmic chanting. I did not yet know the source of his grief. I was too young, but as I grew old enough to walk, he led me through the woods to the bluff at the edge of the sea and told me stories of my Grandmother Bianca. He spoke to me of angels who sang songs composed in heaven. He taught me about angels who danced, and as he pointed to the light that frolicked in the leaves of the trees above us, he said it was the angels dancing.

I believed him then, and I still believe him, even though, here in Lisbon, there are no angels singing or dancing. As Ana and I walk through the streets to the *feria* to purchase food for our Sabbath supper, we lower our heads as we pass the monks dressed in black, their crucifixes swinging like obscene members before them. In their world, there are no angels, though they insist they do the Lord's work. They smell very bad, and Ana says they do not bathe. Though I am only twenty, I know I will never understand what is happening to my people. I only know that I must survive, and I must help Ana survive. She still believes she is my servant, and I am hard-pressed to convince her that this is no longer true and that she is now my beloved friend.

Raul says we will leave soon, but he has not decided where we will go. I am afraid to stay in Lisbon, but with Raul, I will go anywhere fearlessly.

5

⁜

They began eating in silence. Several times Bianca offered various dishes to Amahl, but when he attempted to make eye contact with her, she lowered her eyes. Secretly, Bianca was pleased that Amahl was really as handsome as he had appeared in the stables. His black eyes were fathomless. His long black lashes created deep shadows beneath his eyes, adding to their depth, and his weathered complexion revealed his years of living in open fields. His face was deeply tanned, except for a small white scar on his upper right cheekbone.

Naphtali watched his daughter, surprised at her reticence. Usually, she launched into a lengthy report on the activities of the stables. Soon the silence became uncomfortable.

"Bianca, General Cozar is our neighbor. It is his intention to raise horses on his estate. He hopes to surpass the excellence of the bloodlines in our stable."

Bianca glanced doubtfully at Amahl. She smiled at him, but Amahl did not smile in return.

"You are the eldest son of the old general?" Bianca looked at Amahl graciously.

"No, I am his youngest son."

"How is it you inherit his estate? I was taught one cannot inherit as the youngest son?"

The smile was still on her face, but her eyes were cool. Disconcerted for a moment, he answered her.

"It is true, the tradition of the *mayorazgo* dictates that the oldest son inherits his father's entire estate, but my brothers died defending Spain's honor. I am the only surviving Cozar now."

The smile disappeared from her face as she calmly studied him.

"Our horses are not for sale."

"Why not?"

"My Lord General, I do not raise horses so that they can be abused by the military."

"But they would not be sold to the military."

"I do not believe you. Your father sold his horses to the military."

Amahl looked at Naphtali for guidance. Though Bianca's appearance was enhanced and softened by the pink silk gown, her demeanor was as rigid as it had been in the stables. Naphtali smiled at Amahl, but said nothing. He realized he was about to enjoy a very entertaining evening, and he wished his friends had remained for dinner. A little wagering on whether Amahl could win in his struggle with Bianca would certainly have been in order. He would have wagered in favor of his daughter, though his sympathies were with Amahl.

Amahl resumed his bargaining with Bianca.

"I would offer your father a fair market price and add ten percent to the total."

"We cannot consider any offer, Señor."

"I wish to breed my own horses, Donzella. I have no intention of providing horses to the military."

"There are farms farther up the coast, near Cadiz. They will surely trade with you."

"I want only the best bloodlines. I believe they are here in your stock."

"My Lord General, I do not wish to be rude to you, as you are a guest in my father's house, and I am grateful to you for the help you gave us last week in the village, but you must understand that even if we could reach an agreement, I love the horses. I cannot begin to choose the ones we would sell."

Bianca turned away from Amahl, who was dumbfounded at being spoken to in such a manner by a woman. He watched as she rose from her chair.

"Father, I will excuse myself now. Two of my mares foaled today. I must see to them before I retire."

She reached over and kissed Naphtali, who beamed at Amahl. His enjoyment equaled his pity for the man.

"Sir, welcome home to Tarifa. I hope that you will be happy here."

She left the room, but the scent of her perfume remained, further confusing Amahl. Naphtali waited for his new friend to speak. He was a patient man. This was not the first time his daughter had dismissed a man so summarily. Bianca had never been a woman to observe ceremony.

"She is——!"

"Yes, I know. She is impertinent, disrespectful, willful, beautiful, and too intelligent for our own good. She is impossible, but she knows horses. I am beginning to think you should marry her!"

Naphtali rose from the table and carried the decanter of marc into the library. Amahl followed him as a captain would follow his general into battle. His instincts told him he was about to be ambushed.

"I mean you no disrespect, your Grace, but I could never marry your daughter. She is beautiful, yes, and it is obvious she is intelligent, but I do not seek such a wife."

"Why not?"

"I have had a long life in the military. It was not an easy life, and I want to rest now. I am tired of killing and raiding—tired of living in the fields. I want comfort and a silent wife. In the Koran is God's word, and on the subject of women, it says, 'Men are in charge of women, because God has given some bounty over others, and because men shall expend of their wealth on them. So righteous women obey God, guarding unseen what God has guarded. As for women whose rebellion you fear, admonish them or banish them to their own beds or beat them. . .' Naphtali, I do not believe it is right to beat a woman, which is why I could not marry your daughter."

"But you want horses from Tarifa, and not Cadiz?"

"Yes."

Amahl sighed and continued, "If you have any influence on your daughter, please persuade her to sell me the stock I need. I will pay double your asking price."

"I have no influence on Bianca. I never have."

"There must be a way to do this, some way to convince her?"

"You mean coercion? It will not work. There is nothing with which I could coerce her. She is unafraid, fearless. She cares for nothing but her horses. That is why you must marry her."

"You would agree to a marriage between your daughter and a man of another faith?"

"Yes, for if she does not marry, what is to become of my land and my holdings? Before her brother died, there was no concern in my heart for my children's inheritance. Benjamin was to inherit the land, and Bianca would marry well. Her dowry is exceptional. It grows every year, but she insists she will not marry. This is so unorthodox that even the matchmaker has withdrawn her services."

"I don't think I can marry your daughter. She is beautiful, but, as you say, she is willful. Today she dressed as a man to disguise herself, and covered my robe with horse manure. When I told her

I was looking for her, she did not identify herself to me. I thought she was a stable boy."

"Yes, my friend, she may be all of those things, but she knows horses, and she will not go anywhere without her horses. Think about it. You would receive the entire herd, champion stock, regal bloodlines. Her dowry. Her horses! And when I die, this land."

"I do not want your land, your Grace."

"Oh, but you must take it. You must marry my daughter. It would be the most advantageous alliance when both our estates are joined, and I will be proud to call you my son-in-law."

Amahl walked over to the shelves and studied the books in the candlelight. He turned and looked at Naphtali, then began pacing in front of the shelves. So many books, all leather bound, the colors of jewels. He took one from the shelves and glanced again at Bianca's father.

"Perhaps you are right. Certainly, I wouldn't have to take the time to search for another to be my wife. I could begin training horses sooner."

Naphtali smiled. "And having children."

"Yes, certainly I want children. Many children."

Naphtali waited.

"Yes, I accept the offer of your daughter in marriage. You are a very good and generous friend."

Naphtali rose from his chair and embraced Amahl.

"I am very pleased. Congratulations! Tonight you have made a most important decision, and the battle is now half won."

"What do you mean 'half won'?"

"Now, my friend, we have only to convince Bianca."

✠

6

Late that evening, the discouraged and crestfallen Amahl began his return to his estate. He considered traveling to Cadiz to purchase horses. The journey would not be too far. Surely, it would be much easier to endure the hardships of travel than to convince Bianca to marry him. She was headstrong, an attribute that did not bode well with Amahl. He remembered his mother as a proper and docile wife to his father. How could a man conduct his affairs otherwise? He must know that everything in his home is as it should be when he returns from his travels. There was no other way. Still, Bianca was so lovely, and there were the horses to consider. At no time on his journey home did Amahl Cozar consider love. Such an emotion had little or nothing to do with marriage. Bloodlines mattered. Responsibility to one's forebears was of utmost importance. Religion was also important. A strong faith in Allah and the teachings of Muhammed was paramount.

He had always imagined that his children would continue the Moslem tradition for generations. His youngest son would be raised in the military life, as he had been raised. His daughters would further augment the fortunes of the family through their marital alliances. He had believed in these traditions until he first laid eyes on Bianca.

As a young man, he had resisted his parents' efforts to arrange his marriage. He remembered his father's many long absences, and even as a young boy, Amahl had understood his mother's loneliness. Now, in his retirement, he wanted the presence of a family and the comfort of a loving wife. As he thought of Bianca now, he pictured her, her head covered by a white shawl, chanting the benediction of her Sephardic heritage. He saw the candlelight reflecting the integrity in her eyes, the kind he hoped to see in the eyes of his children someday. Slowly, he surrendered his intention to follow his parents' wishes for a traditional marriage, for he was intrigued by the challenge of Bianca's resistance. Content, he realized he would abide by his decision to marry Bianca de Lucena.

As he traveled along the beach, the sky was almost without light. The moon was merely a sliver, and the stars had disappeared behind the clouds of an approaching storm. Soon it would begin to rain, so he hurried his horse along the water. Ahead of him, through the rising fog billowing in mists from the sea, he heard the sound of muffled voices. He knew the fog could be deceptive, causing noise to echo from the surrounding hills, carrying voices and sending them over the water from long distances. He slowed his horse and dismounted.

He followed the sound of men calling to one another, their voices ricocheting and fragmenting in the fog. It was nearing midnight as he crouched in the rocks and approached the source of the voices. The fog was thicker there, as if concentrated into a solid white mass against the darkness. The voices were stronger as he came to a small clearing protected by large boulders standing like sentinels along the water.

He waited, listening as he unsheathed his sword. The fog shifted, and in the suddenly clear ray of starlight, he saw three men standing together looking out at the water. They were searching for something amid the dissolving mists over the ocean. Amahl followed their gazes and spotted the faint outline of a galleon floating on the water. A longboat was coming toward them, and

Amahl estimated it would soon reach the shore. He crept back into the rocks and waited.

As the boat neared the edge of the water, the three men ran to it and caught the rope that was thrown to them. They pulled the boat to the sand until it was sitting out of the water. They turned in Amahl's direction just as a small, slight woman left the sanctuary of rocks and met them halfway between the shoreline and the cliffs behind her. She wore a dark blue woolen cloak with the hood pulled closely about her face, protecting her from the cold. She spoke to the three men and then turned back to the cliffs and beckoned. Five people, three of them children, hurried from the rocks to join her and the men. Because of their clothing, Amahl recognized them as Moors. They escorted the people to the boat, and when the five had boarded, the longboat pulled away. The woman and the three men watched as the boat neared the rocking ship. Fog surrounded the galleon as the occupants boarded. Suddenly, the massive white sails billowed from their masts, gracing the galleon with a ghostly shroud as the anchor was seated in its place against the side of the ship. It heaved about and disappeared into the heavy mists, beginning its voyage toward the open sea.

As the woman turned and walked back to the rocks, the hood of her cloak fell from her face for a brief moment, and Amahl, startled, saw that the woman was Bianca de Lucena. She quickly pulled the hood back around her face and waited as one of the men brought a horse to her. He helped her mount and followed her, his feet leaving deep prints in the sand. Amahl could hear them bid farewell to the two men who ran down the beach in the opposite direction. Bianca directed her horse toward her father's estate, and the other man followed her. As they passed Amahl hiding in the rocks, he watched them, and he recognized the man as Khalid al-Hassan, who had brought Naphtali de Lucena's invitation to him the day before.

As he continued along the shoreline to his estate, the fog began to lift and the clouds disappeared, leaving a clear sky and an abundance of stars to guide his path. He gave his horse the reins, falling asleep in his saddle. When he awoke, the horse was standing before the entrance of the castle. Amahl dismounted and entered his home with a clearer and more accurate estimation of Bianca de Lucena's character. She was a woman willing to take dangerous risks to defend her beliefs. Despite her apparent aloofness toward him, she was capable of loving to the point of sacrifice to aid the dispossessed, even though they were not sure of her religion. Bianca de Lucena was a young woman of unselfish integrity, and Amahl was determined to make her his wife.

7

✢

Amahl took gifts to Bianca. He carried to her father's estate all the silken fabrics he had gathered in his years of battle. He did not ask to see Bianca, but instead left his presents with Naphtali. When Bianca returned from the stables that afternoon, the gifts were in the drawing room awaiting her acceptance.

"Father, what is this?"

Naphtali was standing in the room, a delighted expression on his face.

"These are for you, Bianca. The general brought them this morning."

Bianca examined the goods. She picked up a piece of material, cloth of gold, and dropped it with disdain. She knew she was forbidden to wear such fine fabrics.

"Why?"

She waited as her father hesitated.

"You have not answered me, Father."

"Please, Bianca, sit down. I have something wonderful to tell you."

She did not sit, but looked at her father with distrust. A nervous Naphtali embraced his daughter.

"I have arranged a marital alliance for you, my darling, with the general, a very fine man. He will care for you and your inheritance. I will die a contented man."

"Father, what are you talking about? What have you done?"

"You will be protected, and loved—I know he will love you,

and you will love him in time. Such a fine man, Bianca."

Bianca remained calm as she spoke to her father. Her determination and confidence were her most effective weapons against
him. She had learned this as a small child.

"I do not wish to marry, Father. I cannot, and will not. I know
you have done this because you love me, and I am grateful to you,
but you must not concern yourself with my welfare. I will live here
in the villa with Sara and Khalid to take care of me. I will be
happy, Father."

"No, no. You cannot live here alone after I die. It is
unseemly, and there will be scandal. You must not invite scandal.
It is better that you have a husband, and not a duenna, for the
rest of your life. You will be lonely, as I have been lonely. Please
accept this offer, my darling. The general is a good and honorable man."

"He only wants the horses, Father. He does not care about
me. You must send my regrets to him, and we must return these
gifts. I will call Khalid. He will take them to the general."

She left the room to return to the stables, Naphtali following
behind. He continued imploring her as she searched for Khalid.
When she found him, she gave him his instructions, then she
returned to the villa. She left her father sitting in the drawing
room staring at the gifts. He was not defeated yet. When Khalid
arrived, he placed the jewels and fabrics in the carriage and
returned them to the Cozar estate.

The following day, Amahl journeyed to Naphtali's estate and
implored the old man to accept the gifts. Naphtali agreed and
stored them in the warehouse at the back of his villa. He did not
tell Bianca they had been returned. He did not want to distress
her. He advised Amahl to be patient with her. Naphtali was keenly

familiar with Bianca's stubborn nature, and did not want to incite her to refuse Amahl indefinitely.

"There must be something I have overlooked, your Honor."

"It will take time. When I told her of our agreement, she did not say anything. She believes she can live here after my death and never marry. Of course, this is not true. She does not understand that she will be unprotected. In our culture, this is unthinkable."

"I have never heard of a woman refusing the marital arrangements of her father!"

Amahl paced the room until his eyes rested on the bookshelves.

"You have many fine books."

"Since Bianca was a child and learned to read with her brother, she has loved books. In the evenings, she is here in the library long after I have gone to bed."

A vision of Bianca sitting before the fire, peacefully reading by candlelight, was incongruous to Amahl, especially juxtaposed with the image of Bianca on the beach wrapped in a cloak against the cold.

He examined the books, taking them from the shelves and turning their pages. There were books of poetry, history, and mathematics, handwritten by students of the Torah. The title pages were embellished with gold filigree lettering and decorated in brilliant vermilion ink. Amahl felt he was holding a precious work of art as he realized that he had not seen a single book in his own home. What had become of his father's books?

He turned to Naphtali. "Where is your daughter?"

"In the stables, of course."

"I will see her before I return to my estate. Thank you, your Grace. I bid you good-bye."

"Please forgive me for the failure of my daughter to accept your proposal. It is not her intention to insult you. She is just a foolish young woman. If her mother were here, I know we would not have such difficulty with Bianca."

"I am not insulted, and I have not lost my determination. I have laid siege to entire villages and waited until the people surrendered. I can wait for your daughter."

Naphtali, relieved, escorted Amahl from the villa.

"You must return often. Visit her, court her. Women, they are not like us, poor things. They do not know their weaknesses. Every morning in my prayers, I thank my Creator that I was not born a woman. It is our custom, you understand? Have you a similar custom in your religion?"

"No, but we do not allow our women to own horses. We do not even allow them near our horses!"

He left Naphtali on the path and sought Bianca in the stables, only to find her assisting a mare in labor. The two stable boys were in a state of panic. One hurried past Amahl as he entered the building. He could hear Bianca shouting at the other boy.

"Find the groom! He can help me with this. The foal is breech, and I cannot turn him by myself!"

Amahl entered the birthing stall and found Bianca on the floor beside the mare. Her hands were inside the thrashing horse, and Amahl could see that Bianca was in danger of being injured by the flailing hooves. He knelt next to her and pulled her hands away from the mare. She turned to him with a look of anxiety on her face. Tears were running down her cheeks.

"She is dying, and I cannot help her."

"Move over, and let me see what I can do."

Amahl reached into the mare and could feel the foal. He turned to Bianca.

"Try to hold her head for me. Be careful of her hooves. Place yourself out of their range."

She did not hesitate as she crawled around the hooves and took the mare's head in her arms. She began speaking to the mare in a soothing voice as Amahl waited for another contraction. He reached in and turned the foal. Within moments, the infant rushed out of its mother and lay for a moment in front of Amahl. The mare began hemorrhaging, and Amahl knew he could not save it. The foal was trying to stand. Amahl lifted it away from its mother and laid the struggling animal at Bianca's feet. He wanted to focus Bianca on the new life, but she was crying as the mare struggled for its last breath.

The foal raised itself unsteadily, then fell to the floor and nudged its mother's neck, then stared at Bianca. She met its gaze and placed the mare's head down on the floor of the stall. She then wrapped her arms around the foal's neck.

She wiped the tears from her cheeks, and with an expression of resolve, she carried the foal from the stable. Amahl followed her as she took the foal to another horse that had given birth five days earlier. They watched as the mother began licking the face of the newborn. Bianca made sure it did not reject the foal and then turned to Amahl.

"I am so sorry the horse died, Donzella. I tried my best."

"It is not your fault. I am so grateful to you for helping me. I would have lost the baby if you had not been here."

"I came to say good-bye. I am to return to my estate."

Bianca looked at Amahl, an expression of sadness on her face. "Will you come back again?"

"Yes, if you will permit me."

Bianca turned back to the stall where she had placed the newborn. It was drinking milk in loud, greedy gulps.

"What will you call him?"

"I don't know yet. I must check my records. He is out of my best mare, and I will miss her."

"Which stallion sired him?"

"Zilis, of course. Do you not recognize his conformation? His son has the same white face. He will be a fine stallion."

"I must go now, Donzella, but I will return next week."

"I wish you a safe journey home, General."

He looked at her, startled. She had never spoken to him with such kindness.

"The mare must be disposed of. May I help you do that?"

"No, but thank you for your offer. Hernando, my groom, will see to it. The stable boys will help him."

He could see the fatigue on Bianca's face.

"You are tired. Will you allow me to escort you to your father's house? The newborn will be all right with his new mother. There is nothing else to be done here."

Bianca wavered between exhaustion and her desire to stay with the mare until the groom arrived.

"Please, Donzella?"

She allowed him to take her to the villa, and bid him farewell as he mounted his horse. Bianca stood in the doorway for several moments, watching as Amahl rode away. Her father stood behind, and Bianca turned to kiss him.

"He is a fine man, isn't he, Bianca?"

"Yes, Father. He is very fine. He helped me birth a new foal, but the mother died."

"Is the foal all right?"

"Yes."

Naphtali could hear the exhaustion in his daughter's voice. He watched her as she looked down the lane. Amahl was a faint dot in the moonlight flooding the road. Bianca forgot her father as she watched Amahl disappear into the darkness.

Amahl traveled along the beach, the path now well-worn by his frequent visits to the de Lucena estate. He waited in the rocks for Bianca and Khalid to arrive, watching for signs of a ship, but as there were none, Bianca did not come. He remained there until dawn, and then continued his trip home in the gray light.

8

✢

Amahl was unable to sleep when he got home. He rode through the woods hunting rabbits with his falcon on his arm. His catch was good, and with the falcon flying from tree to tree above him, he returned to the castle with fifteen hares tied to the sides of his saddle. He spent the rest of the morning cooking the hares, submerging them in crocks filled with rich green olive oil. He stuffed them with thyme and garlic harvested from the herb garden. The treated rabbits would be stored in the cold room next to the pantry to keep through the winter. He relished the memories of his mother's cook as she had done this with the catch brought home by his father and brothers during so many autumn mornings.

When he finished preserving the rabbits, he went out to the garden behind the castle and cleared the weeds where Zoraya's servants had grown the root vegetables. He began digging in the rich soil and soon found what he was looking for. Gradually, mounds of carrots, rutabagas, and turnips emerged from the edges of the vegetable plot. He brought a wooden box from the pantry beside the immense wood-burning stove in the kitchen and filled it with the roots and tubers, carried them into the pantry, and dropped them in a corner on the stone floor. He brushed himself off and went to his bedchamber. Exhausted, he fell into a deep sleep.

He awoke to the sound of rain pounding on the casements. It was the first cold morning of winter, and he shivered as he burrowed deeper under the quilts for warmth. He was thinking of Bianca when he suddenly remembered he had not searched for his father's books. He hurried out of the bed and into the cold. He went down the stairs to the kitchen, approaching a door behind the pantry. It was a large door, heavy and cumbersome, and Amahl had to lean on it to open it. There before him were stone steps that led to the cellar beneath the castle. As he started down the steps, an icy draft swept up to meet him. He paused at intervals to light the large wax candles that were placed on heavy iron sconces in the stone wall of the circular staircase. Light flooded the cavernous ceiling as the stairs widened, until he found himself in a large empty room.

He took a candle from a dusty wooden box and lit it from the flame of the last sconce, and walked to the far end of the cellar, where he faced another stone wall. During his final visit with his father, Atiq had instructed Amahl to come to this area of the cellar when he returned home. There had been no wall then.

He approached the stones, touching them, and found the wall damp with sweat. The new stones were held together with fresh plaster. Amahl chiseled the mortar with a small knife. He removed many of the heavy stones until he made an opening in the wall large enough to enter. Holding the candle above his head, he crawled through and looked around the room his father had created.

There were paintings leaning against one wall. They were framed in gold leaf, which glistened in the candlelight. He saw furniture, carved and delicate, the upholstered seats covered in rich brocades and satins. Rugs were rolled and stacked along the opposite wall. What intrigued and delighted Amahl the most lay behind the rugs—wooden crates of leather-bound books.

He crossed the room and opened a wooden chest. It was filled with gold coins and jewels. He knelt before the chest to uncover necklaces and rings. As they fell through his fingers, he recognized his mother's jewelry. It must have taken his father several days to secure this treasure here. Amahl realized his father had wanted to hide this wealth from possible raiders until his return. Atiq had been trying to protect his family even at the end of his life.

Amahl spent the rest of the morning taking the crates of books to a circular room that stood at one corner of the edifice. There a large fireplace dominated one wall, and encircling the room at mid-height were windows, the panes of glass imported from France. Sunlight flooded the chamber with its warmth. Amahl was still placing the books on the low shelves when he realized he had not yet eaten.

He went to the kitchen and started a fire in the stove. The flames crackled, and as the heat wafted toward him, his fingers outspread before the fire, he slowly knelt on the floor and hugged himself. He stared dully into the light from the stove as his loneliness overtook him. Soon he roused himself and ate a piece of cheese and several olives he found in the cook's pantry.

When he finished his meal, he returned to the cellar. At the back of the large room, he found the opening to a dark tunnel in the corner. The first ten feet of the tunnel was lined with stones, and farther along, the walls and floor were packed with dirt. It took several minutes for Amahl to traverse the tunnel to its exit. The floor of the tunnel rose in places and dipped in others. It turned many times before Amahl saw daylight ahead of him. When he emerged, he was standing high on the rocks above the water line, and as he looked about, he saw that the tunnel's mouth was still well-hidden. The path leading down to the water was overgrown with weeds.

He sat at the edge far above the surf and the white beach below, reminiscing about his childhood. In the midst of his melancholy, he suddenly thought of the one thing he could offer Bianca de Lucena to persuade her to accept his marriage proposal.

✢

From the memoir of
Meschianza de Lucena Cozar-Velasquez
May 9, 1494
Lisbon

This morning I arose to the rocking of the ship. The sea is in turmoil, and the waves are lapping against the stern. Ana is ill from it. We've been on Raul's ship since just before Pesach. We have lived in Lisbon's walled community for safety, but as Passover approached, our safety diminished. As in the past, the Blood Libel began, and the rumors fired their way through the city. I do not know if we will ever return.

The Cardoza family has disappeared. I went to their house early on our last morning in the community. The door was ajar. I saw many of their belongings strewn about the main room of their small house. I entered, calling their names, but it was as if they had vanished. I had just spoken to Señora Cardoza the previous night. Her child, Ramon, was ill, and I prepared a tisane for him to drink. He was feverish, his face flushed and damp. What has become of him?

The soldiers of the Inquisition often come in the night. They are always led by an odorous friar, his eyes aflame with furious accusations. Sometimes we hear them, their voices rising above the walled tenements, echoing their hatred for us through the grated windows of our homes. There is a thunderous knock on a door, followed by screams of fear and outrage, then silence. It is always the same. Entire families disappear. Inquiries are made, but to no avail. Our leaders are helpless.

When I returned to our house and told Raul of the Cardozas' disappearance, he decided that we must flee to the ship. We have been here for almost two months, and in Lisbon for two years. The hardships have overwhelmed us.

We long for the pastures and meadows of our home. It is spring again, but all we see is the surrounding sea water. At home, the orange blossoms bloom. If I close my eyes, I can see the purity of the petals, waxen and heavy, with their deep emerald-green leaves. In my reverie, I walk through the orchards, my feet avoiding the violets that peek from beneath the deep grasses that form long corridors between the rows of trees. The ewes are birthing their tiny white lambs, whose silky fur matches the purity of the blossoms.

The land comes alive in the spring. Birds call to one another, boasting of the birth of their young. Bees drink in the nectar of the orange groves, their fat yellow and black bodies bobbing through the warm sunlight. They find their hives with the deftness of seasoned mariners. Soon my mother and I will begin gathering the honey, placing the heavy combs into the smooth white crocks, and setting them on the shelves in the pantry.

Raul says I must not think about these things now. He does not want me to be sad, but sadness is the melody we all hear. There are no other songs for us. Ana cries almost daily—she is sick again. The confinement of the ship is beginning to wear on all of us. We are safe here, but what is safety? One can only exist in safety, but one does not live.

9

∻

Amahl attended to his preparations for winter and could not return to the de Lucena estate for many weeks, though he continued to put aside gifts for Bianca. The wooden jewelry chest contained a sapphire necklace, as well as his mother's exquisite necklace of pearls. Amahl knew he would present it to Bianca on their wedding day. The one hundred and fifty lustrous pearls were perfectly matched, and their silken cord elaborately knotted between each pearl. He placed the strand in its velvet case in the top drawer of the oak chest in his bedchamber.

Early the next morning, Amahl was awakened by a loud knocking on the front door of the castle. He hurried down the stairs to find Khalid al-Hassan and a large group of men waiting for him.

"Good morning, my Lord General. We are here to help you prepare your estate for the winter months. There is little time, but his Grace wishes to help you. Where would you like us to begin?"

Amahl surveyed the group of men. Many carried their farm implements on their shoulders. Some had shovels, others scythes. Behind the group stood two wooden wagons pulled by tall, heavy plow horses. Their furry hooves pawed the frozen ground impatiently.

"I think we must begin in the groves. The irrigation system must be dismantled, and the clay pipes stored at the back of the stables. There is a shed there."

Khalid turned and shouted orders to his men.

"Juan, Hernando, Luis, see to it!"

He turned back to Amahl. "What else, my Lord General?"

Amahl watched as the three men drove one of the wagons from the courtyard toward the olive groves.

"Perhaps, sir, we will clean the rotted fruit from the orange groves?"

"Yes, yes, it would be good to do that."

"In two months, we will come and harvest the oranges. I have studied the crop, and it will be successful."

"I will join you in a moment, Khalid."

Amahl went into the castle to his bedchamber and put on his robes. When he returned to the courtyard, three men were left waiting with Khalid. Amahl beckoned them to follow him, leading them to the cellar, and the hidden room. Together, they spent the rest of the morning carrying the remainder of his father's legacy to the upper floors of the castle.

In four days, the work in the orchards was completed and the estate was prepared for the cold, wet months ahead. Amahl was resting comfortably in the great room, a roaring fire wafting clouds of warmth about his chair, when he heard a loud knocking at the door. He opened it to find Khalid standing there with a broad smile on his face.

"My Lord General, come quickly. There is a gift. The Donzella de Lucena has sent you a gift."

Amahl looked out the front door to find a large wooden cart in which stood the foal that he and Bianca had birthed weeks before. Bianca's groom, Hernando, stood beside the cart waiting for Amahl. He handed him a note written on thick white paper. It was sealed with Bianca's crest pressed in red wax. Amahl opened it and began to read.

My Lord General, here is Fiero, the white-faced roan you helped me bring into this world. He is weaned and ready to be adopted. I give him to you and ask for your forgiveness. I cannot marry you. I cannot accept your gifts. He is a fine youngster, and will grow up to be a wonderful addition to your farm. He has excellent bloodlines and will bring to your mares many fine children. I know you will care for him well.

Bianca de Lucena

Amahl examined the colt. He was a beautiful, spirited animal. He turned to Hernando and Khalid.

"Come in before the fire and warm yourselves, then we will return the colt to Donzella de Lucena."

Distressed, believing he had done something to displease the general, Hernando began to object, but then thought better of it. He followed Khalid into the castle as Amahl entered the great room.

"My Lord General, I have taken very good care of this colt for you, according to the Donzella's instructions. He is beautiful, isn't he?"

"Yes, Hernando. He is beautiful."

Bewildered, Hernando watched Amahl leave the room. He looked at Khalid, who shrugged his shoulders. Amahl returned shortly, carrying a book he had retrieved from his bedchamber.

They took the colt back to the de Lucena estate, and when they arrived, it was already quite dark. Amahl took the rope from Hernando and led the colt to the stables. Bianca was saddling one of her horses as he entered. She was surprised to see him, and more surprised when he handed the reins to her.

"Donzella, I wish to thank you for your kind and generous gift."

"Why do you return Fiero to me?"

"Because I know and understand your intentions. You believe I will stop asking you to marry me, that it is only the horses I want."

"But isn't it the horses?"

"Donzella Bianca, there was a time when I would have accepted your gift, but having this horse is no longer enough for me. I want you, Donzella. I want you for my wife. If you had no horses, I would still want you to be my wife. I do not want another woman. Only you, Bianca."

Bianca did not reply with words. She merely stared at him, and resumed saddling her horse. Amahl placed the colt in a stall and returned to Bianca. She was putting her booted foot into the stirrup to mount her horse when Amahl took out the book of poetry he had brought from his bedside. He had read it each night by candlelight after finding it in the cellar. Now he read to Bianca.

Open the door to me,
Open it, face like a flower . . .

Bianca, her foot still in the stirrup, stared at him as he continued reading.

You have been mine since you were a child,
How much more so now.

He waited for her to speak, but she said nothing. Undaunted by her silence, he stood in front of her horse.

She with the face like a flower
Went down and opened the door;

They went to the garden
Hand in hand together.

She lifted herself onto the horse, never taking her eyes off him. He reached for her reins and held the horse steady.

"Donzella Bianca, tomorrow I will journey to Cadiz to buy horses. I will no longer ask to buy your stock."

She gently pulled the leather reins from his hands. She turned her horse, and without speaking a word to Amahl, rode the horse at a gallop out of the stables. Amahl followed on foot, calling to her, but she raced the horse to the path that led to the cliffs. Soon she and the horse disappeared down the path to the water.

Amahl, pleased that she hadn't laughed at him, found his horse at the front of the villa and followed her down to the beach. He caught up with her as she neared the water, and almost missed her but for the large and glowing harvest moon that was already beginning to rise. Bianca moved along its gentle radiance as the water reflected on her and her horse.

She dismounted and sat on the sand. Her horse played with her hair, trying to bite it. She pushed it away. She had to think. Bianca hugged her knees to her chest and studied the waves. She could feel the beginning of a strong breeze. She was sitting beneath the cliffs, and they offered some protection, but she was still cold. She should have brought her cloak. He loved her . . .

Bianca called to her horse, and as she began to mount the mare, she caught a glimpse of Amahl waiting at the water's edge. Startled, she hesitated, then settled herself in the saddle to wait for him. She did not speak as he brought his horse next to her. She was shivering from the cold, so he took off his cloak, and reaching across the distance between the two horses, he wrapped it around her. He was tying the cords to secure it at the base of her throat when she finally spoke to him.

"You will get cold, sir."

He sat back in his saddle and studied her for a moment before he replied.

"Donzella, I am quite adept at dealing with coldness."

Disconcerted for a moment, she pulled the cloak about her, grateful for its warmth.

"Where are you going?"

"For a ride along the beach. Where does it look like I am going?"

"Without your duenna?"

"She has gone to visit her family at the *aljama*."

"Does your father know you are riding?"

Impatient with him now, Bianca replied curtly.

"He has retired early. I did not want to disturb him."

"May I ride with you?"

"It appears that is what you are doing."

They rode along the water in silence. The tide had risen, forcing them to move their horses closer to the cliffs. It was growing colder as the fog floated off the water and surrounded them. Amahl led Bianca's horse into the rocks and dismounted.

"Why do you stop here?"

"To build a fire. Here, bring your horse next to mine. I will tie them to this bush."

He helped her dismount, and the two gathered driftwood. Bianca sat on the sand and watched him light moss beneath the kindling. Soon a flame appeared, followed by a small spiral of smoke. Amahl bent forward and blew on the flame until the wood caught fire. When he was satisfied by the strength of the fire, he sat next to her.

"When did you say you are to go to Cadiz?"

"Tomorrow night?"

"For horses?"

"Yes."

He stared at the fire, indifferent to her questions. Her next question was spoken in a near-whisper. He almost missed what she said.

"Will you take me with you?"

At first, he didn't answer her. Amahl was startled by her question. She repeated it.

"Please, will you take me?"

He turned to her, her face bright and eager in the light of the fire.

"Of course not! Your father will never agree. And . . . and . . . your duenna. She would not like the journey. There are many hardships."

Uncomfortable now, he moved away from her, searching for more driftwood to feed the fire. She stood up to follow him.

"I don't want my duenna to go, and I do not intend to tell my father."

Amazed by her declaration, he turned to her suddenly with a piece of driftwood in his hand. She backed away from him, staring at the piece of wood. He followed her glance, and realizing she was frightened, he threw the wood into the fire.

"Donzella Bianca, how can you say such things?"

Nervous, he walked away from her again and stood by the water. Bianca came up behind him and reached for his hand. He could not believe her sudden forwardness.

"Sir, please listen to me. I have never been to Cadiz. I have never been anywhere but Tarifa on the Sabbath, or to the *feria* with my father and Señora Martinez."

"There would be a scandal! Your poor father could never save you from that!"

"But he would not have to. Señora Martinez will be gone for five days. That is enough time, isn't it?"

"Yes, but I cannot do this. Your father trusts me."

"Exactly, he trusts you, and when he reads my note, he will know I am in safe hands. Please?"

"You will be recognized!"

"No. I will not. I will be disguised."

"Disguised as what?"

"I don't know. I will think of something."

"No, Donzella. This is foolish. I will not encourage—"

"I know! I have thought of something! I will dress as a stable boy."

"It will not work."

"I fooled you."

"Yes, and that was very rude of you."

She walked back to the fire and waited for him to join her. He remained at the water, struggling with himself. How had he gotten himself into this? If he refused her, she would probably not speak to him again. Her father would never forgive him for risking her safety, not to mention her reputation. When he returned to the fire, he was still without a solution.

As he neared her, she stood up and ran to Amahl, throwing her arms around him. He tried to push her away from him, but she was too eager.

"You have decided to take me? Thank you, Amahl. Thank

you. I am so happy. I cannot believe I will see Cadiz. Will we go to a horse auction? Father has never let me go, but Benjamin always went with him."

She continued like this, overwhelming him with her excitement. He tried to tell her it was impossible, but she was already untying her mare and climbing onto the saddle.

"Donzella, where are you going?"

"To get ready. I have so much to do! I will write Father a note telling him not to worry. Tomorrow night, I will meet you here, and then we will begin our adventure."

She raced down the beach toward her father's villa. Amahl, flabbergasted, stood by the fire and watched her go. He paced around the burning logs, and then looked up again at her as she and the horse disappeared into the fog.

"Oh, this is not good. Not good. What will I do? Maybe I should have kept Fiero. Yes, that is what I should have done. How did I let this happen?"

He kicked sand onto the fire until there was only a small wisp of smoke rising from it. He mounted his horse and started to follow her, but then he realized he would rob her of her joy if he refused to comply with her plans. At once troubled and happy, Amahl rode his horse through the fog to his estate.

✤

10

꧁

The following night, Amahl waited for Bianca on the beach, hoping she had changed her mind. Perhaps she would see the folly of their plans. Maybe her father would catch her as she tried to sneak out of the villa. Surely, Naphtali would stop her. Amahl had one of his packhorses with him, loaded with provisions for their journey. He knew he could not take her to a *hostal*; it would be unseemly. They would sleep on the beach or in the woods, whichever was the safest. He was armed with his sword, and his crossbow was packed on the mare. His falcon, hooded now, was asleep on his wrist.

He heard Bianca's horse before he saw her. He was hidden in the rocks, so he left the packhorse and rode out to meet her. As he neared her, she held out his cloak. He took it from her and could see that she was wearing a plain brown one that was too big for her.

"I was afraid you would not wait for me. I am so happy you are here."

Her face was shining in the moonlight. She had tucked her hair into the same hat she wore when she was cleaning the stable stalls. Her trousers and shirt were dirty. Looking at her, happy and eager for their journey to begin, Amahl relented and gave her a welcoming smile.

"Are you ready, Donzella?"

They rode along the water, Amahl leading the packhorse.

"You must not call me that."

"What will I call you?"

"I don't know. Think of a name! Any name. A man's name."

"I will call you Abdallah. You will be my groom, traveling with me to the horse auction in Cadiz."

"Oh yes. That will do, won't it?"

He nodded to her. "What is in that large bag attached to your saddle?"

"Food. I have brought food with me for our journey. The cook is so fussy. I had to sneak it out of her kitchen this morning. I have some small pies, and rolls, and I even have candy."

She smiled at him and held out her hand. He took the candy and put it in his pocket.

"Thank you, Donzella, for bringing the food. When it is gone, I will hunt. We will not go hungry."

"That will not do."

"What do you mean, it will not do?"

"Unless the meat is killed by a *shochet*, I cannot eat it. It is forbidden."

He pulled his horse closer to hers and stopped. She went ahead and turned around. They were facing each other, their horses nose to nose.

"Donzella—"

"Abdallah."

"Abdallah, will you explain to me what you have just said?"

"I can only eat what is allowed by my faith."

"Why is it forbidden for you to eat meat that I have killed?"

"Because it must be killed gently."

He leaned forward in his saddle, challenging her.

"It is not possible to kill something gently. The very nature of the act is not gentle."

"Our *shochets* do it!"

"How?"

"Well, they talk to the animal. They talk gently so that the animal feels safe, then they cut its throat."

"So you want me to walk up to a deer and talk to it so it feels safe?" Amahl was trying not to yell, despite his exasperation.

Affronted, Bianca became aloof and quiet. They continued down the beach in silence. Soon they came to a group of boulders. Amahl stopped to dismount, but Bianca remained in her saddle.

"We will stop here and sleep until dawn." He walked to the packhorse and began unloading blankets.

"But I am not sleepy. Can't we go farther before we sleep?"

"No, we cannot. This is a good place. My father, brothers, and I always slept here on our first night. In the rocks, there is a clearing protected from the wind. There is room for the horses. Come, I will show you."

Bianca dismounted and led her horse after him. They entered the clearing, and Amahl began laying the blankets on the sand. Bianca watched him as he made two beds side by side. When he had finished, she took the side of her pile of blankets and pulled it away from his until there was about five feet of sand separating them. She unsaddled her horse and placed the saddle between them. Without looking at Amahl, she crawled into the blankets and prepared to go to sleep.

Amahl did the same, and when they were each in separate beds, there was silence except for the sound of the horses eating from their feed bags. He lay on his back and watched the moon in its path as it crossed the sky. Try as he might, Amahl couldn't fall asleep until almost dawn.

✦

II

✤

Amahl and Bianca continued to travel along the beaches until they were well past Tarifa. Amahl did not want to risk anyone recognizing Bianca. At nightfall of their second day, as they approached the outskirts of Cadiz, the two rode along the main road. His falcon no longer sat on his wrist. Instead, the noble bird chose to ride on Bianca's arm. He tied the leather guard to her wrist, but as they neared Cadiz, the bird perched itself on her shoulder.

Amahl and Bianca were used to each other by this point. The two led their horses into the trees and set up their discrete camp. Amahl watered the horses in a nearby stream and led them back to the camp. Bianca was preparing a meal for them both when Amahl noticed she had fallen asleep on her bed. The falcon, unhooded, was perched near her head. When it saw Amahl approach, it flew off into the trees in search of its dinner.

Amahl sat on the ground near Bianca and watched her sleep. Her hair was disheveled and her face dirty, but she was still the most beautiful woman he had ever seen. He took a blanket and covered her, and ate his dinner. He sat for a long time watching the sun go down behind the trees. He knew he should perform his *salats*, but he did not want to leave her there unprotected, so he stayed where he was. The fire had almost burned out when he fell into his own exhausted sleep.

They entered Cadiz before dawn on the day of the weekly *feria*. Amahl recalled that the horse auction on Cadiz's outskirts began shortly after the farmers' wives set up their wares outside the walled city.

As they passed through the sleepy town, their horses' footfalls echoed through the many small cobbled squares. A rooster crowed as Amahl and Bianca continued through the narrow streets of whitewashed tenements. He led Bianca's horse, careful to avoid the centers of the lanes, trying his best to keep them under the wrought-iron balconies, as the women of the city were emptying their families' chamberpots into the ditches on the streets of Cadiz. During the day, the women also threw out pieces of refuse that even their pigs wouldn't eat.

Amahl and Bianca emerged from the city and traveled to the auction. Along the main road, they passed fields of women who were plowing. There were also women who followed their husbands, helping them fertilize their fields. Bianca tried to see everything before her, often turning to Amahl in silence and smiling at him in gratitude. He did not speak, letting her drink in the sights around them.

As sunlight broke over the land, women hauled water for their families, or gathered kindling for their fires. They passed women walking toward Cadiz, carrying their wares for the *feria*. Amahl and Bianca dismounted when they encountered an elderly lady offering to sell them freshly baked rolls. As Amahl gave her a coin, she reached into a basket and opened a crock of newly churned butter. Using a worn wooden knife, she spread the golden cream onto one of the rolls and smiled a toothless grin at Bianca. The two continued on their way, Bianca watching a young woman openly nursing her infant as she led a cow to market, her three small children rubbing their eyes as they trailed behind her.

It was broad daylight when they arrived at the auction. A man who purchased horses for the military greeted Amahl. He recognized him, having known Amahl during his military days.

"Ho, my Lord General. You are here to buy horses, I see. I was told you were returning to your estate. Welcome home! Señor Dominguez is offering one of his white stallions for bids this morning. Come, he is over here. Bring the boy."

Bianca looked at Amahl, a satisfied grin on her face, as the man led them to a large group of men. At the center of the crowd stood the white Andalusian. Excited, Bianca started to walk over to the horse, but Amahl held her back. They joined a group of men who were discussing the stallion's attributes and speculating on the opening bid when the owner stepped to the bidding platform and asked for silence. Bianca watched an old man sitting alone beneath a nearby tree as he played flamenco music on his polished guitar. He stopped abruptly and adjusted his straw hat so that he could watch the bidding without the sunlight blinding him.

"My friends, today I will sell this excellent stallion to the highest bidder. He is only three years old, and a fine, spirited horse. Look at him!"

The men nodded in agreement as a murmur traveled through the crowd.

"In honor of my daughter's approaching marriage, I begin the bidding with only two hundred maravedis!"

Several of the men politely shook their heads and left the group standing before the white horse. The soldier, who was next to Amahl, turned to leave, patting Amahl on the shoulder.

"Good luck, sir. I go now to look at horses I can afford."

"Perhaps I will join you."

Just then, Bianca grabbed Amahl's elbow. He turned to her as the bidding began, but she did not take her eyes off the auctioneer.

"Bid!" she hissed at him.

"But this is an expensive horse—"

"Bid! You need him!"

Already one of the men in the crowd had raised the bid by twenty-five maravedis. Amahl signaled the auctioneer and raised the bid by seventy-five more. Amahl let out a soft groan as several more men left the bidding. The sale now stood at three hundred maravedis. Amahl waited. A man, well-dressed and obviously more prosperous than Amahl, raised the bid by another fifty maravedis. Amahl sighed with relief and turned to leave just as Bianca pulled on his arm.

Resigned, Amahl bid again. "Five hundred maravedis?"

The other bidder raised his hands in good-natured defeat and smiled at Amahl.

"Sold to General Cozar!"

The horse reared back, and Bianca, in her duties as Amahl's stable boy, walked up to the horse without fear and pulled the stallion into her control. Amahl paid the auctioneer from a leather bag he took out of his tunic. When he turned to Bianca, she was already on the back of the stallion, leading her mare. He mounted his own horse and rode away from the auction, Bianca following after him on the white Andalusian. She caught up to him and joined him on the road.

"This is a wonderful stallion. He will sire many fine colts."

"I hope so, Donzella. He was very expensive."

"Didn't you want him? I thought you wanted him. Everybody wanted this horse!"

"Yes, of course I wanted him, but I had not planned to spend so much on a horse."

"At five hundred maravedis, he is a bargain. Zilis cost my

father twice the amount."

"Then I suppose I should thank you," he replied sarcastically.

"Oh no, of course you shouldn't. Where are we going now?"

The sound of the bells ringing from the cathedral in Cadiz carried to the outer walls of the village where the market was still taking place. As they entered the city again, people bustled about and bartered loudly with the vendors.

"Would you like to go to the *feria*, Abdallah?" He smiled at her as he saw her eyes light up.

"Can we?"

"Follow me. It is better if we walk and lead our horses. Here, you take mine, and I will lead the new stallion."

She reluctantly dismounted and handed over the reins. They entered the fair, and Bianca forgot Amahl and the horses, joining the crowd of people filling the marketplace.

The walls of the surrounding buildings were whitewashed with lime, glistening in the sun. The light reflected the bright colors of the awnings that shaded the wares in each stall. Bianca stood between two of the stalls watching a middle-aged woman. Next to her, a young man with callused fingers strummed a viol. The woman began to sing.

Amahl was familiar with the folksong she sung, but it was the *cante jondo*, the deep song of Spain that he truly loved. These tremulous laments, expressing loss and piercing grief, touched his heart. The *siguiriyas* were the songs he heard his mother sing while he lay in his cradle, and as he performed his *salats*, he could not help but incorporate the fragmented tones and cries into his prayers.

He searched the crowd surrounding the singing woman to see Bianca giving her rapt attention to the music. She looked up and gave him a smile so brilliant that he was stunned for a moment by the lack of inhibition in her eyes. Her reserve was gone, and in its place was a woman Amahl did not recognize. He continued to watch her after she returned her gaze to the singing woman.

When the song ended, they walked their horses between the stalls until they joined a small crowd surrounding a *gaditana*. The young woman danced an impromptu *baile*, her heels tapping on the wooden platform beneath her. Her bright skirts twirled about her as she flashed her eyes at a soldier. Standing beside Bianca was an old woman who clapped her hands to the rhythm of a man accompanying the dancer with his guitar. Bianca joined in the clapping as the man, his voice high-pitched and lilting, exulted with the *saeta*, the arrow of song that was always a part of the *cante flamenco*.

They stayed at the *feria* through the rest of the morning, moving from stall to stall, talking to people as Amahl renewed his acquaintance with his childhood friends. Bianca stopped at one stall to examine the brightly colored fabrics on display.

"I would like to be a gypsy, or a peasant."

"Why?"

"I don't know." She thought about her answer for a moment.

They mounted their horses and left the marketplace.

He nodded toward the beggars who sat leaning against the stone walls of the cathedral as Bianca followed him to the city gates in silence. As she contemplated Amahl's question, she waited several moments before she spoke again.

"Gypsies are free. They can go wherever they wish."

"That is not true, Donzella. They are poor."

"There is no true freedom, is there?"

"No. We are all imprisoned by something. Our cultures create prisons for us."

"If that is true, then we are our own jailers."

He stopped to turn to her. She was sitting on her horse and did not look at him, but instead continued to study her hands.

"I suppose you are correct. But then, perhaps we are the only ones who can determine the degree of our imprisonment, or our freedom."

"Yes. I have been attempting to do this all my life."

"And have you succeeded, Donzella?"

"No."

He nodded at her, and they resumed their journey. They had traveled several miles along the main road when Amahl directed Bianca to a wide lane that veered right. They followed the lane until they came upon a crowd of festive people. Astride her horse, Bianca could see that the people were entering through a gate that was decorated with bull horns.

"My Lord General, where are we going?"

He turned to her with a look of anticipation.

"It is time for *la fiesta brava*."

"A bullfight?" She looked at him, excitement like a sunrise lighting her face.

"*La corrida!* Come. There may be some good seats left."

They followed the crowd to the arena's entrance, and Amahl offered an old man a gold coin to watch over their horses. As they entered the area of spectators, Bianca's excitement was heightened by the circuslike atmosphere that surrounded them. Amahl wanted her to have a favorable view of the bullfight, so he bribed two occupants of the seats he chose close to the edge of the ring. Surprised that a man of his stature would deign to sit next to his servant, they left, happy with their earnings. The horns sounded for the *paso doble*, the march rhythm music that accompanied the matadors' entrance. Bianca, her eyes large with the thrill of the spectacle before her, watched in awe as the procession began. There were three matadors, and each wore a silk jacket heavily embroidered in gold, skintight pants, and a *montera*, a bicorne hat.

Bianca spoke in a near whisper. He leaned close to her to hear.

"Their clothing! They are so beautiful!"

"Yes. They wear the *traje de luces*, the suit of lights. It is an honor reserved for only the best matadors."

"They look like angels from heaven."

She turned back to the ring and was silent for several moments. The matadors' assistants, the banderilleros and the picadors soon followed them into the ring. They all proceeded across the arena and took their places behind a large wooden wall. The crowd's cheers were deafening as the first bull was released out of the *toril*, the bullpen gate, and one of the matadors stepped out from behind the wall and began a series of maneuvers with his cape.

"What is he doing?"

"He is performing the *veronicas*, greeting the bull."

"He is very brave."

Her eyes returned to the scene before them as the bull instinctively charged the bright red cape. As it twirled above his head, Bianca could see that the underside of the cape was made with a golden silk fabric.

The bullfight lasted for only fifteen minutes. The second phase began soon after the greeting of the bull. The picadors, bearing lances and mounted on horses, wore flat-brimmed beige felt *castorenos* on their heads. Their jackets were embroidered with silver threads, and their chamois trousers were covered in steel leg armor.

"What are they going to do?"

"They will protect the banderilleros. Watch!"

A trumpet blew, and the banderilleros, carrying brightly adorned barbed sticks, advanced on the bull. Working on foot, they placed the sticks into the bull's shoulders.

"Why have they done that?" She turned to Amahl, her cheeks flushed with her distress.

"To cause it to lower its head for the kill that is coming."

A trumpet sounded again and signaled the final phase of the bullfight. The bull was wary, for it realized that its true enemy was behind the red cape. The matador, aware that most gorings took place at this time, paced cautiously toward the bull. In his right hand, he carried the muleta, a cape made of serge cloth. It was draped over the *estoque*, the sword with which he would soon kill the bull. As he began the last act of the bullfight, the *faena*, a hush fell over the crowd. In the silence, the matador fell to one knee and began the *trincherazo*. The bull, confused now, stood dumbly and stared at the graceful bullfighter. It pawed the ground, and the matador stood and held out the cloth to it. He performed the *pase de la firma*, remaining motionless as he moved the cloth in front of the bull's nose. The crowd roared its excitement.

Amahl and Bianca stood with the rest of the spectators and watched the matador continue to make passes at the tiring bull, until finally he took the sword out of the muleta and performed the *natural*. This act increased the danger to the matador, for when he took the sword out of the cloth, he created a smaller target. Now the larger target attracting the bull was the matador himself.

The bull thundered toward the man who was tormenting it, but the matador remained where he was and took careful aim. As the bull neared him, he waited, the sword above his head. When the bull's front hooves were together, he plunged the sword straight over the bull's horns and between its withers. The bull fell in a cloud of dust at the feet of the matador.

The crowd was in a frenzy as he took a small knife from his pocket, reached over the bull's head, and cut off the ears of the dead animal. He turned and held the ears over his head for the crowd to see. Years of discipline, training, and raw courage had brought him to this "moment of truth." He walked to the crowd, his bearing erect and proud, his suit of lights dusty with his triumph.

Bianca, her eyes saddened, turned to Amahl.

"Thank you for bringing me."

"Would you like to see more? There are five more fights yet. Each matador must kill two bulls today."

"No. I have seen enough."

"Then we will continue to our homes."

They left the arena and found their horses. As they rode away from the festivities of the bullfight, their horses were beginning to show signs of fatigue, and Amahl knew they must soon find a place to spend the night. Bianca was quiet, and Amahl realized she was near exhaustion, adding to her distress at the brutal killing of the bulls. It had been a long day for both of them.

"We will return to the beaches, Donzella. It is not safe here on the main road after dark."

✢

12

⁂

Amahl remembered a small cave in the rocks that lined a large segment of the cliffs south of Cadiz. When he found it, he and Bianca dismounted and gathered wood for a fire. It was dark, and the sky was brilliant with stars. At the mouth of the cave, he started a small fire. He went to the packhorse and took a net from his belongings. As he was leaving the cave, Bianca questioned him.

"Where are you going? It is dark. You will get lost."

He paused and turned to her. She was sitting by the fire, warming her hands.

"I am going to talk to the fish, Donzella. Are you afraid to stay alone? Why don't you come with me?"

"No, I will wait for you here."

"I won't be long. I must go and be gentle to the fish."

She watched as he walked down the beach to the water. He disappeared in the rocks, and Bianca went through their provisions.

Amahl found the spot he remembered from earlier journeys home. He secured the fishing net to the edge of a rock that stood in solitude near the water. He threw the rest of the net out onto the water and watched it sink slowly beneath the waves. He waited, and soon the net began moving in short jerks. He pulled it toward him and saw that it was full of fish. He chose the largest one, throwing the rest of the fish back into the sea. Carrying his catch wrapped in the net over his shoulder, he returned to the campsite.

As he neared it, moonlight washed the beach in front of the cave, and in the golden light he saw Bianca standing at the edge of the water, dressed in a many-colored skirt and red blouse. She had removed her cap, and her hair was flowing about her shoulders. It fell below her waist in gentle waves and appeared golden in the moon's reflection.

Amahl stopped, not wanting to approach her. She seemed to be entranced by the waves washing at her feet. She was barefoot as she stared at the sea. She began to sway. Bianca did not see him when she turned, and he was afraid to move, to break the spell that had entranced her. He felt like an intruder, but he could not stop watching her.

Bianca began to dance before the water. She turned in a circle, once again facing the water, as if she was testing her abilities. She raised her arms to the moon, dancing a paganlike ritual for the water as Amahl watched, enchanted. She was absorbed by the moonlight and appeared to float in it, her bare feet peeking out from beneath the skirt as it twirled and wrapped itself about her legs.

Tears came to Amahl's eyes, and as he wiped them away, he was bewildered by their appearance. As he watched her, it occurred to him that this was a Bianca he had never known existed. He realized that this was a woman he could never have seen on her father's estate—her father's daughter, confined and restricted by a watchful duenna, and a more watchful community.

She continued her dance for several moments. Amahl caught his breath and held it, waiting to see what she would do next, but she only sat on the sand before the water, her celebration over. Amahl was bereft. He wanted her to dance again, but he was aware that he must not let her know he had seen her, so he waited. Soon she got up from the sand and returned to the cave. He followed her, carrying the fish like an offering.

Amahl entered the cave and found her sitting before the fire. She was flushed, her face moist from her exertion. Bianca watched him as he prepared the fish for the fire.

"Did you kill it gently, sir?"

She whispered her question, and when he looked at her, there was mischief in her eyes.

"Yes. We had a long conversation before I brought him in. He told me about his life in the ocean. He said he was tired of it, so I accommodated him. He came with willingness."

He threw the fish onto the rock at the center of the small fire. It sizzled and crisped as the stone steamed beneath it.

"Are you hungry?"

"Yes. I am starving."

She wrapped her arms around her knees and watched the flames char the tail of the fish, then she looked up at Amahl.

"When will we arrive?"

"In two days. We will ride all day tomorrow. You must go to sleep early, so you will not be tired."

She did not say anything, but instead continued to study him.

"Are you tired, Donzella?"

"No."

He turned the fish over to cook the other side.

"I have liked very much coming here with you. I thank you for bringing me. You have made me very happy."

He took two wooden plates from a leather knapsack. With his knife, he lifted pieces of the fish onto the plates. He gave one to her, and the two sat back against the wall of the cave, eating their dinner with their fingers. When they finished, he stood up to rinse the plates in the water. Bianca intervened, offering to take them. After she left the cave, Amahl lay down on his blankets, overwhelmed by fatigue. He quickly fell asleep.

He awoke to find Bianca leaning over him, her hair forming a curtain around their faces. He reached up, startled, but Bianca intercepted his hand. Her eyes were intent on his, and he watched as a single tear traced her cheek. She spoke to him in a whisper.

"Thou art fair, my love; thou art fair."

He tried to sit up, but she placed her hands on his chest and pushed him back against the sand. Before he could stop her, she kissed him on the mouth. Amahl put his arms around Bianca, pulling her against his chest. He turned her over onto her back and kissed her again. He examined her face, looking for an indication that he should continue. He knew he must stop, but he was helpless as he looked into her eyes.

"We must not do this. Not now."

She reached up and placed her arms around his neck.

"Now is the only time, Amahl, don't you see?"

He put his head down against her breasts.

"I love you. Do you know this? I love you. I want you to be my wife."

She pulled his face away from hers to look at him. She continued to whisper:

"Then I will marry you. We will tell my father when we get home, but for tonight, pretend we are as free as gypsies, or peasants. Please, Amahl?"

"We will never be free. Don't you see?"

"But you said that we must create our own freedom."

"This is not what I meant. I cannot free you if I dishonor you."

"Amahl, for the rest of our lives, you can be the gentleman, but for tonight, I would be very happy if you would forget your manners, and call me by my given name."

"Bianca, I have a deep foreboding that somehow you are going to make me forget my very name."

"That will be all right, as long as you don't forget mine."

13

The following morning, Amahl and Bianca continued their journey home, riding along the beach when they could. When they were blocked by towering cliffs of rock and sand, they returned to the main road. It was important to Amahl that they arrive at the de Lucena estate before Señora Martinez ended her visit with her family. They rode through the night on the last leg of their journey. When they arrived at Amahl's estate, he led Bianca up the path to the stables, where they placed the horses in stalls. They did not speak as they cared for their mounts. She followed him up the path to the castle, the now waning moon lighting their way.

When he opened the front door and led her inside, she stopped at the entrance to the great room. Unaware, he continued into the kitchen, only to discover she was not behind him. He retraced his steps to find her sitting on a bench, holding one of his mother's illuminated manuscripts. It was displayed on the table next to Bianca, and as he entered the room, she looked up at him with an awed expression.

"My grandfather took that in a raid. There are more in my mother's chamber."

"It is very beautiful. The artistry is exquisite."

"I believe they were drawn by monks. My grandfather found them hidden in the ruins of a church. Come with me. There is something I want to show you."

She placed the manuscript back on the table and followed him to the kitchen. She hesitated as he opened the cellar door. He lit a candle and beckoned to her, but she held back, looking down at the deep pit before them. Amahl took her hand and gently led her down the stairs. The shadows formed by the lit sconces lent an eerie cast to their descent, and Bianca tightened her grip on Amahl's hand.

He led her to the opening of the tunnel and began walking into it. She drew back again, and he turned to her.

"What is this? Where are you taking me?"

"To the ocean, Bianca. Be quiet and follow me."

He took her through the winding, dipping excavation until they reached the opening. A cold wind raced toward them from the mouth and chilled their faces. He placed her at the mouth of the tunnel, and as she shivered in the wind, he placed his arms around her.

"Do you see this path below us? At high tide, the water covers the path. It almost reaches the tunnel this way, which is why it dips downward to the opening. The water will not flood the tunnel."

"Yes, I see."

"Do you see the iron rings imbedded in those two boulders? A longboat can be tied there, for boarding."

"How long has this tunnel been here? Did your father create it?"

"No. It has been here for generations. Before the land was granted to my family, the castle was owned by a caliph. He smuggled his soldiers into Spain through this tunnel."

"What happened to him?"

"He was hanged, along with his son, from the ridge beam in the stables. His wife and daughter were raped and murdered in the castle."

Bianca turned and looked at Amahl with distaste.

"Now let's go back to the castle. We have much to talk about."

✥

14

❖

Amahl filled the fireplace with wood, and as the fire warmed the room, he placed two chairs before the flames and motioned Bianca to one of them. He took the chair opposite her and began speaking.

"Tell me about the smuggling. Who is involved, how did you come to help these people, how often does the ship arrive, where does the ship take them . . . "

"How do you know of the smuggling?"

"I have known since the first night I visited you and your father. Will you answer my questions?"

"I cannot tell you! Why did you wait until now to ask me this? Why didn't you say something on our journey to Cadiz?"

"I didn't want to distress you."

"So you distress me now?"

"I am sorry, Bianca. Will you forgive me?"

She didn't answer him.

"Bianca, you must trust me. I cannot help you if you do not have faith in me, and you cannot continue doing this by yourself. It is too dangerous!"

"Have you told my father?"

"No. I thought about it, but then I realized that your father cannot stop you, and neither can I. That is why I want to help you."

"Why should I trust you?"

"Because I love you, and I cannot have you in this danger."

"That is not good enough."

He stood up, exasperated with her. Bianca sat calmly and

watched him stand before the fire. She waited. Finally, he sat down again and faced her.

"Tell me about the people you help, Bianca."

"They are Moriscos, converts who have been forced to abandon their Islamic religion. Some have lost their families to the purgings. There is nowhere for them to turn. They hold to their faith and practice in secret. When they are suspected by the priests, they are burned to death, Amahl. Even the children are murdered."

"Before I returned here, I believed this area was purged of my people."

"Then you and all who believe like you are fools. The persecutions have never stopped. Your people continue to die."

"So they came to you?"

"No. They came to Khalid."

"Khalid is Moslem."

"Yes, he is, but his wife, Sara, is my father's cook, and she is Jewish. They have helped people for many years."

"How did you become involved in it?"

"I overheard Sara and Khalid talking in the stables one evening. I insisted on joining them."

He looked at her without speaking. His concern for her was evident, so she continued her story.

"Someone must help them, Amahl. My father's estate is one of the few farms along the coast. From the beach, we can meet the ships. The people are taken to Morocco and Constantinople. It is the only way they can survive."

She was pleading with him now, her eyes begging him to understand.

"Bianca, you must not continue smuggling people from the beach. You are all too exposed. I want to offer you the tunnel. The people will be safe waiting there, and at high tide they can board the longboats without the risk of being seen. Please let me help you?"

"Do you mean after we are married?"

"No, I mean now, before our marriage. The people can come here, instead of waiting on the beach. Do you realize the danger you are in, Bianca?"

She did not answer, for she was bewildered by his proposal. Why should he risk his own safety to help the Moriscos when he had once fought for the King who was driving them out? She rose from her chair and walked to the door. Amahl followed her, and as he opened the door for her, she turned and looked at him.

"I must discuss this with Khalid and Sara. There are others involved. I cannot make this decision alone."

He began to object, but seeing her resolve, he surrendered to her determination. Silently, they walked to the stables and saddled their horses. As they rode their tired mounts along the beach to the de Lucena villa, Amahl wanted to continue their discussion, but she changed the subject to address another concern.

"There is something we need to discuss that I feel is of greater importance than the tunnel, Amahl."

She saw him nod in agreement, so she continued.

"We do not share the same faith."

"Others have married and overcome these differences."

"You must not be very devout to your faith, Amahl."

"I believe you are right."

He sighed, looking out to sea as the dawn rose. The moon was across the sky and now hung suspended like a white ghost above the horizon.

"I have seen so much violence in the name of God. So many have died. All my life, I have witnessed, and even participated in, this violence. I am not proud of many of the things I have done. I cannot even excuse myself and blame my ignorance. But I believe there must be something more—something to give meaning to my life. Perhaps I will have the opportunity to redeem myself in the sight of Allah. There are so many burdens on my conscience, Bianca. I seek peace for my soul, and a family and wife I can love. If you love me, Bianca, then surely God and His angels must love me, also."

He looked at her with longing, but she was silent for several moments.

"And our marriage will give your life meaning, Amahl?"

He studied her, considering his answer.

"I want the family that was taken from me. I want children, and I want to be here to raise them. I want sons to stand by my side, and daughters to cherish, and I want you to love me, Bianca. I know we are of different faiths, but I believe we both love God, and that, together, we can teach our children to love God. Isn't that all that matters?"

"You imagine simple solutions to difficult problems, Amahl."

"Where is the difficulty?"

"How would our children be taught, and what faith would we teach them?"

"They would be taught according to your wishes, Bianca. I promise you that."

"Would you give up your faith?"

"No. I could never abandon my beliefs, but I would not expect you to abandon yours. It is a mother's duty to teach her children, and while I would help you fulfill these duties, I would never interfere, nor will I allow anyone else to interfere."

"It is going to rain. Do you see the clouds, Amahl?"

Gilt-edged clouds were dissipating as an orange sunrise began to emerge.

"We must hurry, Bianca. I hope your father is not too angry with us. Will he be waiting, do you think?"

"Look up there, Amahl. He is coming toward us. See, on the bluff? He is coming down the trail. Hurry, we will meet him."

Bianca spurred her horse and rode to greet her father. Amahl followed slowly, for he was reluctant to meet Naphtali, anticipating his anger. When Amahl caught up with Bianca, she had her arms around her father's neck. Naphtali looked at Amahl with consternation as he held his daughter.

"I see you are safe, Bianca. How foolish of you to run off like that."

"Father, of course I am safe. I was with the general. You said yourself that he is a man of integrity, so I felt it would be all right for me to go to Cadiz with him. Surely, you did not worry, Father?"

Bianca smiled at her father, charming him into compliance.

"Your duenna has not returned, or there would have been a terrible scandal. But you are safe, I can see. I was worried, Bianca."

He turned to Amahl, a stern expression on his face.

"Señor de Lucena, forgive me please. We didn't wish to distress you, but I wanted to show your daughter her first horse auction."

"And the *feria*, Father. We went to the *feria*. It was so wonderful. I saw many things."

Naphtali was silent, still holding his daughter in his arms. Then he glared again at Amahl.

"Your Grace, again, forgive me. I had no intention of causing scandal . . . "

"Father, I have decided to marry the general, as you have requested. We wish to be married before Pesach."

"Marriage! You have agreed? Oh, this is good news."

He reached out and grabbed Amahl's outstretched hand. He shook it so hard that Amahl found it difficult to sit his horse. The rain began as the three rode toward the villa. Naphtali was so happy and forgiving that he lifted Bianca from her saddle and sat her in front of him on his horse. She laughed and hugged her father and, grinning, looked back at Amahl.

The gloom of the storm-darkening sky was momentarily lifted by lightning. The brightness of dawn disappeared completely as the three raced their horses up the hill, the rain pelting them. Naphtali shouted to Amahl and Bianca.

"Come! We have plans to make. Before Pesach, eh? There is not much time. A party must be planned for after the wedding. Food must be prepared!"

He reined in his horse and turned to Amahl, still holding Bianca with one arm. He pointed his finger at Amahl.

"No more kidnappings before the wedding, eh, General? I will forgive you this time, as I know you are an honorable man, but no more! We are lucky. Señora Martinez was not here. By now, the entire *aljama* would know! She is such a gossip. Now she will need another position!"

He turned and spurred his horse, shouting for Hernando as they entered the courtyard in front of the villa. The three of them stepped into the entryway and shook the rain from their clothing. Naphtali went ahead of them, and his voice could be heard throughout the house.

"Sara, Sara, where are you? Prepare a feast! We must celebrate. My daughter will wed the Moor. Hurry, bring the wine!"

Bianca stood in the foyer and looked at Amahl with relief. Her eyes reflected fatigue as she went to him. He placed his arms around her and held her for a long moment.

"Bianca, my love. Will you really marry me in the spring?"

"Yes, Amahl, and I will be a good wife to you."

"Your father is very happy."

"He loves us both. We are so fortunate."

"Will you give him my apologies? I must return to my estate and care for the animals. I will come back this afternoon. We will discuss our plans."

"Yes, I will tell him."

Amahl left the villa, and Bianca watched from the window as he mounted his horse. The sudden rainfall had stopped, and the puddles in the small courtyard reflected the brilliant sunrise as he rode his horse through the gate. The lane leading away from the courtyard was slightly flooded, and as the stallion moved through the water, its hooves splashed golden droplets behind Amahl.

✣

15

⁕

Naphtali understood that the news of his daughter's approaching marriage would reach the ears of the community rather quickly, but he did not expect the rabbi to appear at his door within the week. He arrived one morning as Naphtali finished his morning prayers.

Moses Rodriguez, the chief rabbi, was a poet of great sensitivity. His family, like Naphtali's, had been in southern Spain since the first Moslem conquest of A.D. 711. Uriah Rivera, who accompanied him, was Naphtali's fellow merchant and brother-in-law. They had often journeyed together, each in separate ships. They had offered each other protection as they evaded the marauding Moorish pirates that plied the Mediterranean. The two had been friends since childhood.

Naphtali called for refreshments as he motioned his visitors into his study. He was grateful that Bianca was at the stables.

"You honor my house, Rabbi. And my dear friend and brother-in-law, as always, I am so pleased to see you. How was your latest journey? Successful, I hope? I must come soon to your warehouse. Perhaps we can do business again."

"We have come on an urgent mission, your Grace. We are here because of our friendship and love for you and your daughter, the Donzella Bianca."

Naphtali turned to Moses and waited in silence.

"We come to your house today, because we have been advised of your intention to marry your daughter to the Moor, Amahl Cozar. Is this true, your Grace?"

"Yes, it is true. They will marry in the spring just before Pesach."

"I am saddened to hear this." Moses paused and looked at Uriah, but Uriah, embarrassed by their intrusion, stared at the floor before him. Moses continued:

"We have come to implore you to abandon these plans, Naphtali. The Donzella must not marry the Moor."

"Why? He is an honorable man. He has become like a son to me, and Bianca loves him."

"Yes, I understand this, but it must not take place."

Uriah went to him, his arms outstretched and imploring.

"My brother, you know we must protest. Our community grows smaller because of the many interfaith marriages that have taken place over the years. Whether these alliances are with Moslems or Catholics, the children are usually lost to our community. We must not allow this to continue."

"Moses, Uriah, we have lived and intermarried with the Christians and Moslems for generations. I agree that many times the children are lost to us, but this will not be our experience with Bianca's children. She would never fail to teach her children our religious rituals."

"How can you be certain of this? Do you not concern yourself with the heritage of your grandchildren?"

"The happiness of my daughter is much more important to me, Moses."

Undaunted by Naphtali's disagreement, Moses continued:

"How can we be certain that the Moor will allow your daughter to teach their children?"

"Because he is an honorable man. He loves my daughter. During the winter months, the General and I have had many long conversations about his and Bianca's children. Do you think I would give my permission if I thought he would care little for Bianca's happiness?"

"She can be happy married to one of our young men in the community!"

"If that was true, Rabbi, she would have married long ago."

"If you had not made the tragic mistake of educating her, she would have married and taken her proper place in our community."

"And she would not have been happy, Uriah. You have known Bianca since she was a child. You know she is a good and kind woman, a very virtuous young woman. She is outspoken, of course, but she would have been that way whether or not I had educated her."

"If her mother had lived, Bianca would be a mother now. She would attend temple and sit in her proper place with the women."

"I don't believe this is true, Moses. In any case, her mother is not alive, and Bianca is still a virtuous young woman. She will marry the Moor, and that is as it should be. My daughter's happiness is very important to me. I feel it is a blessing that, when I die, I will die knowing Bianca is loved and cared for."

"Your Grace, you must concern yourself with the *halakhic* unity of our people."

"Yes, of course, and I do. I just do not believe my daughter's marriage will affect our solidarity. Someday, we will see Bianca's sons celebrate their Bar Mitzvot. Even you will be proud of them."

"We beg you to reconsider this alliance. The Christians are slowly succeeding in driving the Moors from Spain. It is only a matter of time before the last Moor is defeated. Have you thought of the next victim of this religious zeal?"

"You are not suggesting that it will be the Sepharad, Moses?"

"On the contrary, the persecutions against the Sepharad have continued since the horrors of Seville!"

"I cannot believe this. Uriah, do you agree with Moses?"

"The stories reach us. The forced conversions have not stopped."

"But our people have contributed so much to Spain. By trade alone, we have shared our wealth with the Christians. And you, Moses, a poet. Surely, you can appreciate the contributions our people have made to literature and music. We are the educators in the great universities. Drive us out, and what would the Christians do to educate their children? No, no, I cannot believe you fear persecution from the Spanish King. Why, we have financed his war against the Moors. He will never betray us!"

"You must not be naive, your Grace. As long as he needs our gold to pay his armies, he will leave us alone, but what about when the war is over? What then? You must think about this. You are one of the leaders of our community. You must not let your daughter set an example of intermarriage."

"My friends, I understand your concerns, and I have heard your advice, and I tell you now, with love and respect, that my daughter will marry the Moor. I do not share your fears. My only concern has been for my daughter's happiness. Perhaps it is selfish of me, but you must indulge an old man who has suffered many losses in this life. Bianca's children will be my heirs. They will be raised in our faith, and Bianca will be happy."

As Naphtali walked out of the room, he added, "You would honor us if you would stay to share our evening meal." He stopped at the door and turned, waiting for his visitors' response.

Moses and Uriah understood that their conversation was over. As they gave him their regrets, Bianca burst into the hall. Her hair was disheveled, and her clothes were smudged with sand.

"Uncle Uriah, how good to see you." She turned to the rabbi and bowed respectfully, all the while trying to rearrange her errant curls from beneath her cap. She had been riding her favorite mare along the beach, and had fallen from the horse as she jumped over a large piece of driftwood. Bianca tried to keep the three men from seeing the back of her dress. It was split up the middle again, and she was attempting to get around them so that she could go to her room to change.

"Father, did you tell them about my wedding?" She smiled at her Uncle Uriah.

"Of course, my darling. That is why they are here. To congratulate you, and to help you with your plans for the ceremony." He looked at Moses, and waited.

"We wish you happiness, Donzella." He was stiff in his formality.

"Thank you, Rabbi." She turned to Uriah.

"I understand Amahl Cozar is a fine man. Your Aunt Rycha also sends her best wishes to you. Your happiness has always been important to us."

Bianca reached up and hugged Uriah. Since her earliest memories, he and Rycha had been like a second set of parents to her. They had objected to her being tutored with her brother, but Bianca had persevered, and in the end had won their approval.

"Come to my home with your father next week, Bianca. We will choose a most auspicious day for the marriage ceremony."

Moses turned to Naphtali. "Your Grace, we will take our leave now. Thank you for the dinner invitation. Another time, perhaps."

He held out his hand to his host, and then turned and walked out the door, Uriah following, kissing Bianca on the cheek as he left. As they mounted their horses, held steady by the groom, Naphtali placed his arm around his daughter. They waved their guests away, and Bianca turned to enter the house. She ran up the stairs, and her father spotted the tear in her dress. Shaking his head, poured himself a glass of wine and went into the dining room to await his dinner.

✠

16

※

The people of Tarifa spoke of Bianca de Lucena's wedding for many generations. It was treated with the care of legends, and each listener was certain that he had been told a fantasy.

Sara oversaw a crew of women as they cleaned the castle. Every room was aired, swept, and dusted. Floors were scrubbed, carpets and rugs were hung beneath the olive trees on great frames built by Khalid. In every room of the castle, the stone walls were scoured.

Seven seamstresses were at work creating Bianca's wedding gown. Bolts of silk organza were brought from the warehouses of Bianca's uncle. A dress was designed under the supervision of Aunt Rycha as Bianca endured hours of standing for the head seamstress.

"Donzella, stand still. If you keep moving about, the hem will be crooked!"

"Aunt Rycha, I am tired. Can we do this tomorrow?"

"No." She turned to one of the seamstresses.

"Help me place this over the Donzella's head. Be careful of the pins."

They lowered the underdress and secured the lacings at Bianca's back. The bodice of the silk organza dress was forced into hundreds of tiny pleats, each one hand-stitched and pressed. The pleats ended at the empire waist as the gown fell into voluminous folds to her velvet and brocade slippers.

Rycha stood back and admired the creation. The seamstresses

gathered around Bianca's stool and began pinning the hem. Bianca swayed as an overdress of heavy ivory silk, embroidered with French knots in white and silver threads, was placed over the organza gown. The silk threads caused the dress to glisten and shimmer in the light.

At Bianca's shoulders, a train of silk brocade was attached. It stood free and trailed down to cover the floor behind her. She felt like a wilting flower under the weight of the dress. Losing patience with the seamstresses' attention, she stepped down from the stool, holding the gown with both hands to keep it from dragging on the floor.

"Enough, I feel like a pincushion!"

"Donzella, you must get back on the stool. We are not finished."

"Aunt Rycha, I am finished. The gown is beautiful. All of you have worked so hard, and I am grateful, but the hem is marked. You surely can finish it now without me. Please, Aunt Rycha?"

Her aunt dismissed the seamstresses and helped Bianca take off the dress. In her shift, the young woman collapsed onto a chair. Already the weather was warming. It was an early spring, and she and Amahl would have a beautiful day for their wedding.

Rycha pulled a chair over to Bianca's seat, and faced her niece.

"My dear, your father has asked me to talk to you."

"About what?"

She placed her hand on Bianca's knee and brought her face close to the young woman.

"About your wedding night?"

"My wedding night?"

"Yes. If your poor mother were here, she would have this talk with you. Since she is not, it has fallen on me."

"What about my wedding night, Aunt Rycha? Is there something I must know?"

She looked at her aunt with feigned innocence.

"Bianca, you may not mock me. There are things you must understand before you are married."

"For instance?"

"Well, for instance, do you know how babies are made?"

"Nooo, Aunt Rycha, only how horses are made. Surely, it can't be the same for people!"

Bianca was trying to resist a laugh. She wanted to take pity on her aunt, but her sense of mischief overcame her.

Rycha looked at her niece, shocked at what she had said.

"You have seen horses?"

"You forget, Aunt Rycha, I breed horses."

"That is shameful! Doesn't your father know better?"

"Father does not know at all. He thinks Hernando takes charge of that."

Aghast, Rycha stood up and backed away from Bianca. She started crying. Bianca followed her aunt and put her arms around her.

"Aunt Rycha, I should not have spoken to you like that. Please forgive me."

"Oh, my dear, I have failed your mother. You must forgive me."

"No, Auntie, you have been very good to me. I have always been grateful to you. Now what is it you want to tell me?"

"Just that your will is to your husband. You must always remember that."

Knowing she must not upset her aunt anymore, Bianca answered with as much solemnity as she could muster.

"Yes, Aunt Rycha. To my husband. I will remember that."

Rycha held her niece for several moments before releasing her.

"We are all very proud of you, Bianca, and we love you very much."

Still solemn, Bianca kissed her aunt and left the room. Pulling her robe about her, she muffled her laughter as she hurried down the hallway to her bedchamber.

17

꩜

The morning of her wedding day, Bianca answered her aunt's call to dress for the ceremony, standing obediently as Rycha fastened her veil.

"A gift arrived this morning from your betrothed."

Rycha reached behind her to a small table and took out a package wrapped in red silk. She handed it to Bianca.

"The General brought this? Where is he? Is he still here?"

"No, he has left already with Khalid and Sara. They are waiting for you at the synagogue."

"What is it?"

She looked at her aunt, her eyes lit with excitement. Rycha helped Bianca untie the silk to reveal Amahl's gift: a necklace of pearls. Bianca gasped as she lifted the pearls and held them to the light.

"These are mine? Are they not beautiful? Here, help me put them on."

She handed the pearls to her aunt and turned around. Holding her veil to the side, she waited with impatience as Rycha secured them at the back of her neck. Bianca went to the mirror and stared as the pearls shimmered against the pleated bodice.

"Such a beautiful gift, Bianca. These are pearls fit for a queen. This man must love you very much."

Bianca was still staring into the mirror when she heard a commotion beneath her bedchamber window. She went to the window and opened the casement. In the courtyard below was a carriage drawn by four white Andalusian horses. Her father stood by the open door of the carriage and looked up at his daughter.

"It is time for your wedding, my daughter. Come, we must go now to the synagogue."

"I am ready, Father."

She left the room, moving as quickly as her heavy garments would allow. The pristine whiteness of the carriage nearly blinded Bianca as she entered with the help of two of her seamstresses.

Naphtali looked at his daughter with pride as Rycha and Uriah entered another carriage to follow behind them.

"You look beautiful, Bianca. Such a happy day for you. I am so proud, and your mother, may she rest in peace, would be proud of you, also."

"Oh, Father, my gown is so heavy." She began laughing at her father. "Do you think I will be able to move in it? You and Aunt Rycha will have to carry me down the aisle, or else I will fall to my knees before I ever reach my groom."

Naphtali joined her in her laughter, tears streaming down his face.

"No, Bianca, you will float down the aisle like the angel you are."

"Father, there are not wings strong enough to lift me from the ground."

"Bianca, do you know how pleased I am for you? The general loves you so much."

"And I love him, too, Father. You were right about him. He does not seek to imprison me. I have always been afraid of that."

"But you are not afraid anymore?"

"No, Father. I am happy."

At the synagogue, Bianca looked for Amahl among the guests

gathered outside waiting for her as she was being helped out of the carriage. When she couldn't find him, she allowed herself to be led into the temple to wait until it was time for the ceremony to begin.

The four corners of the *huppah* were held by Bianca's aunt and three women from the community as Rabbi Rodriguez performed the ceremony. There was a hush at the end as Amahl broke the glass beneath his heel. The *huppah* was dropped by the four women, and the beautiful fabric floated down, enclosing Amahl and Bianca within its symbolic protection.

The entire congregation was smiling, wishing the couple happiness. Bianca hugged her father, her Uncle Uriah, and her Aunt Rycha, who had tears in her eyes. Even the rabbi broke into laughter as he congratulated the pair.

Fifty carriages escorted the guests to the Cozar estate for the wedding feast. The lane leading to the castle's entrance had been planted weeks before with hyacinths and roses. Crushed white marble was spread on the drive.

In their carriage, Amahl and Bianca waved to the guests as the white Andalusians raced ahead of the conveyance line.

"You look so beautiful, Bianca. Do you like the pearls?" asked Amahl.

"They are the most elegant gift I have ever received. Wherever did you get them?"

"The pearls belonged to my mother. I know she would want you to have them."

Bianca put her hand to her neck, fingering the pearls.

"I will cherish them forever, Amahl."

He reached across the carriage and kissed her as they arrived at the front door of the castle.

"Is everything prepared? I should have come this morning to help Sara, but Aunt Rycha said that I mustn't see you on the morning of the wedding. I looked for you anyway."

A footman opened the door, and Amahl left the carriage. He turned and lifted Bianca to the ground.

"Sara has been here all morning. There were many women helping her. I think you will be pleased."

They entered the castle, Bianca on the arm of her new husband. In the great hall, the scents of pale blue hyacinth and tiny white roses intermingled with orange blossoms and pale pink carnations. The flowers were banked about the room behind great trestle tables covered with white linen cloths.

Bianca gasped with pleasure as they entered. The guests followed to find a tremendous feast. There they enjoyed cheese-filled pastry turnovers, cheese soufflés, and small crystal pots trembling with golden flan, the caramelized sugar dripping over the rims, staining the linen cloths. Loaves of *challah* were placed among fruit jellies and various cheeses for the guests. Children reached into large silver bowls filled with *huevos haminados*, eggs cooked all night over smoldering coals of braziers. One elderly couple, dressed in their finest, admired carved mahogany bowls of apples, grapes, oranges, olives, and figs. Nestled on small platters were heaps of quince, simmered long hours until they crystallized into candy, served in squares.

As Bianca and Amahl enjoyed the feast, the guests began serenading the newlyweds, singing *romanzas*. The sound of the Spanish ballads filled the room. The old women of Bianca's congregation came to her and wished her well. Not wanting the day to end, the bride, the groom, and their guests celebrated through the night. No one noticed when Bianca and Amahl stole up the stairs. He

led her into the circular room where, several days earlier, the two
had unpacked her books. Now, exhausted and happy, they reveled
in the silence of the isolated room.

A pale dawn reflected its lilac colors onto the whitewashed
wall opposite the windows as Amahl and Bianca fell into a deep
sleep.

Downstairs, the carriages left one by one, the guests sated and
sleepy. The sky was fully lit when Simon and Uriah drove a very
happy Naphtali home to his bed. The servants would not serve
the wedding breakfast until late morning, when the newly married
couple would ride to the de Lucena estate to retrieve the horses.

From the memoir of
Meschianza de Lucena Cozar-Velasquez
March 3, 1495
Lisbon

My earliest memories are of my grandfather telling me of his marriage to my grandmother. He spoke of it often, and it seemed that he would revisit this time when he described it to me. I do not believe he was aware of the tears that filled his eyes. Telling the stories comforted him.

I know they became a legend in the community as they drove the forty-two horses from the de Lucena estate to the stables behind the castle.

Dressed in dark green velvet, my grandmother shocked the countryside and rode beside my grandfather as the stable boys from the de Lucena estate joined together to herd the horses along the water, the hooves of the horses kicking up sand and disturbing great flights of birds along the shore. The mares, their manes flowing in the wind, were chest high in the water. My grandmother rode behind my grandfather and the stable boys, herding the colts that fell behind their mothers. The ocean air was invigorating, and her cheeks were glowing. My grandfather said she was glorious in her green velvet gown, the ocean spray falling on her dark hair. She sat her horse with a certainty that he had never felt, even in the height of battle.

As they entered the castle, Sara was in the kitchen preparing their evening meal. She and Khalid had agreed to live there and work for my grandparents.

The great hall was filled with trunks and wooden crates containing my grandmother's dowry. Gifts from the Sepharad community spilled over the large wooden rectory tables that lined the walls of the immense room. My grandmother walked from table to table, discovering a pair of chairs, gilt gesso framed and upholstered in Genoese velvet. There were vessels worked in gold and silver, bolts of woolen fabrics, jewels and spices, timepieces and potpourri vases.

As Amahl watched her, Bianca began searching through the heavy crates from her father's villa.

"Bianca, what are you looking for?"

"My ledgers. My lists."

"I have secured them in the cellar. It is not wise to keep them in the castle."

She looked at him and nodded in agreement.

They went into the sitting room, where he moved a chair closer to the fire and led Bianca to it. He covered her with a deep purple down-filled quilt that Sara had placed on the chair earlier that day, while he sat across from her and watched Bianca as she fell asleep.

I wonder if my grandmother's dreams were filled with the scent of hyacinths and roses as her exhaustion carried her into her own blessed oblivion.

18

✢

From the earliest days of her marriage, Bianca often left the castle in the gray dawn to go to the stables. Sometimes Amahl accompanied her, but one morning she awoke to find Amahl had already left their bed. She dressed and went downstairs to the kitchen to find him sitting at the breakfast table, talking to Khalid. As Bianca joined him, Sara brought her a cup of steaming coffee. She had prepared it the way Bianca liked it, with hot milk and honey.

"Why have you risen so early? It is not yet dawn."

"The orange trees have shed their white blossoms, and new, tiny green fruit is beginning to appear. Khalid and I will be very busy now. Today we will start rebuilding the irrigation system."

Sipping her coffee, Bianca looked at Khalid, then at her husband.

"Khalid, have you been contacted by Captain Morales? With summer approaching, and warmer weather, the sea is growing calm."

"Yes. Two nights ago, his man came to the stables to tell me that the captain will arrive next week. Sara will speak to the rabbi today. Is that correct, Sara? You will not forget?"

"I have already sent a message to him. He is alerted."

"Good!" He turned to Amahl and grinned. "My Lord General, I am grateful to you that you offer the tunnel for the people. Last night, I saw the first soldiers patrol the beaches. The tide was in, and the water too high for them to venture near the tunnel. Your plan will work."

Amahl nodded and arose from the table. He bent forward and kissed Bianca on the cheek, then turned to leave the kitchen, Khalid following him.

"Sara, we must go to my father's estate today and bring more linens and blankets. We have much to do before the first group of refugees arrive. We must have more food on hand. You will send for the *shochet*?"

"It is done. He will arrive tomorrow morning, and his wife will come to begin the baking. I have forgotten nothing."

She cleared the table, and Bianca left the kitchen. Satisfied with her work, Sara went to the stables to tell Hernando to prepare the wagon.

Within days, she and Bianca, Khalid, and Amahl were smuggling the frightened families onto the waiting ship during the nights when there was only a sliver of a new moon.

Sara harvested the vegetable garden, and soon the pantry shelves revealed her careful cultivation of the herbs that grew next to the kitchen door. The scent of some of the elixirs she created drifted throughout the castle as the two couples went about their daily lives.

Hernando was proud of his new responsibilities as he helped Bianca care for the horses in the stable. He and the two stable boys from the de Lucena estate lived in the stables and continued in their duties caring for the horses.

Amahl spent most evenings in the circular room with Bianca, writing in the ledgers and recording the activities of the farm they were restoring.

"We will have good crops this year, Bianca. Already the olives are fat, and the oranges cause the tree limbs to sag from their weight. There is plenty of water in the wells."

"Do you miss your travels, Amahl? Do you miss being a soldier?"

He looked at her with adoration. She had changed into a pale green silk gown and was sitting on the floor, pillows at her back and books surrounding her. A ledger was in her lap, and she was waving her feathered quill about as she spoke to him. Even when Bianca was sitting still, she appeared to be moving.

"I should have come home years earlier. I would have found you long ago."

"Perhaps not. Perhaps we would never have met. You were there to help us when we needed you. Father believes it was fate that brought us together."

"Yes, surely it was fate."

"Amahl, when will we go to the auction again? And the *feria?* Will it be soon?"

"Yes, soon."

"Can we sleep on the beach?"

"We don't have to. I don't need to hide you. We can stay in the *hostals.*"

"I like the beach better. We can pretend we are peasants again."

He stood and lifted her to her feet. His arm around her waist, he led her from the room.

"You like that, don't you—being a peasant? Will you dance for me on the beach?"

"I will dance for you anywhere, Amahl."

Their life continued in this manner for three months, until one morning when Bianca stayed in bed later than usual. When she did not come downstairs for the spartan breakfast Sara prepared for the household, the older woman went in search of her.

"Señora Cozar, are you awake? Forgive me for disturbing you, but I was concerned, as you did not appear for breakfast. The general and my husband have already left for the groves."

Bianca was lying on her pillows, her arm shielding her eyes from the light as Sara opened the draperies at each window. Her head hurt, and her stomach was upset.

"I am ill. I believe I have a fever."

Sara went to the bed and placed her hand on Bianca's forehead.

"Your brow does not feel hot. Would you like me to bring you something to drink? Perhaps a biscuit?"

Bianca made a face and rolled over onto her pillows as Sara watched her. She pulled a chair to the side of the bed and sat on it. She took Bianca's hand and found it cold and clammy. Sara left the room, returning several moments later, carrying a tisane.

"Señora, drink this."

Bianca looked at the cup and began to turn away in revulsion.

"It will make you feel better. I promise you. Trust me."

Bianca could barely lift her head, so Sara helped her up. Holding the cup before the young woman's lips, she helped her drink, then lowered her back onto the pillows and waited. Slowly, the color returned to Bianca's face. She opened her eyes and looked at Sara with gratitude.

"What did you give me?"

"Something for the baby," Sara said smugly.

"The baby?"

"Yes. The baby! Your child."

"How do you know? You can't be certain."

Bianca lifted the blankets and stared at her stomach. She sat up, the nausea overwhelming her again. She reached for the cup on the bedside table and drank the remainder of the tisane. She waited for the nausea to pass, and then rose from the bed and went into her dressing room.

"Where are you going?"

"To tell the general."

"Madam, you can tell him when he returns. Now you must go back to bed."

"Why? I feel fine now. The horses must be fed and watered."

"Hernando is doing that. You must rest now and think of the baby. Why are you taking your riding crop?"

"To ride, of course."

She dodged Sara and ran from the room.

19

✤

Bianca continued to ride until her fifth month of pregnancy. She finally had to surrender to Sara's admonitions. When Bianca arrived at the breakfast table, she was pulling at the waist of her riding habit. It was too snug, and she was not comfortable.

"My lady, surely you will not ride again this morning!"

"Well, perhaps not, Sara. I am getting fat, aren't I?"

"No, it is not that you are getting fat. It is that the baby is growing. You must not ride until he is born."

Amahl, sitting at the table drinking his coffee, had not said anything yet. He had been uneasy all week, watching Bianca ride through the orchards.

"Bianca, my darling, come. I will walk with you. The meadows are in full bloom."

"Don't you have to go to the orchards?"

"No. Khalid is in charge there. The baby and you are important now. The oranges will grow by themselves."

She began taking daily walks through the meadows, and Amahl, wishing to protect Bianca and their child from the harmful influences of the *jinn* Al-shaytan, would accompany her.

"Who is Al-shaytan, and why are you afraid of him? I cannot imagine you being afraid of anything, Amahl."

"My mother was taught by her grandmother that the demon *jinn* are made of fire, unlike the angels, who are made of light. She taught me that the *jinn* are earthbound, cast out of heaven, but the angels' light falls from the sky with every drop of rain."

He smiled at her and took her hand, helping her over a rock that jutted out of the ground in front of them.

"Oh, Amahl, I feel like a great cow about to give birth."

"But you are not a cow, Bianca, and this baby is not a calf. He is my son!"

"Tell me more about demons, Amahl."

"The *jinn* will be jealous of our unborn child, but the angels will protect him."

Bianca watched the sunlight fall through the olive grove, imagining the angels safeguarding her children.

Later that day, Bianca and Sara gathered fabrics for the baby clothes. Sara went to work sewing the clothing with the tiny stitches she had been taught by her grandmother.

"How do you do that, Sara? Show me."

"You mean no one taught you to sew, madam?"

"No. I didn't want to learn. My Aunt Rycha tried to teach me, but I would not sit still."

She chose one of the garments and sat next to Sara. Watching her, she picked up a needle and tried to thread it.

"Here, let me show you. You must wet the end of it first, like this. Now see. Place it in the hole and catch it as it goes through."

Bianca, a look of accomplishment on her face, was quick to despair as she poked the needle into her finger.

"Now you are a true seamstress."

Bianca was holding her finger in the air, trying not to let it bleed on the fabric, when her father entered the room.

"At last, the cradle is finished. I thought the craftsman would not have it done in time, but I hurried him. Every day, I have gone to the village and checked on his progress, and now we have the cradle!"

He placed it in front of Bianca with a satisfied grin. Bianca, delighted, started rocking the cradle as her father looked about the room.

"This chamber needs paint. I will find Khalid. He will paint this room tomorrow. Everything must be ready for my grandson."

He started to leave the room, but instead he turned back and went over to his daughter. Placing his hand on her cheek, he asked her, "How are you today, my angel? And the baby, does he do well?"

By late summer, the household prepared for the birth of Bianca's baby. Amahl wagered with Naphtali whether the baby would be born before or after Hanukkah. As her time neared, Bianca could no longer navigate the stairs without help, so Amahl brought many of her favorite books from the small library and piled them onto the floor around the bed in their bedchamber. There Bianca spent the last autumn days reading and napping.

"Amahl, you were right. I am not a cow. I am a brood mare."

Amahl was relaxing in a chair across from her. The olive harvest had been as successful as he had predicted. The oranges were almost bursting on their branches. He looked at his wife, and in his contentment, he could not resist teasing her.

"A prize mare, my darling. A prize mare."

Their son, Rafael, was born two days before Hanukkah, and Naphtali lost his bet. Cheerfully, he doled out the winnings to the victor. Unable to leave his new grandson, Naphtali took up residence in one of the bedchambers on the third floor of his daughter's home. His loneliness had been acute after Bianca's wedding. Semiretired, he did little business with the merchants.

"My father, you must come and live with us. Bianca needs you, and I need you, too."

"Perhaps you are right, Amahl. With Bianca gone, I eat alone.

I have even lost my joy in the creativity of my new cook. My staff keeps my house running efficiently, and now that the horses are in your stables, my life at the villa has changed. Yes, I will come and live here. You are too generous."

Soon his life was centered around his grandson. In the early morning hours, Naphtali was the first to enter the baby's room. He stood by Rafael's bed and watched him sleep. It was only now, since the death of his son, that Naphtali was at peace as he waited patiently for his grandson to awaken. The silence of the room was broken only by the baby's soft breathing.

Often Bianca joined him. She entered with the sunlight, opening the drapes and bringing warmth to the chamber. As she stood by the cradle, Naphtali smiled as she whispered her morning prayers over the child. Soon Rafael stirred, and it was a contest to see who would pick him up. Usually, Naphtali deferred to Bianca, but there were mornings when he could not wait to nuzzle the sleepy baby against his neck.

"He purrs like a new kitten, doesn't he, Bianca?"

"Yes, Father. He is wonderful, and so tiny."

He handed the baby to his daughter, and waited as she sang him awake.

The wetnurse took the baby from Bianca. She hurried him into dry clothing and returned him to his mother for his morning feeding. Naphtali descended the stairs and watched as Sara prepared the family's morning meal. The family ate breakfast together, then Naphtali hovered over the nurse as she prepared the baby for an outing. He handed her Rafael's clothes, and as she dressed him, Naphtali, in his eager clumsiness, often got in her way. She tolerated the old man's interference, for Rafael smiled at his grandfather, delighting in his attention.

With lunch in a basket, a bottle of Naphtali's favorite wine tucked in next to the chicken, he and Sara took the baby out to the meadow below the stables. There, while Rafael napped in the warm sunlight, Naphtali taught Sara how to read.

"Why do you drink so much, your Grace?" Sara asked him.

"Often I believe I do not drink enough."

"You set a bad example for your grandson!"

Naphtali looked down at the baby with tenderness.

"He is asleep. He cannot see his grandfather drinking this fine wine."

"As he grows, he will see. With all respect, sir, you must stop drinking the wine."

He picked up the bottle and emptied it onto the grass. Sara watched him, then reached into the pocket of her skirt and took out a leather thong with a small brocaded pouch. She offered it to Naphtali.

"What is this, Sara?"

"It is a token, an amulet that will bring you peace. I made it for you. You must wear it around your neck."

"What is in it?" Naphtali took the amulet, lifted it to his nose, and sniffed it.

"I have placed the light of the angels in it for you."

"It must be a very small light."

"Your Grace, don't blaspheme. Do not insult the messengers of God when they offer their light to you. If you intend to stop drinking wine, you need the help of the angels to do it."

She took the amulet and tied it around Naphtali's neck, then leaned back and admired her work. Naphtali looked down at the red and gold pouch.

"Sara, how is it that you practice this magic? How old are you now?"

"I am forty-six, and my father taught me the magic. His grandmother taught it to him, because he had no sisters."

She smiled at the old man. Naphtali placed the amulet into his shirt and reached for the wine bottle again. Remembering that he had emptied it, he looked at Sara.

"The sun is beginning to go down. We must return Rafael to his nurse, or she will be unhappy with us."

Sara lifted the baby to her shoulder while Naphtali gathered up the basket and blanket. When they were ready to walk back to the castle, Naphtali looked kindly at her.

"Thank you for giving me the amulet, for your gift of the angels' light."

As they walked back to the castle, their shadows led them up the path. A haze was forming above the sea cliffs, and in the distance came the sound of Amahl's chants. The fog would come in tonight, and the air was beginning to chill from it. Soon spring would be upon them, bringing warmth and new life.

✢

20

In less than two years, Benjamin was born, and then Mathias a year later. Benjamin was sturdy and strong like his older brother, but Mathias was a fragile baby, slow to gain weight. Bianca awoke before dawn one morning. It was still very dark when she entered the baby's room. A dark premonition prompted her to hurry to his cradle. When she touched the baby's cheek, he was cold. She tried to rouse him, but to no avail. Her screams woke the household, but it was Amahl who found her first.

She was sitting in a chair next to the cradle, the baby in her arms. She was rocking Mathias and calling his name. Amahl knelt before her and tried to take the baby from her, but she would not let go of him. Terrified, the nurse ran from the room.

"Bianca? Bianca, what is wrong? Why—?

"He is sleeping! Only sleeping. He will wake up soon. Go away!"

Amahl turned to Sara as she entered the room, followed by Naphtali, and then Khalid. They all watched in shock as Sara tried to take the baby from Bianca, but she held him more tightly and began rocking the chair back and forth.

"Go away! All of you, go!"

Sara turned to the three men and ushered them from the room, then she stood in front of Bianca and watched as tears streamed down the young woman's face.

"My Lady, may I hold the baby? Please, give me Mathias."

Bianca looked up at Sara and shook her head, her face pleading and her eyes red with tears.

"He is so cold, Sara. I cannot warm him."

Sara got a blanket from the cradle and offered it to Bianca.

"Let me have him. I will wrap him in this blanket. Let me help you," she whispered to the stricken woman and held out her arms.

Bianca looked at the blanket, and nodding her head, offered the baby to Sara, who held out the blanket and wrapped him in it.

"I will take him downstairs by the fire. He will be all right with me, my Lady."

As she opened the door to leave the room, Amahl saw she had the baby.

"What has happened? What is wrong with Mathias?"

Sara went to him and hesitated, then uncovered Mathias's face. Her hand shaking, she felt his forehead.

"I fear he is dead, my Lord."

Amahl looked at his son and saw that he was very still. He placed his head against Mathias's chest, but there was no heart-beat.

"I believe you are right, Sara," he whispered. "My poor little son."

She nodded to him and hurried down the stairs. He entered the room and found Bianca studying her hands. She looked at him, her eyes tormented.

"I knew, Amahl. I knew. When I woke up, I came in here, and he was dead. Our baby is dead."

"He is alive with Allah now, Bianca."

"But I don't want him with Allah, I want him here with me."

"He plays with the angels, my darling. And he is happy!"

Tears streamed down Amahl's face as he reached for his wife. She continued to whisper against his shoulder.

"I want him here, Amahl. Here, with me."

They stayed together in the baby's room for most of the morning.

Naphtali's grief was overwhelming and placed him in such emotional darkness that even Sara could not reach him. There seemed no time for Sara to indulge her own grief, for the entire family was devastated by their loss.

They buried Mathias next to his grandparents, Atiq and Zoraya. The small family cemetery stood protected from the winds and storms of winter amid a grove of poplar trees beside the meadow.

Amahl did not go to the orange groves, and the fruit of the olive trees fell to the ground. He spent his days caring for Bianca and overseeing the daily supervision of his two older sons.

Mathias's grave, according to custom, was unmarked for the first year of mourning. Bianca could not rouse herself from her grief to go to the stables, and soon Hernando was in full charge of the horses. During the first year of her mourning, Bianca cared for her two sons, and at the appropriate time, a ceremony was held and a marker placed on Mathias's grave.

The evening after the family observed the ceremony, there was a light tapping at the front door of the castle. At first, Bianca thought the sound was imagined, but when it was repeated, she sent Khalid to the door with Amahl following him. The new rabbi from the *aljama* stood there in the cold. He was well-dressed. A boy stood behind him.

Khalid opened the door wide, welcoming the rabbi and the lad into the foyer of the castle, and then he escorted them to the room where Amahl and Bianca waited. Bianca turned to her husband.

"My Lord General, this is Rabbi Mendez and . . . ?"

"This is Efraim Velasquez. He is the son of Israel and Deborah Velasquez."

Amahl and Bianca nodded their welcome to Efraim.

"Forgive me, General, for our intrusion. We are in urgent need of your help, and of yours, Señora."

They led the visitors into the great room, where the four of them sat before the fire.

"Have you heard the news?"

"What news, Rabbi?"

"Constantinople has fallen to the Ottomans. Forced conversions are taking place, and many of our people are dying. I received word this morning that refugees will arrive soon, but they have no way to enter the country. If they come in through the ports, the guards will imprison them. Many have families here in Andalusia. We are appealing to our people who live on the coast to help the refugees."

Since the birth of Rafael and Benjamin, Bianca had ceased smuggling Moors out of Spain. What Amahl could not accomplish with his efforts to convince her to stop, the birth of their children had. Their safety and future were more important to her now.

"Rabbi, I am sorry, but we cannot help."

"But you must help us."

"Please understand, taking the people out of Spain is very different from helping them enter. I don't know how to do that. I have no contacts for relocating them."

Amahl sighed his relief.

"Señora Cozar, Efraim's father and I will concern ourselves with the arrangements, but we need a place to hide the people until their families come for them."

"You mean the tunnel?"

"Yes, the tunnel."

"How do you know of the tunnel?"

"Señora, many of us know."

She looked at Amahl, silently pleading with him. Amahl addressed the young man.

"You want to smuggle them in, hide them in the tunnel, and then smuggle them out again?"

"Yes. They would be here for only a few days until their families are notified they have arrived, and come for them."

Amahl thought about this for several moments in the now silent room. Finally, he gave his consent, and Bianca looked at him with relief.

The four talked late into the night until the rabbi and the boy left. Thus began their new endeavor. They helped the refugees enter Spain and resettle. The frightened people arrived on the longboats and disembarked on the shore, and Efraim, who was only eleven years old, led them up the path to the mouth of the tunnel.

The people were housed in the cellar of the castle, cared for by Bianca, and did not see daylight until their families came for them. It wasn't until the approaching Pesach that Bianca was confronted with what seemed to be an insurmountable situation.

✤

From the memoir of
Meschianza de Lucena Cozar-Velasquez
March 17, 1495
Lisbon

"Why is this night different from all others?"

In the year of 1455, my grandmother, pregnant with my mother, Justina, had many guests living in the cellar of the castle, the second spring after the fall of Constantinople. Bianca sent my Great-grandfather Naphtali to the de Lucena villa, instructing him to bring her mother's special china, silverware, and crystal used exclusively for the Passover meal. He returned with it carefully packed and loaded onto a wagon. It took him most of the afternoon to deliver it, for he drove the wagon slowly to prevent breakage. I remember my grandfather telling me, when I was very small, that the devil hates the sound of breaking glass. It attracts his attention, and in revenge, he spoils joy.

Bianca and Sara worked together as they prepared the Seder meal. The grand dining table that crowded the castle's dining hall was dismantled and carried to the cellar piece by piece. The night before Passover began, my grandmother led four small children and her two sons by the hand throughout the castle to collect and burn the *chomets*, ensuring that not a crumb of leavened bread remained.

Bianca gathered the refugees. Some of them protested for fear of discovery, as they had been denied the freedom to observe

Passover. The penalty upon discovery was death. The first edict about the Jews had been handed down by Pope Clement IX, two hundred and fifty years before. He had ordered the prosecution of all Christian heretics and extended the Church's authority so that professing Jews, like my grandmother, could be prosecuted if they were suspected of influencing Christian converts. The Inquisitors called it judaizing, and the Pope declared it an act of heresy. Many of the people hidden in our cellars were Marranos, converts to the Christian faith who practiced their Jewish religion in secret. My grandmother, knowing the risks she was taking, gently coaxed her guests to the meal she had prepared. She sent the same four children around the table with silver bowls of water for the ritual hand washing, creating a purified and holy circle of love in the cold, musty room.

When my grandfather told me of this, I was quite small, though my child's mind completely understood his love and pride in my grandmother. He worshipped her as we worship our Creator. Perhaps that was his crime, to love her more than God.

✦

21

$\maltese$

Several weeks after Justina's birth, Sara insisted that she heard singing coming from the walls of the room. She looked at the midwife and realized the woman didn't hear anything.

"Perhaps it was your angels, Sara."

Naphtali and Sara were in the baby's room, looking down at her through the white gauze that surrounded her cradle. It was late spring, and the mosquitoes were already out. The irrigation in the groves created pools of water where they joyfully bred and multiplied. Sara made smudge pots of vile-smelling smoke and placed them in the windows to keep the mosquitoes from the baby's room. Sara still kept Justina's crib swathed with the white fabric for extra protection.

"Look at her, sir. She is born with God's grace, don't you think? My father would say she is born with the gift of knowing."

Naphtali gazed down at his granddaughter, and nodding in agreement, turned to Sara.

"Stay with this baby. Do not leave her alone."

"Yes, sir, but you must not fear for her. The angels protect Justina."

Naphtali left the room and went in search of his daughter. He found her in the meadow beside the stables. She was exercising a new colt, the offspring of her best mare and the Andalusian stallion. Rafael and Benjamin were perched on the rails of the outdoor paddock built recently by Amahl and Khalid. When Bianca saw her father, she dropped the lead rein and walked over to greet him.

"Good morning, Father. I see you have managed to take yourself away from Justina."

He placed his arms around his daughter and felt the sense of well-being flowing through her body. He could see the happiness on her face. He turned to greet his two grandsons. Rafael, six years old now, was helping his four-year-old brother from the fence. He gathered the two boys into his arms, lifting Benjamin.

"My daughter, I believe your sons are old enough to begin joining the men with me at the temple. They are too old to be sitting with the women in the balcony. Do you agree?"

Bianca looked down at Rafael. He smiled at her eagerly, agreeing with his grandfather. As much as Bianca disliked releasing her son from her guidance, she could not deny the pride she saw in Rafael's eyes.

"Yes, Father. I know you are right, but it is so hard for me to give them up."

"You are not giving them up, Bianca, but they must begin learning the Talmud. They need tutors. It is time for their education. You have many duties here on the estate, and now you have Justina. I cannot teach her what she will need to know, but I can teach my grandsons. Will you allow me to do this?"

Bianca reached for Benjamin, took him from her father's arms, and buried her face in his warm little neck. Nuzzling him, she held back her tears and handed him to her father.

"I know you are right, but I cannot let them go. Also, their father has much to teach them. Someday, Rafael and Benjamin will own this estate, and Justina will inherit your property."

Naphtali concurred, though his disappointment was evident. Bianca, relenting, offered her father a compromise.

"Father, I would like you to arrange for Rafael's tutor.

Someone from the *alhama*? I trust your judgment in this more than my own. Would you take him there for his lessons?"

Beaming his pleasure, Naphtali eagerly agreed.

Bianca knelt before her oldest son and addressed him directly.

"Rafael, you are to go with your grandfather now. You are to be obedient to your tutor, and set a proper example for your brother. Beginning today, you must ask your grandfather's permission to join me in the stables. You are to study hard and make me proud of you."

"Yes, Mother. Father said I am almost a man now, and that I must take care of Benjamin and Justina."

"Yes, my darling. You are almost a man."

Bianca watched her father return to the castle, leading her son by his hand. She picked up the lead rein, but did not move toward the colt. She looked up at where her father and Rafael had disappeared around the corner of the stable, then she dropped the rein and called out to Hernando, who was cleaning the stalls.

"Yes, madam."

"Would you brush down the colt and stable him? Benjamin and I are going to the castle."

"Yes, madam. Will you be back today?"

"No, Hernando. We will return in the morning."

✠

22

꘎

Bianca found Sara kneeling in her garden, pulling weeds, Justina beside her in a small basket. Bianca hesitated for only a moment, and then she and Benjamin joined Sara on the ground. Startled, Sara turned to her as Bianca surveyed the plot. She reached for a large weed and began to pull it up from the ground, but Sara stayed her hand.

"That is my angelica. Please, madam, do not pull it out!"

She guided Bianca's hand to a straggly, forlorn clump of grass. "This is a weed."

Bianca pulled it out as a bewildered Sara watched her.

"How can you tell the weeds from the plants, Sara?"

"I have known the difference since childhood. Did no one teach you?"

"No. I only know about horses."

"That is a pity."

Sara returned to her weeding, glancing with concern at Bianca as she sat on the ground, watching.

"What is wrong, madam?"

"I don't know."

The older woman stopped what she was doing and turned to the younger one. She sat next to her and waited in silence.

"Sara, did you ever feel that, as a woman, you are without choices, without will?"

"Why do you say this?"

"Today my father has taken charge of my eldest son."

"Yes. I see what you mean. I have not been blessed with children, and I have not questioned this, but I observe, madam, and what I have learned is that women are only for the birthing of their sons. We are not for the teaching of them."

"But Sara, they are still babies."

She watched Benjamin, who was digging into the dirt around Sara's onions.

"Did the child cry as your father led him away?"

"No. He seemed eager."

"Then he is not a baby anymore."

Bianca studied the ground before her as she tried to understand what Sara was telling her.

"How am I supposed to bear this, Sara?"

"You have a daughter. Justina belongs to you forever; your sons never belong to you. Look to your daughter, madam. Look to your home and to your husband. That is all there is for you."

Bianca rose and went to her younger son. She lifted him and returned to her place on the ground beside Sara. She held him, almost in desperation, until he struggled away from her. She watched him as she continued questioning Sara.

"Is that why you spend so much time in this garden, Sara?"

"There is healing here."

"Father says there are physicians for healing, and that this is witchcraft, the healing with herbs."

"I suppose it is, but not as he believes it."

"I don't understand."

Sara reached toward a large bright green bush and broke off a small leaf. Taking Bianca's hand, she crushed the leaf and placed it on Bianca's palm.

"This is basil. If one of the children has an upset stomach, you make a tisane with it. The stomachache will go away."

Bianca examined the leaf in her hand as Sara added another.

"This is borage. It is for fevers. And here. Costmary. For swelling."

Sara continued to pick small bunches of leaves from the plants surrounding her and placed them in Bianca's hands.

"When I was pregnant with Rafael, this is how you made the tisane that relieved the nausea?"

In response, Sara plucked a long branch from a fernlike bush, and smiling, offered it to Bianca.

"Fennel."

Delighted, Bianca took it in her other hand.

"Did you think I was a witch, madam?"

Nodding her head, Bianca confessed.

"Can you forgive me?"

"Of course. I don't know about foolish old men, though."

She turned back to her weeding as Bianca dropped the herbs into the basket Sara always carried with her.

During the following months of summer, Bianca spent many hours away from her horses, walking the fields with Sara, each of them carrying a basket. With the older woman's instruction, she learned to mix the salves and ointments, the perfumes and elixirs.

Through the long winter, she administered to her children's sore throats and fevers, and often sat up with Sara during a cold night, watching over a sick child.

When Benjamin was five, he was bright and inquisitive. He and Rafael spent all their time with their father. At Benjamin's insistence, Amahl fashioned a small wooden sword. Often his younger son spent his afternoons running through the groves, brandishing his weapon at the trees, pretending they were the enemy. Rafael, now seven, was beginning to learn the workings of the vast estate he and his brother would someday inherit. Unlike his brother, Rafael had no interest in war.

The following spring, Justina began walking. Holding Naphtali's hand, the little girl followed Bianca and Sara into the woods. As the two women gathered plants and mushrooms, Justina filled her small arms with wildflowers. Sometimes Bianca took her daughter's hand, while Naphtali and Sara followed.

It was a time of contentment and prosperity for the family, as if the estate were a great ship floating upon a calm sea, gently rocking and lulling the inhabitants.

From the memoir of
Meschianza de Lucena Cozar-Velasquez
December 24, 1495
Lisbon

Ana is recovering slowly now that we have returned to the community. The King ordered the end to cruelties against the Jews, and
finally Raul deemed it safe for us to leave the ship. Still, there is
fear, and so many of us are missing. We hope for their release, but
our prayers for them are unanswered.

Yesterday Raul accompanied me into the hills so that I could
search for the herbs I know Ana needs to recover from her illness,
but I could find little. The meadows are barren now that it is winter. I do not know what to gather for her malaise. It is an illness of
the spirit from which she suffers. Mother would have known the
proper herbs and how to prepare them. I wish now that I had paid
better attention to her instruction. I feel useless to Ana. I have
searched the community for another woman schooled in the use of
herbs, but if she exists, perhaps she is frightened of the stigma of
witchcraft that hovers over all the people of Lisbon. Only the
physicians are allowed to heal without censure.

The auto-da-fés continue. Our *aljama* is located near the plaza
where the burnings take place, and though we hover in terror with
the rest of the community, the sounds of the penitents' screams
and the cheering of the onlookers penetrate our silence, mocking
our horror and fear. There are rumors that in some provinces of

Portugal, there are forced conversions, and families that refuse the Christian faith are robbed of their children, who are taken and given to Christian families.

We no longer live in a world of reason. Ana no longer participates in our reality. She has retreated into her dreams.

23

Naphtali waited for the nurse to dress Justina, but at the active age of four, she was squirming and wriggling about. As a shoe was placed on her tiny foot, she removed it while the other shoe was being adjusted around her ankle.

"Donzella, stop that. Leave your shoes alone."

The little girl giggled and pulled her cotton blouse over her head as Sara was fastening the buttons on her velveteen dress. The nurse did not scold her, but she learned determination in caring for Justina, and eventually, she won the battle of dressing her. She handed Justina to Naphtali, then left the little girl's room.

"Grandfather, I had a dream again last night."

"The one where I died? You had that one again?"

No longer giggling, Justina looked into her grandfather's eyes. He returned her stare and marveled at how much she looked like Bianca when she had been a child.

"Grandfather, are you going to die?"

"Not for a very long time. Let us go downstairs and look for your mother. It is time for our walk."

Naphtali took his treasured granddaughter by her chubby hand and led her down the stone steps of the castle. He did not find Bianca waiting at the bottom of the stairs, so he took Justina into the kitchen. He continued until he saw Sara in the garden by the kitchen door. She was bent over and having difficulty rising. He let go of Justina's hand and helped Sara straighten her back.

"Are you all right, Sara?"

"Yes, your Grace. I am growing old, I suspect."

"No, Sara. You must not say that. If you are growing old, then I must be one of the ancients. I remember when you were born. Do not say you are old. Where is my daughter? We are ready for our walk."

He looked about for Justina and found her uprooting the irises. He rushed over to her and took the plants from her hands. Justina hurried to another cluster of the fresh blooms, and looking helplessly at Sara, he picked up the girl and held her against his hip as she struggled to get down.

"My Lady should be back by now. She left early to gather mushrooms, and asked that we wait for her."

He handed Justina to Sara. The little girl placed her hands on Sara's face and left smudges of dirt on her cheeks. There were pieces of grass at the corners of Justina's mouth. Sara took her to the well to clean her face as Naphtali went into the kitchen to search again for Bianca, but he did not find her. He climbed the stairs, and as he reached the last step, he stopped, short of breath and perspiring. He rested a moment, and then searched Bianca's bedchamber. Not finding her, he went back to the garden and spoke to Sara.

"Did she say which grove had the mushrooms?"

"I think she said the orange grove. The one along the cliffs. There is always fog, and the dampness gives us the best mushrooms. She may still be there. The crop is plentiful this year."

"I will leave Justina with you while I find her. Then we will take our walk."

He left by the back gate and started down the path to the grove. The morning was gentle, and light floated in the open spaces on the fog-laden path. As he neared the grove, the mist grew heavy and rested on his clothing, dampening him with a light spray. It was difficult to see the path as the fog closed about him.

Naphtali entered the grove, and the mist became a light rain. He was indifferent to the scent of violets, his foreboding intense as he searched the orchard for Bianca. His breathing was labored, and there was a sharp pain in both of his ears. He could feel his heart pounding in his chest, and as the throbbing in his head intensified, he turned to walk back to the castle. Twice he stumbled before he finally fell to the ground, his left leg and arm numb. He lay there staring up at the leaves of the orange trees before he lost consciousness. The pain disappeared, and Naphtali was at peace.

When Bianca found her father, she thought he had stumbled and fallen, knocking himself unconscious on the rock where his head was resting, but as she reached for him, she could see that he was dead. Devastated by this discovery, she sat on the ground next to him and took him into her arms. She gently brushed grass from his cheek and forehead, taking a silk handkerchief from her pocket to remove a grass stain from his face. She placed her hand on the side of his face.

"Oh, Father," she whispered.

She looked around the meadow. The mists were slowly lifting. Her basket of morels had spilled on the ground next to the tree behind the rock. Cradling him in her arms, she continued talking to him.

"Father, how can you leave me like this? Don't you know how much we need you? How much I need you?"

She lifted his head onto her shoulder and held him tightly. Through her sobbing, she begged him.

"Don't leave me, Father."

She did not move again until the sun had risen above the trees. The fog had burned away, and the meadow was clean and bright. The flowers had defied the mist and were now staring at Bianca. Crocus and daffodils mocked her, and tiny yellow roses hung over her in the trees. She could hear the cicadas sing a dirge for her father. She looked at his face again and took out a comb from her pocket and began combing his hair.

"The angels wait for you, Father. They wait for you with joy, and they will sing new songs for you."

She straightened his clothing, brushing bits of grass and violets from his cloak, then she paused and looked about, whispering to Naphtali, "Who will teach my sons now?"

When Amahl found them, Bianca was leaning against a tree, her arms wrapped tightly around her father's body.

From the memoir of
Meschianza de Lucena Cozar-Velasquez
February 12, 1496
Lisbon

My grandfather often spoke to me about my Great-grandfather Naphtali. As a young man, many years before he married my Great-grandmother Rosalia, he sailed his ship south through the Strait of Gibraltar and then east, past Barcelona, then north through the Mediterranean to France. There his love of fine and beautiful things—fabrics, delicacies, wines, and spices—led him to the marketplace to trade. He continued east to Italy and Greece, trading and buying, and I was told that on one of his journeys, he traveled as far as Istanbul.

My great-grandfather was an innocent. The first time my grandfather told me this, I didn't understand, so he explained it to me. He said that innocents are God's chosen. They are placed here on this earth to remind us of our beginnings. The innocents come into the world with patches of light on their souls. These patches are the windows to heaven. It is through the windows that the rest of us behold a glimpse of God.

The innocents do not see evil, for they cannot recognize it. In this way, their souls are not at risk. They take a true delight in the beauties of our lives, and experience every moment as if it is a precious jewel they hold in their hands. They examine it with a look of wonder, and they try to share it with us.

My great-grandfather was full of love and joy, and as I listened to my grandfather speak of him with longing and veneration, I knew that his sudden death was like an abrupt extinguishing of a beautiful and wondrous light.

When the Cortes of Madrigal decreed that all Jews in Spain must wear an identifying red badge on the right shoulder, and further decreed the prohibition of silk and fine scarlet clothing, my great-grandfather, in defiance of this edict, still wore these fabrics in the privacy of his home. His boots were of soft black leather, and his capes of velvet. He kept this finery separate from the permitted colorless clothing, as my mother had done with her dishware; one set for dairy, and the other for meat. In his home, Naphtali was the *maja*, but in public, he was a soberly dressed man.

My grandmother and Sara prepared my great-grandfather for burial, as is our custom. They cleansed a sinless man, and prepared him for his place in heaven. Bianca, in an act of defiance she learned from her father, dressed him in his finery. They buried him, according to our laws, before sundown. As my Uncle Rafael, a mere boy of nine, sang the Kaddish for his grandfather, my Grandfather Amahl stood on the bluff chanting his own prayers for the man he revered as much as his own father. He chanted his gratitude for the daughter given to him in marriage without hesitation and in a spirit of love and generosity. When the service ended and the mourners returned to the castle, it was Amahl and his two sons who, with their hands, replaced the dirt that would close the grave of Naphtali de Lucena.

I did not know my great-grandfather, but today, in my memoir, I remember him for my children.

24

⁜

After Naphtali's death, the persecutions against the Jews increased. Rafael's and Benjamin's tutor was invited to live with the family, as it was not safe for him to make the daily journey from the *juderia* in Tarifa. Amahl no longer permitted Bianca to take their children to the village for the Sabbath. Even he could no longer protect them.

Justina was eight years old when she learned of the full danger under which they lived. One night she was awakened by a dream, and she heard sounds that echoed from beneath the castle. As she listened, her dream overshadowed her. She had a vision of her brother Benjamin in a land she did not recognize. He stood on great mounds of sand, but there was no water about. An animal was beside him, but it was not a horse. The animal had two large mounds on its back, and its face was sad.

She had been aware from a very young age that there were people who lived in the darker regions of her home. She was not allowed to venture there, having been admonished by her mother to stay upstairs with Sara, but, on this night, there was no one to restrain her as she snuck down the stairs and went through the kitchen. She had difficulty with the large oak door that led to the cellar, but, after much struggling, she was able to push it open just enough to fit her small body through.

She stood at the top of the stone stairs, their centers worn and rounded. She was barefoot, and the cold stones shot chills up her legs to the base of her spine. She edged her way down. She did not look at the shadows cast by the large white candles set in their iron sconces. She wanted to be brave and follow the voices that had roused her from sleep.

It was Efraim, now a young man of nineteen, who discovered her as she crept down the stairs. He spent most of his days on the Cozar estate, acting as an older brother to Rafael and Benjamin, often riding with them along the beach. On many late afternoons, he appeared with Justina's brothers for their evening meal. Efraim often noted to Justina that Benjamin had the look of a wanderer.

Her oldest brother, Rafael, was the quiet one. Fourteen now, he spent most of his days with their father, taking care of the estate. Twelve-year-old Benjamin was noisy and full of mischief. He teased all of them, including their mother, Bianca. Justina could always tell that Benjamin was their mother's favorite. It was as if Benjamin were a celebration, taking his happiness with him wherever he went.

He was messy, and even Sara did not scold him for this. Justina often heard her exuberant brother running through the castle. He rode the fastest horse in the stables, swinging their father's military sword at the tree branches in the groves. Often he succeeded in lopping them off, leaving the severed limbs to lie on the ground for Rafael to gather. In the late afternoon when Justina sat with her father as he performed his *salats*, it was Benjamin's voice she heard over the sound of her father's prayers as he shouted war cries and drove his horse along the beach below them. Though she loved her brothers, Justina was concerned about Benjamin, for sometimes he sat his horse quietly, staring at the golden sea before him, silently watching the horizon. On those evenings, he appeared pensive at the table throughout the meal. When they were finished, and the family retired to the great room for the duration of the evening, Benjamin would kiss his mother on the cheek and go to bed early.

Efraim confronted Justina on the stairs and saw that she was dressed in her nightgown. He removed his jacket, placing it around her shoulders.

"Why are you down here, Donzella?"

"I heard a noise."

"You should go back to bed."

"Why? What are you doing? Is Mother with you?"

He tried to lead her back up the stairs, but she broke from his grasp and ran around him. He could not catch her as she raced down the steps.

There was a large group of people entering the cellar from the opening of the tunnel. Some of them were carrying valises, but many had their belongings wrapped in blankets and shawls. Bianca was at the opening of the tunnel, speaking a few words to each person as he entered. She turned and saw Justina.

"My darling, you must not be down here. I want you to return to your room. I will have Benjamin lead you back to your chamber."

Bianca turned and looked for Benjamin. Not finding him, she queried Efraim:

"Have you seen him?"

"Yes. He left with the general to greet the first group of people. He is at the water waiting for the longboats. Shall I bring him here?"

"No. It will be too difficult. I will take Justina back to her room. Will you wait for me?"

"Yes, Señora. Do you think the captain will be able to deliver all the people tonight? The wind is rising. Already the waves are high."

"I don't know. Wait here for the general. He will know soon."

"Mother, please let me stay? I will not get in the way. What are you doing here? Who are these people?"

"Justina, I want you in bed."

"No, Mother. If you put me to bed, I will come back."

Impatient with her daughter, Bianca took her by the hand. She had begun to lead her up the stairs when Amahl appeared at the opening of the tunnel. She released Justina's hand and went to her husband.

"The captain has sent the first longboats, but it does not look like he will wait. The storm is already beginning, and I do not think they can bring any more to the shore tonight."

Slowly, the cellar filled with people as Efraim ushered them in. Bianca joined him, offering comfort and reassurance to a frightened old woman. She searched through the last of the people for her son, but he did not appear. Forgetting Justina, she turned to Efraim.

"Where is Benjamin? Has he come back from the longboat?"

"No, Señora. I have not seen him yet."

Efraim searched through the group of people milling about in confusion. Disappointment emanated from them in a collective sigh. Many of them still had relatives waiting on the ship. Amahl was assuring them that they could stay with his family until the seas calmed and the ship could return.

Bianca hurried to her husband, her anxiety heightened. She understood her youngest son's restlessness. Often during the previous year, she had seen Benjamin standing in the mouth of the tunnel long after the last longboat had cut its way through the waves to the great ship that waited in the natural harbor.

"Have you seen Benjamin?"

"What do you mean? Is he not here?"

"We cannot find him. Come with me, now!"

Together, they hurried through the tunnel. They did not speak, and all that could be heard was their labored breathing as they ran through the myriad turns until they reached the opening that overlooked the water.

The night was black, and the stars were hidden by the dark clouds that hung over the galleon as it rocked from side to side. One sail was torn and falling to the deck. The ship appeared as light as a walnut shell, bobbing and floating precariously on the cobalt sea. As Bianca and Amahl watched, the water already at their feet, the longboat crashed against the hull of the galleon. The two seamen who had rowed the boat to the ship were now clinging to the rope ladder. They were tossed against the hull as they made their desperate climb to the railing. Between them, they gripped the arms of a boy that Bianca realized was her son.

"Benjamin! Benjamin!"

Amahl reached out and grabbed Bianca by her waist, fearing that she was going to jump into the waves to retrieve their son. She continued to scream as Amahl pulled her away. Horrified, he watched as the first seaman climbed over the railing and reached for Benjamin. He caught his arm as the ship heaved and turned. The man beneath Benjamin lost his grip on the boy and fell into the greedy waves. As the sailor above yanked Benjamin over the railing, the other one disappeared beneath the water.

"He is safe, Bianca. I saw it! He is on the ship!"

Bianca pulled herself away from Amahl and ran back to the opening. Amahl tried to bring her away from the water, but she pushed him from her. She fell to her knees, clawing at her clothing. The front of her dress was in shreds as she cried for her son. Amahl tried to lift her, but she had curled her body into a tight ball of agony. He fell to his knees beside her and begged her to listen to him.

"He will come back, Bianca. He will come back."

She turned on him, her face transformed by grief and rage. She began hitting him, Amahl intercepting her fists in his effort to stop her.

"Your fault! Your fault! You encouraged him."

"No. No, my darling. I would not do that. I don't know . . . "

"You gave him your sword. You talked to him of war and killing!"

"No, Bianca. Never did I speak to him of war. He asked me about it. About my youth, but I did not speak to him of war."

"You filled his head. Why didn't you keep him close to you, as you did Rafael?"

"I could not, Bianca. Benjamin did not want the estate. He never wanted it."

She was standing now, facing him. Her grief ravaged her. She bent toward him as sobs racked her body.

"I will not forgive you for letting him go! I will not forgive you!"

He reached for her as she ran past him into the tunnel, but she shook him off. He stood, helpless, and watched her as she disappeared into the darkness. Amahl turned back to see that the galleon was a small black dot on the horizon. Lightning broke the sky, cutting through the clouds in a sharp angle, as if to accuse him of his failure. It illuminated the ship, the sails appearing as ghosts. Suddenly, the sky was black again, and the galleon disappeared.

Amahl stood for a moment in the darkness, searching the horizon. Defeated, he followed his wife.

✤

From the memoir of
Meschianza de Lucena Cozar-Velasquez
May 19, 1496
Lisbon

After my Uncle Benjamin stole away on the longboat, the persecutions against the Jews began to escalate. The auto-da-fés continued in cities north of my family's estate as more and more refugees traveled south to leave Spain. Word of my grandmother's activities spread slowly, and Efraim Velasquez became a permanent presence within our family. At Bianca's insistence, he now accompanied the sea captain on his voyages to help the refugees find sanctuary. Efraim searched the seaports and markets for Benjamin, asking the people of the great caravans if they had seen him. After his inquiries, he returned to the galleon, dejected.

My grandmother waited for him, often spending her days sitting in the mouth of the tunnel in search of the great ship. In her grief, she turned away from my mother, leaving Justina to grow up in a state of fear and insecurity. During those years, my grandfather said that Bianca was like a shadow as she avoided him. Bianca's condemnation of Amahl was an act of grief for the loss of her son.

Amahl's prayers were full of entreaties to Allah in hopes that Efraim would find Benjamin, or at the least bring back word of him. My grandfather needed this redemption so that he could offer it to my grandmother as a peace treaty, but as the months and years passed, this gift was denied to both of them. A cold estrangement soon filled the void my grandparents now shared. It pushed their love aside, burying it in the recesses of Bianca's heart. My grandfather entered a long, dark night in his melancholic soul.

Tragedy lies in wait for a cowardly ambush. My grandfather once told me that tragedy, in its glee, shames itself. Lacking integrity, it is the true marauder of our souls. Tragedy is patient and has the power to wait for us. In their estrangement, my grandparents forgot this.

25

For seven years, there was no word from Benjamin. There were few persecutions against the Sephardim during these years. Edicts were passed to protect the Jews for a time, only to be overturned. The hatred and the fear, the ignorance, would reemerge. Peace was desultory and unreliable. The cruelties would begin, especially in the larger cities to the north, and often during Pesach. It was usually during this time that the rumors of the *Niño de La Guardia* surfaced. One such rumor alleged that Jews stole Christian babies and sacrificed them for their blood as part of the Passover ritual. Justina often asked her father about the origin of this rumor, but he could only shake his head as he placed his arm around her.

Justina, her intelligence acute, was keenly aware of their danger. She listened to everything, often hiding in rooms where Bianca and Efraim discussed his search for Benjamin. When Justina questioned her mother, she was relegated to her place as a child. But Justina was always concerned, and always frightened.

Bianca's quest to recover her son had become the focus of her life. Amahl's, in the meantime, was to care for his family, and the estate. Rafael had recently married Hannah Dominguez, as arranged by Bianca five years after Benjamin's disappearance. Not even the loving Rafael had time for his sister.

It seemed to Justina that Efraim was the only person in the household who listened to her. His kindness had been consistent since Justina's infancy. Still, she felt awkward, and was always in somebody's way. One day, Efraim found Justina sitting in the mouth of the tunnel, looking out at the sea. It was winter, so the cellars were empty, for the ship could not anchor close to the rocks. He searched for her throughout the castle, finally finding her in the tunnel.

"Donzella, what are you doing here? Are you having visions again?"

She turned to him, her cheeks coated with tears. At the age of fifteen, she was very beautiful and delicate. She had an ethereal quality about her, and because of her pallor, she often appeared as a wraith to Efraim.

"I always have the dreams, Efraim. Why does this happen? What is wrong with me?"

He knelt down before her and touched her arms. She was shivering from the chill of the tunnel.

"It is too cold for you."

He reached for the driftwood at the mouth of the tunnel to prepare a fire. As he piled it in front of them, he continued speaking to her:

"You should not be here. You will catch a draft and be ill again. Your mother will worry."

He took out his flints and started a flame burning beneath the wood. Justina watched him as he blew on the tiny spark, the smoke curling through his light brown hair. She didn't quite grasp her feelings for him. Lately, she became confused and shy when she was in his presence. He was part of her life, and he filled her earliest memories. Efraim had been there when she took her first steps. It was Efraim who had picked her up from the ground when she fell, and it was Efraim who had placed her on her first horse.

"Did you bring a blanket with you?"

She answered him with a muted whisper.

"I did not think it would be this cold, but I have my cape."

He found it and put it on her. He wrapped his own cloak more tightly around himself and sat next to her, pulling her close to him. He rubbed her arms until they warmed, and fed more wood into the fire.

"I suppose you didn't bring anything to eat?"

She reached under her cloak, and from the folds of her skirt, she brought out a parcel containing bread, some cheese, and olives. He took the food from her and sliced the cheese with his knife.

He offered it to her, but Justina refused it.

"You have to eat. You never eat enough. This is why you are so pale and so thin."

She took the bread and cheese and bit into it. He watched her until he was satisfied, and began eating his own sparse meal.

"What are you doing down here anyway? We have been looking for you everywhere."

"I come here to think, Efraim."

"About what? What do you think about?"

"I think about everyone, Mother, Father, Rafael, and Hannah. I think about Benjamin all the time. Do you believe he will ever return to us?"

"Yes, of course he will. He will be homesick, and he will come back."

"But he has been gone for so long. Maybe he has forgotten us."

"No, he will not forget."

She took another bite of her sandwich and looked out at the sea. It started to rain, but Efraim's fire protected them from the damp.

"I want him to come back so that Mother will love Father again—so that we can all be happy, as we once were."

"Your mother loves your father. How can you think she doesn't?"

"They hardly speak. She blames him, doesn't she, Efraim?"

"Perhaps, but she is wrong. Benjamin would have run away even if the longboat had not been there. He was restless. He often asked me about the places the ship visited. He had so many questions. I did not have enough answers, so Benjamin went to find the answers for himself."

She looked at Efraim for a long moment, then sat silently staring at the water.

"Donzella, tell me what you think about, besides the family."

She turned to him, a look of profound sadness on her face.

"How long do you think we will be safe, Efraim?"

"What do you mean?"

"How long will the Jews be safe in Spain? How long do you think it will be before we will have to get into the longboats and sail away to nowhere, Efraim?"

Disconcerted by her question, he did not answer for several moments. He tightened his arm around her and held her close.

"Are you afraid?"

"Aren't you? It is only a matter of time before we will have to leave. I dream about it, and I am scared."

"I don't think we will have to leave. Our King will not allow it."

"You have more faith than I, Efraim. I envy you."

"Faith is all we have. Faith is the one thing that makes me persevere."

"So you believe we are protected? I don't."

"But you must believe."

"I cannot. The Fates are against us; they have always been against us."

"Why do you think that? We are protected here. We have always been."

"No, the Fates won't allow it. You see, Efraim, I think about this all the time. The Fates are the dark angels of God. They obtain joy from our misery."

"But what about our happiness?"

She laughed with irony at his naive question.

"Our happiness? The Fates are imps who dangle happiness in front of us as they would a golden apple. It is glowing, full of promise, if only we will reach for it. They allow us to believe that happiness is there for us to take. I try to ignore that golden apple, for I know that when I reach out for it, they will pull it away from me. They are patient, Efraim, and when they have my attention and my faith, they rob me of it."

He turned to her, shocked by her words.

"Donzella, are you afraid to be happy?"

"No. I am too smart."

"And you are frightened?"

"Yes, I am terrified."

"Don't you know I will never let anything happen to you?"

She looked up at him, her nose level with his chin, her cheek pressed against his.

"How can you protect me, Efraim?"

"I will marry you, and I will take care of you. No one will harm you."

"You want to marry me? Why?"

"How else will I keep you in my life? If I don't marry you,

your mother will marry you to someone else. How will I take care of you then?"

She moved away from him and wrapped her cloak around herself as if to ward him off.

"You mustn't say those things. Haven't you heard what I just said to you? About the Fates?"

"Oh, must I whisper, so that they don't hear me? Can it be that you know you will be happy with me and you don't want the Fates to learn this? If so, don't say it. Don't say you love me, and I won't say I love you. Just tell me that you will marry me. I know your mother and father will approve."

She moved farther away from him, tears flooding her eyes. Shaking her head, she tried to push him away as he reached for her. Her body broke into racking sobs as he cradled her in his arms.

"Don't be afraid. I will never let anyone hurt you. We will be happy. I will even fend off the Fates for you. They will not touch you, ever."

Slowly, she stopped crying. She put her arms around Efraim's neck while he repeated his promises to her. They stayed there, whispering their love, so that the dark angels could not hear. They did not understand the relentlessness of patience, or the timeless endurance of demons. They had only their faith in each other, and in a God who would soon forget them.

✢

From the memoir of
Meschianza de Lucena Cozar-Velasquez
April 21, 1496
Lisbon

My mother and father were married in the deep recesses of the castle per my mother's insistence, and she would not allow my grandmother to embellish the cellar in any way, fearing that this would attract the attention of the dreaded Fates. She wished for a simple dress, and a small wedding. Bianca was granted only one wish. As a result, hundreds of candles washed the cellar walls with their golden light, illuminating my mother's silk dress and veil. She looked like a gilded angel. My grandfather often told me that she lacked only the wings to fly. My father, Efraim, indulged my mother's eccentricities from that day on. He protected her from the questions asked by Rafael and Hannah, my grandparents, and even Sara and Khalid. In his eyes, my mother was the perfection he sought.

Naphtali's estate was offered as Justina's dowry. She and my father lived there, though they spent most of their days at the castle. Their quiet happiness contrasted with the continuing estrangement of my grandparents. Bianca was often found riding along the water, searching the horizon for the ship that would bring her son home. She stopped smuggling refugees from Spain, afraid that she would endanger her other son, indulging his own restlessness.

Benjamin did not return. No one knew if he was alive or dead, but my grandmother never gave up hope. Time had reduced their pain to a dull, but endurable, ache. My grandmother began to accept her loss. In her self-imposed exile, she began to return her attention to her remaining children.

Rafael and Hannah were happy, though they were childless. Hannah was often distressed by this, but Rafael assured her that she must not worry. My parents were already awaiting my birth, and living in their own world, content that they had found the calm to house their joy, safely hidden from the feared black angels.

One day, my mother decided that she and Efraim should raise sheep on the estate. At first, Efraim and Amahl scoffed at her determination. My grandfather argued that the Spanish textile industry had died more than fifty years earlier, leaving the weaving to Flanders and Britain, two countries that prohibited the export of wool. Justina predicted that the prohibition would be lifted by Flanders. When her prediction was realized, they had a place to send their wool, and make a profit.

The King heavily taxed the exportation of Spanish wool, for he needed to finance his ongoing war against the Moors. My mother believed that if we were contributing to the King's coffers through our taxes, we would be able to improve the estate's security. My grandfather finally agreed, and the first lambs were purchased in partnership with a merchant in Tarifa.

My grandfather was seventy years old. He could finally rest from his labors. He happily surrendered his duties at the estate farms, and passed them on to my Uncle Rafael. It was my father and mother who increased our family's wealth when they decided to raise the beautiful Merino sheep.

Efraim and Justina returned to live at the castle so they could care for their growing flock, and await my birth. As long as they paid the exorbitant taxes, they were left undisturbed, and the family lived in peace until the year I was born.

Perhaps it was the serenity of their lives, newfound since Benjamin's disappearance, that caused my grandmother to relent and forgive my grandfather. My mother, Justina, never completely understood what brought Bianca to Amahl again, but in her later years, my mother released herself from her quest for the answer, and again accepted God's mercy.

She told me that the reconciliation happened while my grandfather was singing his evening prayers. He began late that day, for he had helped my mother with the lambs until sunset. It was already dark, so he hurried to his *salats*, and was in the midst of kneeling on the moss when he caught sight of Bianca standing by the wall of the garden watching him. I have often wondered what prompted my grandmother to redeem them both. Perhaps, like my mother, she had premonitions, too.

Amahl, astonished, watched as Bianca walked slowly toward him, her arms outstretched, a smile of entreaty on her face. My mother remembered that Bianca dropped her crop on the moss and stood before him. Amahl did not move, he was so afraid of breaking the spell that held them. Bianca waited, her hands held out to him, until suddenly he understood and took her into his arms. Both kneeling on the prayer rug, Bianca begged him to forgive her. My mother could hear Amahl repeat over and over to Bianca, "He will return to us, he will return. I promise you, Bianca, our son will come home."

My mother told me that the family entered into the most productive and serene time of their lives. She often said that this period began there on the bluff, in the darkness, my grandparents on their knees, holding their love between them like a fragile vessel.

If I close my eyes, I can see them, Amahl and Bianca, wrapped in starlight and clinging to each other.

26

✢

It was Efraim who took charge of the continued smuggling that occurred from the beaches south of Cadiz. The persecutions of the Inquisition were increasing, and the vigilance of the Inquisitor's guards was more oppressive. The risks were greater, as the guards now patrolled the southern coasts of Spain and the borders of Portugal. He often accompanied the captain to the coast of Morocco, for the King's Armada sailed constantly in the small channel that separated the Andalusian coast and the ports of Morocco. When he was gone, Justina agonized for his safety until his return, but today, with Efraim home, she felt as if everything in her world was in place. She had not dreamed her visions for many months. Her baby would be born soon, and she and Efraim would have another to love. Living with danger all of her life, she had never expected to be this happy.

In their bedchamber, Justina found Bianca placing new baby clothes into the crib that had once belonged to her. Everything was ready for the birth of her baby. Bianca saw the glow of happiness on her daughter's face and was relieved. She was always aware of Justina's fears for her husband. Surely, the angels were watching over Justina to bring her such joy. As the birth day approached, the entire household readied itself.

Bianca placed the last of the tiny garments into the crib and turned to embrace her daughter.

"I see your afternoon in the ocean air has done you some good."

"Yes, Mother. I feel very well today. The baby is moving. Here, feel the baby moving, Mother."

Bianca placed her hand on Justina's stomach and waited.

"I remember the first day I felt you move. I was so happy. Already I had two boys. I was certain you would be a girl. I wanted you so much."

Justina embraced her mother, then Bianca left the room and went in search of her husband. Hannah was in the dining room, supervising the setting of the table for dinner.

"Hannah, my dear, is the general in the orange grove with Rafael? Have you seen them?"

"I believe they said something about the stables, Madam, but I can't remember if they went there first."

"I'll look in the stables. If I don't find them, I'll saddle a horse and ride to the grove. I see dinner is going to be ready soon. We will return together."

Bianca let herself out the front door of the castle. As she walked around to the path leading to the stables, she smelled burning wood. She glanced at the kitchen chimney as she rounded the corner of the stone edifice. Sara must have a great fire burning in her stove, for there was so much smoke. It traveled before her on the path to the stables and hung in the air, a pall that drifted through the trees. She neared the stables, and the smell grew stronger. She began running toward the entrance, and as she opened the heavy wooden doors, a great billowing of smoke and fire met her. She fell back, but after her initial shock passed, she ran into the stables shouting for Efraim.

Flames and smoke were all about her. She looked up at the rafters and could see that they were on fire also. Bianca began opening the doors to the stalls, and calling for Efraim again, but he did not answer. She hurried to each stall, releasing the horses and trying to stay away from their path. When she came to the Andalusian's stall, the great stallion reared up in terror and kicked the gate as Bianca unfastened the metal hasp. She was struck in the chest and fell backward. She tried but failed to roll away from the horse's flailing hooves.

In its panic, the horse trampled Bianca as it sought to escape the conflagration. Instead of running for the door, it ran into the paddock and was met with a wall of flames. Crazed, the stallion turned and charged into the railing, breaking its front legs. It fell into the soft area of the paddock and died of the smoke as the flames reached it.

Before Bianca arrived at the stables, Efraim had discovered the fire and had run to the groves for help. Soon he returned with Amahl and Rafael. Amahl saw the flames and helped Rafael release some of the horses, then sent Efraim to the meadow to get Khalid. Before Amahl could reenter the stable, Rafael found his mother and lifted the heavy wooden gate off her, but she was unconscious. Smoke filled the air; Rafael crawled beneath it in his attempt to get Bianca out of the building, but the burning roof caved in on them before he could pull her to safety.

Outside, Amahl, Khalid, and Sara waited for the two of them to come out of the stables. When they did not, Amahl tried to go after them, but Khalid and Sara held him back. The building was completely engulfed in flames, and the trees that grew around the building were burning. Dusk fell rapidly, and the growing darkness was enhanced by the black smoke that surrounded them. It billowed above the remaining trees as flames continued to rise out of the paddock area.

Justina smelled the smoke. Looking from her bedroom window, she saw flames rising above the trees surrounding the stables. She hurried out of the castle, calling to Hannah. Together, they rushed down the path, and it was Justina's screaming that brought Khalid, Sara, and Amahl out of their stunned condition.

Efraim went to Justina and pulled her to the ground as Khalid continued to cling to Amahl. Justina struggled with Efraim, and together they lay on the path, horrified, and watched the building burn to the ground. Sara, traumatized as she realized that Bianca and Rafael were dying in the fire, sat dumbly in the path, rocking her body and tearing her clothing. Khalid tried to comfort Amahl, but he was beyond comfort. In shock, Amahl ran around the still smoking ruins, calling for Bianca and his son. Flames continued to eat at the back of the building, but the front was only a pile of black rubble.

Khalid went to Justina and Efraim and knelt before them. Justina looked at Khalid and began crying uncontrollably and pointing to the remains of the stable. She kept thrusting her finger at the ruins as Khalid shook his head in despair. He turned and walked slowly back to the charred remains of the stable as Amahl came around from behind the building. Khalid caught Amahl as he collapsed in front of what remained of the building. Efraim and Khalid carried Amahl and Justina to the castle. As news of the fire traveled through the countryside, women from the surrounding estates began arriving with food.

The women cared for Justina for several days. Khalid and Efraim sifted through the ruins, but there was nothing to be found of Bianca or Rafael. The searchers could not determine where they had been when the roof collapsed. They found the remains of the horse and buried it next to where it died. Carrying water from the well at the back of the castle, they extinguished the many small fires that continued to burn. Ten days after the fire, Justina went into labor. The neighboring women returned and helped Sara deliver Justina's baby girl.

Amahl stayed in Bianca's library, his grief private and terrible. He read Bianca's books aloud, as he had done in the past, as if Bianca were sitting there with him. He discussed the literature with her, while Efraim sat outside the door, waiting for Amahl to become coherent again. He took food to Amahl, but it was nearly untouched. Late at night, in terror, Efraim could hear Amahl crying out for his son, and listened as the general sobbed his grief for his family.

Sara kept the baby wrapped in warm blankets she heated on the stove in the kitchen, for Meschianza had been born three weeks before she was due. She was tiny, but strong. At no point did she ever begin to fail, but, rather, every day she seemed to grow in strength. They put her to Justina's breast, and the little girl drank greedily, a living denial of all the death surrounding her birth.

Days passed, and finally Justina was allowed to leave her bed. She was helped up the stairs to her mother's library, but Amahl would not respond to her knock. Khalid stayed by the door now, his own grief still overwhelming him.

Justina, her mind numb with despair for her mother and Rafael, struggled against a depression that threatened to overtake her. She could not rise in the morning, but instead lay in her bed. She struggled against consciousness as her mind awakened and a sensation of dread filled her. She believed she was struggling upward through a dark tunnel, and as she reached the light, the realization of her loss overwhelmed her. She would awaken with a start, her body braced as if for a physical onslaught. Finally, she grew afraid to fall asleep, so she walked through the castle until early morning. Often Efraim would find her asleep on the floor in the corner of the great room, her candle burned out, the melted wax a hardened puddle on the carpet.

Justina was sitting in the chair by the window of her room, staring at the ocean, her baby asleep in her arms. She was rocking gently, and did not notice when Sara took Meschianza from her. She remained in the chair until Efraim came for her. Justina followed her husband to the dining room and ate the dinner Sara had prepared for her, then she returned to her room and the chair.

Sometimes Amahl would leave the library and search for Bianca in the castle. When Khalid found him, he led him outside to where the stables had been, and patiently explained to him what had happened to Bianca and his son. Both men had aged since the fire, and together, as Amahl again understood his losses, they would return to the castle and try to make sense of their lives.

27

Several weeks passed. Meschianza continued to thrive under Sara's care. Justina left her chair by the window and began helping Sara in the kitchen. One day, when Khalid came for her father's tray, it was Justina who insisted on taking the tray to Amahl.

She entered the room to find all the drapes drawn across the windows. Her father was sitting in the dark, and the room was cold and damp. The winter rains had begun, but he refused to allow Khalid to light a fire. He believed his discomfort should be a penance for Bianca's death.

Justina went to the curtains and ripped them off the windows. Light flooded the room as Amahl squinted and began to protest. She walked to the fireplace and placed wood and kindling in it. She searched for the flints Khalid used to light the fires and found them under the table by her father's chair. Amahl reached out and tried to take the flints from her, but Justina pried her father's claw-like fingers from her hand. He had eaten little since Bianca's and his son's death, and his weight loss shocked her. She lit the fire and felt the warmth begin to permeate the room, then sat in a chair she had placed so that it faced her father.

She began speaking to Amahl. He tried to ignore her, but she continued in her efforts.

"Father, two months ago, we lost Mother and Rafael. I am here to tell you that we will not lose you, too. I am not going to allow it, Father. Do you hear me?"

Amahl did not answer her.

"Father, Hannah is gone. She has returned to her parents' home. She could not stay in this silent house anymore. She grieves for Rafael, but we did not help her. We forgot her, Father, so she is gone now."

Amahl continued to ignore his daughter.

"Father, you are going to leave this room now. Today!"

He shook his head in refusal.

"I will have Efraim carry you out if I have to. I will board up this room with my own hands to keep you out."

Amahl looked around the room at Bianca's books as tears filled his eyes. He looked at his daughter, and his tears spilled down his cheeks. He tried to speak, but words wouldn't form.

"Father, I want you to come with me. I want to show you something."

She pulled gently on his arms, but he resisted.

"Please, Father. Come with me." She began to cry, and then she was sobbing against his chest.

Amahl placed his hands on his daughter's hair. She looked up at him and whispered, "Come with me now."

She led him out of the room and down the stairs. They walked through the front door of the castle and around to the path leading to the stables. The sun was bright and almost blinding in the clean air. The rain had stopped the night before, leaving a new land growing about them. They walked together, the old man and the young girl, down the path to the charred ruins. The blackened timbers of the paddock glistened in the morning light. Puddles of water reflected the trees surrounding the wreckage. Blue sky rested on the ashes, promising an essence of hope.

Justina led her father to the center of what had once been the paddock. He tried to resist, but she determinedly took him by the hand and walked with him.

"Stand here, Father."

He looked at her, puzzled.

"Now listen. Do you hear them?"

They stood in silence listening to the breeze rustling the leaves of the trees. Birds sang and toads chirruped in their wet surroundings.

"There, do you hear it?"

Amahl looked around, waiting and trying to hear what Justina was describing to him, and then he heard them, too. Voices, singing voices. Soft, almost a muted sound of singing. He gazed at his daughter in wonder.

"What is that? Whose voices are those?"

"I come here every day to place flowers in the ashes, and I hear them."

The voices grew louder, the singing more resonant.

"Father, they are angels. Listen. Angels. They are singing for Mother and Rafael."

As the voices gained volume, Justina looked at her father, a smile on her face, as if she were begging for his approval. He began walking around the remains of the paddock, following the sound of the voices. He talked softly to his dead wife.

"Bianca? My darling? Do you hear them? They are your angels, Bianca. They sing for you."

He continued walking about the paddock. As Justina left, she could hear her father talking to her mother, but instead of calling out to her in his grief, he was sharing his joy with her as he had always done.

✢

From the memoir of
Meschianza de Lucena Cozar-Velasquez
July 28, 1496
Lisbon

Raul asks me why I write so diligently in my journal. I tell him that I write so the children we hope to have someday will not forget. He asks me, "Forget what?" And I answer him, "Everything."

My grandfather taught me to read. I was very small, but he took me to the circular room, and there I learned to read my grandmother's books. I sat on his lap and pointed to each word as he guided me. When I was older, he taught me to read in Arabic, the language of his religion, and it opened the world for me. When I was twelve years old, he told me of my grandmother, and he read to me a poem that had been one of her favorites. She could not read Arabic, so she memorized the poem as my grandfather read it to her. Following her example, I was able to memorize parts of it. I write it down for my children.

> *. . . How could the traveler not be delighted*
> *that love is the nearest house to the Lord?*
> *Love is a tree that produces only joy's fruit,*
> *an earth that grows nothing but intimacy's flowers,*
> *a cloud that rains nothing but light,*
> *a wine whose potion is nothing but honey . . .*

My grandfather's grief for my grandmother created the foundation of my childhood. I heard the angels singing long before my grandfather took me to the ruins. I told no one that I could see them, not even my mother.

I know that all light comes from God, and that the angels are His messengers. For the carrying of their messages, angels require wings. I believe this. My grandfather told me that Gabriel, God's most important angel, has seven hundred wings. It is he who carries the throne of God.

And the angel of death, Alzrael. I would think the losses of my family, and of our community, would have tired him. Perhaps he is tireless. Certainly, he is relentless. Does ruthlessness provide an energy that is undying? And where is God now? Even His angels hide their faces in shame.

28

⁂

The following spring, Amahl ordered the hyacinths that had been planted for his wedding over twenty years ago to be cut and banked on the ruins of the stable. Over time, the plants had multiplied, becoming so overgrown that the fragrant white blossoms filled two wagons. Each afternoon, he sat on the bench he placed in the burned courtyard, and in the drowning sunlight, he remembered his wife and son until Khalid came and brought him back to the castle.

Sara and a wet nurse took care of Meschianza, who was growing into a strong and active little girl. In the year since Bianca's death, Amahl had not yet recovered, and he had no interest in the estate. It was natural for Efraim to take charge of the groves and the sheep. With Khalid's instruction, he learned of each enterprise. Justina kept the ledgers, recording the activities of the estate as her mother had once done.

Amahl's days were often spent in the garden, watching over his little granddaughter, who was now piling flowers in his lap. Meschianza toddled over to gather more flowers, pulling out many by their roots. She was placing a new armload on her grandfather's lap when a man appeared from around the corner of the stone wall that bordered the garden. He stopped and looked at the little girl who ran up to him, handing him a rose she had ripped from the branches along the wall. Her thumb was bleeding where a thorn had scratched her. The man bent down and wrapped the little girl's finger with his linen handkerchief. He picked her up and walked toward the old man sitting in the shade, his lap full of flowers.

"Father, it is me, Benjamin."

Amahl looked up at his son and smiled wanly at him. Benjamin knelt before Amahl, still holding Meschianza in his arms. She struggled until he let her go, placing her on the ground next to her grandfather. She turned and ran into the castle through the kitchen door.

"Father, look at me."

Amahl, his hand shaking, reached up and touched Benjamin's face.

Benjamin waited for his father to acknowledge him, but Amahl was rising from his chair.

"Wait, Father."

Amahl stopped and turned to Benjamin, who was still kneeling on the ground before him.

Panic filled Amahl's eyes and quickly turned to despair. He sat in the chair again as if exhausted. The color left his face, and he was suddenly ashen. Benjamin didn't move, but continued to watch his father. Amahl studied his son as the realization occurred to him that Bianca's prayers had finally been answered. Grief overcame him as he examined his son. Benjamin looked so much like his mother, with her dark features and green eyes. He reached out to Benjamin, took him in his arms, and began crying.

"They are gone, Benjamin. Did you know? All of them, your mother, your brother. Gone."

"Yes, I was told in the village this morning. I am here to care for you and for Justina, too."

"But Benjamin, there is nothing to do. They are gone, all gone. The family is dead."

"No, the family is not dead. I'm here, and you and Justina, the baby, and Efraim—we are a family."

"But how will we continue without your mother? Hannah is gone, Rafael is gone. They have all left us."

Amahl's voice drifted off, and he would speak no more. Benjamin walked with him into the castle. Justina was in the kitchen with Sara, and as the two men entered, she and Sara stared in shock at the younger man.

"Father, who—Benjamin? Benjamin, is that you?"

Benjamin stood awkwardly next to his father, and then suddenly Justina was in his arms, laughing and hugging him. Sara, her eyesight weakened by old age, went to the two young people and held out her arms to Benjamin. He pulled her into their embrace and kissed the old woman on her cheek. Justina pulled away from his arms and ran to find her husband. The baby began to cry in the confusion. Her grandfather picked her up and offered her to his son. The little girl, frightened by all the commotion, scrambled from his embrace and ran behind a chair.

Justina entered with Efraim, who looked at Benjamin with disbelief. He held out his hand to the young man and began asking questions.

"All these years, I searched for you. Where did you go? I asked everyone I saw if they had seen you."

"I was in the Far East—oh, we have much to talk about, Efraim."

Sara began herding the happy group into the dining room.

"We will eat, and we will rejoice. Benjamin is home. We will celebrate. Everyone sit down. Come now, it is time."

Benjamin picked up Meschianza, who was still hiding behind a chair. He led his father into the dining room and set Meschianza down in a chair beside him. Sara brought in platters of food, and she and Khalid stood behind Amahl's and Justina's chairs. As Efraim took his place at the head of the table, he lifted the silver wine goblet and looked at Justina.

"Shabbat Shalom, Justina."

"Shabbat Shalom, Efraim."

He looked at Amahl, and then at Benjamin. He turned to Sara and Khalid as they all waited in silence. Then he lifted the cup and began to chant.

Blessed be he who comes in the name of the Lord.

Slowly, Amahl stood up and joined his son-in-law. Together, they intoned:

Blessed Art Thou, O Lord Our God, Ruler of the Universe, who has created the fruit of the vine.

Efraim drank from the cup and passed it to Amahl. He watched as his father-in-law drank from it, and passed it to Justina. When everyone had shared the Sabbath cup, and ritually washed their hands, Efraim continued.

He took the *challah* from the tray, and closed his eyes.

Blessed Art Thou, O Lord Our God, Ruler of the Universe, who bringest forth food from the earth.

He pulled off a piece of the *challah* and dipped it in the salt. He turned to Meschianza, and reaching down, he placed a piece of it in her mouth. He broke the rest of the loaf into pieces, dipped them in salt, and passed the tray to Justina, who rose from her chair and carried the tray to each person at the table.

Outside, the sun was tumbling into the sea. As its golden rays lay across the land, the angels in the copse began their litany for Bianca and her son. Their singing was joined by Efraim's lament as he intoned the Psalm of Thanksgiving.

Oh give thanks unto the Lord, for He is good;
For His mercy endures forever.
So let the house of Aaron now say
For His mercy endures forever.

PART 2

I

1480
Cadiz

The estate prospered under the charge of Efraim and Justina. The textile industry in Flanders created a never-ending demand for wool. The couple hired Andres Davila, a merchant in Tarifa, to be their new associate. This work had benefited their wealth greatly, and today the family was getting ninety-eight new Merinos for their farm. Justina and Meschianza, now eight years old, waited for Señor Davila and Efraim to deliver the sheep from the dock at the Cadiz waterfront. Jaime, born two years after Meschianza, stood next to his sister and mother, eagerly watching for his father.

"Mother, they are here!" shouted Jaime.

A cloud of dust traveled along the courtyard lane, pausing at the great iron gates, resuming movement toward the front of the castle. Soon the dust enveloped them, and Meschianza, coughing and standing behind her mother for protection, was surrounded by sheep. Her father, Andres Davila, and Raul, his nine-year-old son, herded nearly one hundred animals to the meadow below the olive groves. Though Justina tried to stop him, Jaime ran after Raul.

A seven-year-old girl was left sitting sidesaddle on her pony, not knowing whether to follow Andres Davila and the sheep, or to wait for him at the front of the castle. Justina, noticing the child's uncertainty, approached the girl. Meschianza, suddenly shy, remained where she was.

"You must be Pisa Davila. My husband told me that you would come today with your brother and father to deliver the sheep. I am Señora Cozar-Velasquez."

The little girl beamed her delight at Justina and offered her hand.

"Welcome to our home, Pisa. This is my daughter, Meschianza."

Pisa dismounted as Justina turned to Meschianza. She led the two children to the door, and Pisa was awestruck by the size of the castle. She entered the castle, her eyes transfixed on the stone stairs as she followed the steps to the third floor. Sunlight streamed through the glass windows inset in the staircase's circular walls. Dust motes sparkled like tiny diamonds as they floated in the light rays. Pisa turned to Justina:

"Your house is very beautiful, Señora."

"Thank you, Donzella. Are you hungry?"

Pisa did not answer immediately. She was still studying the entry, her eyes traveling over the hanging tapestries on the stone walls and the Oriental carpets that graced the marble floors.

"Meschianza, why don't you take Pisa to your bedchamber, and I will send a servant with some refreshments for the two of you."

Meschianza took Pisa by the hand and slowly led her up the stairs. They entered her room, and Pisa gasped.

She approached Meschianza's bed and stared at the dolls that covered the surface. Meschianza reached out and picked up one of the dolls. She offered it to Pisa, who hesitated and then took the beautiful confection in her arms.

"Oh, I don't have dolls like these. They are so wonderful."

Meschianza watched Pisa as she held the doll.

"I would like to give her to you."

"But I can't take your doll. It is very generous of you to offer it to me, but I may not accept it."

"Why not?"

Pisa was embarrassed now. She hesitated, and then answered Meschianza.

"I don't think my mother will let me keep it."

"Why not?"

"My mother . . . she does not . . . "

Pisa hesitated, and a worried expression came over her face as Meschianza waited.

"You see, my mother . . . does not like . . . Jews."

Pisa looked down at the floor in shame as Meschianza stared at her silently. Pisa offered the doll back to Meschianza without looking at her, her embarrassment heating her face like fire. Meschianza did not take the proffered doll. She merely stared at Pisa distrustfully.

"Do you like Jews?" Meschianza blurted out.

"I don't know any. My mother says I must not talk to Jews, but my father says that she is wrong."

Meschianza watched Pisa. Both girls stood awkwardly for a moment, then Meschianza took the doll from Pisa's hands. With reluctance, Pisa let it go.

"I will keep your doll for you here. I will take care of it, and if you come again, you can play with it."

Pisa looked gratefully at Meschianza.

"I have never had a friend to play with, except for my brother."

"Neither have I. I have a brother, but he only likes to ride horses."

Before the servant arrived with a tray of food for the two little girls, they had already left Meschianza's room and run out the front door of the castle. Justina saw them through the window of the parlor as they rounded the corner of the building and continued toward the meadows. Their laughter carried back to Justina's ears, and then suddenly the sound disappeared as they entered the barn that housed the baby lambs.

There they discovered Jaime and Raul. When Jaime saw Pisa, he handed her a lamb that was only three days old. As she cradled it in her arms, her father entered the barn, followed by Efraim.

"I see you children have met. Good! I have been wanting to bring you to meet Jaime and Meschianza for many weeks now."

Andres Davila looked at his partner, Efraim, with delight. His children had been isolated too long by their mother. He wanted them here in the clean sea air, the meadows, and the groves. He and Efraim had already discussed sharing a tutor for their children, and arrangements had been made for a young scholar of the Sephardic community to begin teaching the four children the following week. Esperanza Davila objected to her children being tutored by the young man because she wanted her son to be instructed by the monks. She didn't want Pisa to be educated at all. Esperanza's mother had died a year after she was born. Esperanza's father had gone bankrupt and disappeared, leaving his small daughter in his sister's care. Esperanza's aunt was bitter about his disappearance, insisting that a Jewish moneylender had robbed her brother of his inheritance. She had never attributed his losses to gambling, or to his lack of business savvy. She had placed Esperanza in a poor and barren convent, paying only a minimal stipend for her niece's care. The little girl had grown up without love. As she matured, Esperanza shared her aunt's anti-Semitic sentiment. Her aunt had arranged the marriage to Andres in an effort to unburden herself of her charge.

Esperanza did not love her husband, nor was she capable of loving her two children. The most important goal in her life was to maintain her social status. She lived in fear that her peers would penetrate the façade she desperately struggled to maintain.

Andres recognized his young daughter's capacity to learn, and he did not intend to refuse her wish to be educated with her brother. He used his authority to override his wife's objections. Now he was content that his children would be happy to visit the Cozar-Velasquez estate and receive an education. Andres's action only heightened his wife's resentment against Pisa.

When Esperanza remembered her own barren childhood, trapped in the convent and subjected to the nuns' cruelty, her jealousy of her daughter's freedom incensed her. She had never escaped her childhood memories. Esperanza was an unhappy woman isolated by her own fears, imprisoned by her hatred.

✤

2

⁜

The four children developed loyalty to one another during their childhood. On the cold winter days, after their lessons, the four of them gathered in the circular room and read to one another from the beautiful, ancient, handwritten books.

When they tired of reading, the children hid from each other in the castle. There were over twenty rooms. When they discovered the cellar, they found even better hiding places. One day, Meschianza led Raul into the long, damp, curving tunnel. They followed its path until they reached the opening. In near whispers, she told him how her family used to smuggle Moors out of Spain, swearing him to secrecy. She told him of her Uncle Benjamin, who ran away and then suddenly returned, only to leave again. Benjamin was forever restless, never having married. He had been gone now for many years.

The two stood watching the sea roil and churn in a black storm. They decided to start a small fire at the mouth of the cave, and ran back to get Jaime and Pisa. The four children raided the kitchen, greatly disturbing the new cook who had been hired soon after Sara's death. Khalid's death had preceded Sara's by a year. Her grief for him had caused her health to fail, until she died peacefully in her sleep.

The two girls took their contraband of food to the entrance, and the boys carried wood from the cook's stove. They spent the rest of the afternoon around their fire, eating candied oranges, cheese, and freshly baked bread. They spoke of their dreams and their futures.

Raul would soon be leaving for the university, and Jaime would follow. Their childhood was coming to an end. One cold, damp afternoon, Meschianza and Raul sought the sanctuary of the tunnel, and as they warmed their hands over the fire, a calm descended upon them. Raul, who seldom took his eyes off Meschianza, was edgy and irritable. He tried to deny his feelings for Meschianza, but now that he was about to leave for the university, his pain at their impending separation was overtaking him. He couldn't declare his love for her. He knew that Meschianza was promised to Mateo de la Vega, a young man who lived in the walled Jewish section of the city. The marriage had been arranged when they were children and would take place when her betrothed completed his education in Madrid.

"Meschianza, when does Mateo return?"

"He will be gone for three years, Raul."

She studied her hands, and then looked out at the entrance of the tunnel. The sea was churning, the great waves cresting and the white foam spraying the base of the cliffs below.

"Will you marry him when he comes home?"

She looked at Raul with an expression of pain.

"I must obey my father's wishes, Raul. Mateo is a good man, and I know that he loves me. Our marriage has been planned since we were children."

Her loyalty was one of the characteristics he loved most about her. Ironically, it was also the characteristic that would ultimately take her from him.

"But is this what you want?"

"How can it be different, Raul? It does not matter what I want. My mother says I will be happy with Mateo."

He stood at the mouth of the cave and stared at the sea. He turned to her.

"When I return from the university, I will build a ship. We will sail away, Meschianza. Together, we could be happy."

Tears came to her eyes as she looked at him. His misery caused her heart to break.

"We could never be happy like that, Raul, without our parents' blessings."

"And they would not give it?"

"We are of different faiths."

"You don't believe in dreams, Meschianza?"

"Mother has taught me that dreams are dangerous, and that we must accept our fate. It is not our destiny to be together, Raul. My destiny is with Mateo. My mother believes I will be safe with him."

"Safe? You do not think you can be safe and happy with me?"

"Perhaps the two things do not go together."

He knelt down in front of her and took her by the shoulders.

"Meschianza, they can exist side by side; safety, happiness, love. I love you! Don't you know this?"

"Yes. I know it. I have always known it."

"You love me, don't you?"

She tried to pull away from him, but he would not let her go.

"Say it! Say it to me, Meschianza. You love me. Say it!"

She began sobbing, and he let her go. He waited for her to answer him.

"I cannot say those words to you, Raul. I am betrothed. I must not say them."

He sat beside her and took her in his arms. She clung to him, whispering, begging his forgiveness.

That day, as they watched the dark sea below, Raul felt a more devastating storm approaching. He could not define his fears, but he would often be awakened in the night by a vision of Meschianza's grief-stricken face. He told no one of his forebodings.

Meschianza was fifteen when Raul left for the University of Salamanca. Andres wanted Raul to study law so that he would be better suited to administer the estate he would inherit. Rather than follow his father's wishes, Raul pursued navigation with Abraham Zacuto, who was famous for his invention of astronomical tables and his astrolabe. Raul intended to use this knowledge for his own explorations someday.

As he read his assignments, Meschianza's face haunted the pages of Raul's books. Her essence rose from the paper as he wrote the answers to his exams. His restlessness grew year by year, until his return, when he sought her out, riding along the coast to her father's estate. She spotted him from the top of the bluff and began riding down the path to meet him. He could hear Meschianza calling his name above the sound of the surf. Each dismounted and fell to the sand as they embraced each other, Meschianza on top of him, laughing and kissing his face over and over.

She had still been a little girl to him when he left for the university, but in three years she had grown taller and more beautiful. The tide was coming in, so they climbed the rocks and sat there for the rest of the afternoon.

"Tell me, Raul. Tell me all about Salamanca. What did you see?"

"I saw so many wonderful things, Meschianza. There is such a world beyond us, so many things we cannot even imagine."

"And the university, what did you learn?"

"I studied ships, and oceans, and navigation. The exams were very difficult, and the professors were sadistic, but I persevered, and I completed my studies."

"I wish I could have gone with you. There is so much I want to know, and so much I want to see."

She looked at him eagerly and listened attentively as he told her of his adventures. When he finished, she told him everything that had occurred while he was away. As the blue shadows on the rocks surrounding them grew longer on the narrowing stretch of sand, they led their horses to the back of the castle. He was welcomed by her family and invited to join their Sabbath meal.

The flame from the candles illuminated Meschianza's face as her father chanted the benediction. Every glance Raul cast her way made him feel as if he were studying a fine painting. He watched her as the plans for building his own ships spun in his head, and Raul realized he could never follow in his father's footsteps. His rebellion came to fruition that night on the eve of the Sabbath, at a table filled with her loving family. Since his childhood, this room had represented the warmth he craved from his own parents. He felt closer to Meschianza's family than he ever could have felt to his own family in his sinister mother's home.

Raul returned to his parents' villa that night, feeling more at peace than he could comprehend. With money his father gave him, he hired the best builder in Cadiz and began constructing his first ship. He was fascinated with ocean travel and the foreign galleons that entered Cadiz's seaport. He desired his own fleet, and spent his days overseeing the building of his dreams, for it was his intention to sail to the North African coast as soon as his ship was finished.

✤

3

❖

Meschianza waited in front of the castle for Pisa to arrive. She watched the approaching carriage, barely able to contain her excitement. The two of them had not seen each other since the beginning of the *fiesta de pan cenceno*. Meschianza's hands were held together as if in prayer as Señor Davila's daughter stepped out of the carriage. Her duenna, Señora Gomez, followed. She was a large, barrel-shaped woman dressed in black, her mantilla shading a face that never smiled.

"I have missed you, Pisa. Are you well?"

Meschianza embraced her friend, her glee impossible to contain.

"Yes, I am very well, and glad to be here with you again. I have been so lonely. There was little to do without you."

Pisa turned to Justina, who had joined them. She was nodding at the duenna and smiling her welcome to the older woman. Señora Gomez stood, her aloof stance a daunting commentary on the joy the two young women shared as they embraced and entered the castle.

Justina led Señora Gomez to the sitting room she had provided for Meschianza's duenna.

"Señora Luna, Señora Gomez is here to join you. Isn't it nice of her to visit with us today?"

Justina looked at the other woman, a pleading expression on her face as she brought Señora Gomez into the room. Señora Luna was working on a piece of embroidery, laboring the fabric with a nearsighted eye and a trembling needle. Neither woman uttered a word as they shared the room in frigid tolerance. Señora Gomez, a devout Catholic, always made a point of sitting down to say her rosary in a low murmur, which provoked Meschianza's duenna to shoot her a distrustful glare.

Justina left the room and closed the door as the two embattled women sat in silence. She turned to speak to Meschianza and Pisa, but the two young women had scurried up to Meschianza's room.

Justina stood alone in the entry of the castle and listened to the quiet. Certain that all was well, she went to the kitchen to direct the new cook in preparing supper for the family and their guests.

As the young women entered Meschianza's room, Pisa ran to open the casement windows.

"Where is Jaime? I cannot see him."

"Pisa, he is probably waiting for us by the water. Did Raul bring your horse? Is he coming?"

"Yes. He should be at the mouth of the cave now. Do you think Jaime is there also?"

"I think he is. See, there is my father. He is coming back to the castle. The sheep must be in the new pasture. Hurry!"

The girls left Meschianza's room and crept down the steps to the front door of the building. After they determined that all was clear, they hurried to the side of the castle. They had to sneak past the windows of the parlor where their duennas were sitting. The two girls crawled beneath the casements, the ground muddy from last night's rain. By the time the two were upright again, they were filthy, with mud clinging to their clothing and faces.

They ran to the edge of the bluff, careful to avoid the spot where Meschianza's grandfather sang his prayers every evening, and began the treacherous climb down to the rocks below.

Meschianza was already at the bottom of the cliff watching Pisa ease herself along the rocks when Raul and Jaime approached them. Jaime dismounted his horse to help Pisa climb the rest of the way to the sand. He pulled her into his arms as she reached up and kissed him. Raul and Meschianza walked, leading their horses to the far end of the cove to give Jaime and Pisa some time alone.

The Passover celebration passed slowly for them, for during the eight days, Jaime and Meschianza were restricted to their father's home because of the unrest in the village. The Catholic community was particularly distrustful of the walled Jewish quarters in Tarifa. For several years, the level of persecution of the Jews had risen again, especially during the time of the Passover. Travel was restricted, as the roads were dangerous for Jewish families.

Raul and Meschianza walked silently along the beach. They watched the light change on the violet water as the sun broke through the gray clouds. Her cloak already ruined with mud, Meschianza spread it onto the sand and sat down. Raul sat beside her, holding the reins of his horse in his hand.

"What will happen to those two?"

"I don't know, Raul." Meschianza began smoothing her dress.

"They cannot continue like this much longer before they are found out. I don't think they understand the resistance they will encounter from my parents and yours."

"They know. They just don't want to think about it."

"Every time Pisa escapes from her duenna, Mother goes into a rage that lasts for days. Our mother will never agree to a marriage between them."

"Yes, she would rather place Pisa in a convent than see her married to a Jew."

Meschianza watched Raul from the corner of her eye. He was

perhaps the most handsome young man in Tarifa. His hair was sun-bleached to near whiteness, and his tanned skin was golden. He exuded health and well-being. When the four of them were children, they had played along the beach after their lessons were finished. As they splashed in the waves, pushing one another, it was Raul who was most compelled by the ocean. He memorized the rise and fall of the water according to the seasons.

"Are they aware of all that is taking place in Spain right now?"

Before Meschianza could speak, he answered for her.

"No, they are not!"

She was studying the sand before her, her hands stuffed into her pockets. She tried to think of a reply, but could only shake her head. She was rendered speechless, as she often was with Raul. He watched as her hair blew across her face, then reached over to brush it away. Meschianza shivered.

"Are you cold? Perhaps we should go back to the castle?"

"No. Let's not disturb them. They have not seen each other since Pesach. It has been more than a week."

Raul was quiet for a moment, but his frustrations overtook him again.

"You know, there is talk of the Blood Libel again. I heard about it in the village during Passover."

"Yes, I know. I heard my father speaking to my mother about the *Niño de La Guardia*. We are all afraid."

"It is such nonsense. How can anyone believe that your people would kill Christian babies for their blood? Even my father is amazed by this foolish superstition. He says people are so ignorant."

He was grabbing handfuls of sand and throwing them out to the sea. Some of the sand blew back in their faces. Meschianza ducked behind Raul and began laughing at him. She picked up a handful of sand and dumped it on his head. He tried to grab her, but she got up to run down the length of the beach. He considered chasing her, but sensed that Pisa must get back to the castle soon.

He called out to Pisa and Jaime as they emerged from the cave, both of them flushed and embarrassed. Raul said nothing as Meschianza approached them, pretending to study the shells in her hand.

He spoke to Jaime as Meschianza joined him at the base of the cliff.

"It is time for Pisa to return before her duenna discovers she is gone."

✧

4

The sun rested on the horizon like a great orange bird perched on a giant tree limb when Meschianza and Pisa reached the top of the bluff. The two young women heard Amahl chant his prayers as the sun bobbed gently, slowly descending beneath the sea. They circled around the kneeling Amahl, and as they approached the castle, they too knelt as they crawled beneath the window. Whispering to each other to be quiet, they muffled their giggles as they rounded the corner of the castle. Suddenly, Meschianza, who was in front of Pisa, stopped and stared at a pair of black shoes peeking out from beneath a black bombazine skirt. The hem of the skirt was slightly frayed and rusty. The shoes were covered with mud.

Meschianza looked up at the person who was blocking their path. Pisa, surprised by the abrupt halt in their progress, bumped into Meschianza, causing her friend to fall forward onto the feet of the duenna. The two young women slowly raised their eyes to meet the faces of Señora Gomez, Señora Luna, and Justina. Frozen in their kneeling position, they could only stare in disbelief at two of the stern, unattractive faces. Señora Gomez's mustachioed mouth was grim and disapproving, while Señora Luna's displayed a shocked frown. Justina was plainly distressed.

She spoke to her daughter with firm authority.

"Meschianza, what is this?"

Pisa's duenna walked around Meschianza, grabbed Pisa by the elbow, and jerked her up to a standing position. She did not let go of her arm while she looked at Señora Luna and Justina. Her anger was piercing out of her small, close-set eyes. Her face trembled, and her jowls shook rapidly as she dragged Pisa to the front of the castle.

Meschianza ran after her friend as Justina reached out for her daughter.

"Meschianza, stay here. I want to know where you have been."

Meschianza pulled away from her mother's grasp and continued around the corner of the castle in time to see the duenna shove Pisa into the dark depths of the black-curtained carriage. The groom started the conveyance down the drive before the door was closed.

"Meschianza, where are Jaime and Raul? Was Pisa with Jaime again? You must explain this," demanded Justina.

"Not now, Mother!"

Meschianza ran from the drive to the back of the castle. Justina and Señora Luna hurried after her, but she was already fleeing down the cellar steps. Justina ran after her daughter, but she had disappeared. Meschianza flew fearlessly down the cellar steps in the dark.

As she reached the dusky light at the tunnel's opening, Meschianza began calling out to Jaime and Raul. She was halfway down the cliff when they rode up to meet her. Breathless, she began telling them what had happened.

"Pisa—she is in trouble—her duenna, Señora Gomez, has taken her home!"

Jaime, grabbed his sister's arm in the heat of his alarm.

"What do you mean, she is in trouble?"

"We were caught! Our duennas caught us trying to sneak back into the castle. And our mother! She was there, too. She is so angry, Jaime, and she suspects you were with Pisa again. Señora Gomez has taken Pisa home. She probably knows, too. She will tell Pisa's mother!"

Meschianza felt helpless as she looked at Jaime and Raul.

"It is all my fault. We should have gone through the tunnel, but I believed Mother would be in the kitchen with the cook, so I thought . . . "

"Meschianza, it is not your fault. You were only trying to help us. I am to blame. I did this to Pisa. How could I have been so stupid?"

"Father must know by now. And Señor Davila. We must return to the castle and face them."

Raul, trying to remain calm, spoke to both of them.

"I will go home and try to calm my mother. Perhaps I can get there before the carriage arrives."

"Yes, Raul. You must go. Please tell Pisa I am sorry. I blame myself. She is my friend, and I love her very much."

He mounted his horse and raced down the darkening beach. Jaime helped Meschianza onto his horse and climbed behind her. Together, they sped up the path to the barn behind the castle.

✣

5

❖

Meschianza and Jaime brushed the horse, hurrying because they knew they were late. The rain was starting again, and they wanted to get to the castle before it began to pour.

"What will you do, Jaime?"

"Marry her, of course."

"Father won't let you."

"Yes, he will. I will speak to him tonight."

"He won't listen. Mother wants you to marry our cousin, Rachel Pereira."

Meschianza thought about Rachel, an unattractive woman. She broke out in giggles.

"You will have very homely children."

"Meschianza, that is not funny!"

She buried her face in the mane of the horse to muffle her laughter.

"And what about you? Always mooning over Raul. Do you think you will marry him? Father will lock you in the cellar first, and then marry you to Mateo."

Meschianza stopped laughing and looked at her brother, a hurt expression on her face.

"Why do you speak to me with such cruelty?"

"Because Raul will never marry you. He is a wanderer just like Uncle Benjamin. He only wants to sail the oceans. Soon he will be gone, and you will never see him again."

"I don't think that is true."

"Don't be foolish, Meschianza."

"I am no more foolish than you are. Even if Father agrees to let you marry Pisa, her mother would rather see Pisa dead before she agreed to let her daughter marry a Jew."

"I will convert. Then she will accept me."

Meschianza stopped brushing the horse's mane. She dropped the brush and backed away from her brother. Her hands were shaking as she stared at him, appalled by his statement.

"You must not say that, Jaime, not even in jest!"

"I am serious, Meschianza. I have spoken to Pisa about it, and we have been to see the priest. He is instructing me."

"Tell me you are lying! Say you are teasing me as you have always done."

He looked at her, his face solemn.

"I am not lying. I love Pisa, and I will not live without her, even if I must live my life dead to my father and mother."

Meschianza backed away from Jaime, and then ran out of the barn. Jaime called after her, but she didn't answer. He placed his head against the side of his horse and tried to find resolve amid his despair for upsetting his sister. He loved Meschianza as much as he loved Pisa. He did not want to hurt anyone in his family, but he knew he could not sacrifice the one person he wanted to spend his life with. He resolved to speak to his father. Dreading the encounter, he entered the castle and prepared for the confrontation.

✦

6

Meschianza raced up the stone steps to the top floor. Her bed-chamber was in the corner of the east wing, directly across from the tower room. Visions of her mother's despair and her father's anger overwhelmed her as she entered her room. She did not want to go downstairs for dinner. She did not want to believe Jaime's confession to her, but then she remembered the expressions on Pisa's and Jaime's faces as they left the cave, and knew that Jaime had every intention of marrying Pisa. Her terror grew as she thought of her friend. How would Pisa's parents react?

Pisa was a brave woman. She had a courage Meschianza could never possess. Pisa had taken risks along the cliffs where they had played as children, while Meschianza had held her breath, her eyes shut, clinging to the rocks in fear. She would wait for Raul to rescue her. It was Pisa who risked her mother's wrath every time she escaped her duenna's watchful eye to meet with Jaime, stealing precious hours with him in the tunnel.

Meschianza went to the water bowl on her large oak vanity. She washed her face and stared at herself in the mirror. She straightened her hair and changed into clean clothes. She had difficulty fastening her dress. She should have called her maid, Ana, but she was already late for dinner.

Jaime's room was at the end of the corridor. She knocked on the carved oak door. When Jaime opened it, she threw herself into his arms.

"I should not have left you in the barn. Please forgive me."

Jaime held his sister, squeezing her too hard as he had when they were children. Her hair smelled of sea water, and her black velvet dress felt luxurious beneath his fingers. She was trembling, and Jaime tightened his embrace.

"Do not be afraid, Meschianza. Everything will be all right."

"No, Jaime. It will not. This will hurt Mother. And Father. He will be so angry. I am afraid for you and Pisa. Her mother . . . She will beat Pisa! She will harm her."

"No. Señor Davila will not allow Pisa to be hurt. And we will be married soon. Pisa will not have to be with her mother much longer."

Meschianza could see Jaime's resolve as she looked into his eyes.

"I love you. I love Pisa, too. I want happiness for both of you, but where will you live? How will you take care of her?"

"Father loves us, Meschianza. He will not turn us away."

She looked at her brother doubtfully.

"We must go down to dinner now, Jaime. Mother, Father, and Grandfather will be waiting for us."

"Yes, I know." Jaime hesitated. He straightened his clothing and asked Meschianza, "How do I look?"

"Handsome, as always. My very handsome brother. No wonder Pisa loves you."

"Meschianza, will you help me talk to Father?"

She turned to her brother and shook her head.

"You must do this by yourself, Jaime. I love you, and I will always love you, but I cannot help you tell Father."

She embraced him again, feeling his trembling body. She took him by the hand and led him to dinner.

✤

7

Efraim Cozar-Velasquez had never raised his voice to either of his children. He was soft-spoken with his wife, and tolerant with Jaime and Meschianza. He had not enforced restrictions on them at the estate, recognizing their freedom to run along the beaches and meadows with their friends, the Davila children. Many citizens of Tarifa had shunned the Jews, but not Andres Davila. He actively opposed his wife's wishes, allowing the children's friendship. As the tax on all commercial transactions, the *alcalba*, had risen each year, it was Andres who helped ease Efraim's burden by offering to pay half on their joint enterprises. When the General Assembly of Mirando de Ebro required Jews to pay an additional tax to support the war effort, Andres contributed his share again. There were many decent, compassionate men in Spain who disagreed with the dictates of the assembly, who secretly aided their Sephardic friends. Efraim often heard rumors of more actions against the Jewish community, many of which seemed incredible.

Efraim looked at his family as they sat around the dining table. Justina had placed her hand on Meschianza's forehead.

"Do you have a fever? You look ill."

"No, Mother. I am just tired."

Amahl reached across the table and patted his granddaughter's hand. He removed a small honey cake from his plate and placed it on hers before he returned to his meal.

Efraim noticed Meschianza's trembling hands as she smiled

back at her grandfather. Jaime was quieter than usual. What were the two of them up to now? His wife was still shaken from the afternoon. Justina had advised Efraim of what had occurred earlier as they waited for their children to join the dinner table.

"Did Meschianza tell you what it was about?"

"No, Efraim. I have not seen either of them since she ran down the cellar steps. Ana said that they are getting ready for dinner and will be with us shortly."

"Perhaps Jaime should attend to his duties as the heir of this estate. He has been home from Barcelona for three months already. I spoke to my cousin Constanza only last month. She agrees to let her daughter marry Jaime. I will speak to her again. The wedding must be planned and the west wing of the castle prepared for the new bride."

"Yes, Efraim. And Meschianza?"

"Mateo's father says he will return from the university soon. He may be home already. I will speak to his parents. Perhaps it is time for two weddings, my darling."

"Our children have grown up so fast."

"Yes, but the time has come, Justina. We must see to our children's futures. We would fail them if we did not."

Now, at the dinner table, he turned to his son.

"Jaime, we must speak of your plans for the future. After dinner, you will join me in the great room."

Jaime glanced nervously at his sister, who, startled by her father's request, dropped her fork on the stone floor. Meschianza stared straight ahead as the serving maid bent down to retrieve it. When Jaime realized his sister was not going to look his way, he replied to his father.

"Yes, Father, I will be happy to join you."

The maids cleared the table, and Amahl retired to the tower room with a book in his hand. Meschianza and Justina went to their sitting room, where Meschianza's eyes blurred over the words of her book. Justina worked on her embroidery.

"Meschianza, we must discuss this afternoon."

"Yes, Mother."

"Where were you and Pisa? With Raul and Jaime? Is that why you left the castle without your duennas?"

Meschianza hesitated, but before she could answer her mother, the two heard shouts echoing from the great room. Shocked, Justina looked up from her sewing at Meschianza. She dropped her embroidery into the basket by her chair and ran to her husband. Meschianza, full of dread, followed her mother.

As Justina entered the room, Efraim was in a furor as he spoke to his son.

"A converso? You wish to become a converso? A traitor? A defector?"

Her father continued yelling as Meschianza went to stand by her mother. Amahl entered the room and placed his arm around the motionless and stunned Justina.

Jaime was pleading with his father, but Efraim was still fuming.

"How can you betray us like this and abandon everything we have taught you? Where does this weakness come from?"

Head bowed, her brother tried to defend himself.

"Answer me! Surely, I am entitled to an explanation! You are my heir, and yet you speak of this ultimate betrayal. You are my only son, and you would renounce your covenant with the Creator? How can you do this when so many have died before they would convert? Our community still has not recovered from the executions in Seville. So many of us died as martyrs asserting the *kiddush ha-Shem*. There are people who refused to become one of the many *anusim* in our midst. And now you intend to become one of these converts? Without even being forced like the rest of them? You shame us! You bring infamy upon our name. Where does this cowardice come from?"

When his father was finally silent, Jaime spoke.

"Father, I love Pisa, and I intend to marry her. I cannot do this unless I convert."

Efraim turned away from his son in disgust.

"I do not recognize you! I do not know you! You betray everyone who has come before you. Every sacrifice and every persecution this family has suffered in four hundred years, you now render meaningless."

He turned back to reproach his son.

"Your grandfather's ancestors have been here since the eleventh century, loyal to the Cid, given this land by the King of Spain. He and your grandmother shared an honorable marriage, and at no time did the old general demand that your grandmother surrender her faith. We have kept his covenant with her. You will force our heritage in Spain to end!"

Justina began moaning, her low voice muffled by her handkerchief. Efraim slumped into a chair, his anger spent and replaced now by despair. Justina bent forward as Meschianza tried to comfort her. Jaime stood by the fireplace and watched his parents. He felt remorseful as he looked at his mother. She was staring blankly and slowly tearing her dress from the shoulder to her waist. Meschianza tried to stop her, but her efforts were useless.

Efraim, silent tears drowning his eyes, watched Justina as she rocked back and forth, Meschianza's arms around her. Her eyes were focused on the floor, but Efraim could sense that she was withdrawn, knowing what was to follow.

He directed his declaration to his wife as Jaime listened with disbelief.

"Justina, our son is gone from us now."

Jaime's mother shook her head in denial. She feared what was coming. This caused her to speak in a muted whisper.

"You must not do this, Efraim. Our son. You must think of the Fates. Do not reward them like this, Efraim."

His rage was such that, for the first time in their wedded life, he ignored his wife.

"Our son, Jaime de Lucena Cozar-Velasquez, is dead."

Justina cried out only once before she collapsed. Her sobbing nearly drowned the sound of her husband reciting the Mourner's Kaddish for their son.

"Do not do this, Efraim. Do not force us to participate in this revenge. Don't you feel them? They are all around us. They celebrate our grief. Efraim, listen to me."

Meschianza held her mother as her father finished the prayer. Efraim looked at Meschianza with a stern stare. She shook her head at him. She knew she was expected to leave the room, but she refused to abandon her brother.

While Efraim condemned his son, Amahl stood next to his daughter in silence. He was appalled. When Amahl heard Efraim declare Jaime dead to them, he castigated his son-in-law.

"What has become of this family? Look at your wife, Efraim. Look at her grief!"

Efraim began to object.

"My Father, Jaime's betrayal will not be tolerated. I condemn it!"

"You condemn it? You condemn love?"

Dry-eyed and shocked, Meschianza ran to her brother's side. He lay crumpled on the floor, holding to the edge of a chair. He looked up at her, his eyes full of panic. Jaime tried to say something, but his words came out in tears. He fell against her. Meschianza managed to pull him onto the chair. As she knelt before him, she began her sin against her father, and consoled Jaime.

"Look at your children, Efraim! How can you condemn them? Have you forgotten what my wife stood for? These are her grandchildren, and they are not dead! Your son loves this young woman. She is good and decent. Raised with your children, by your choice. By your choice!"

He roared at Efraim. Justina reached for her father's arm and tried to calm him, but his anger was beyond her control.

"Love, Efraim. That is what this family stands for. If you had not known Bianca, I could forgive you, but you knew her. You know that what she did for people, she did out of love for them, not for religious principles. If they were persecuted Catholics, she would have helped them."

Efraim got up to leave the room, but not before turning to face his father-in-law.

"Bianca would not consent to her grandson becoming a converso. You know this, Father!"

"No, I do not! She would have defended the love between Pisa and Jaime, and she would condemn you for your rejection. You forget, she married me. She was my wife because she loved me."

Efraim, not wishing to be disrespectful toward his father-in-law, beckoned to Justina. She turned to her father, uncertain what to do. Amahl felt compassion for her predicament.

"You must obey your husband, Justina. I have said all I can."

Justina did not look at her children as she left the room with Efraim.

Meschianza remained. She spoke to her brother.

"I will not desert you, Jaime. I will not desert Pisa. Do you hear me? I love you, and you will never be dead to me."

Jaime's sobs continued, his body racked by his tears. He clung to his sister in desperation.

"Didn't you see, Meschianza? Mother couldn't even look at me. And Father. He despises me."

Amahl went to Jaime and tried to comfort him.

"No, no. Jaime, they love you. Your mother loves you."

"How could he declare me dead when I stood before him?"

"He must. You know this."

"Will Mother ever look at me, Grandfather? Will she see me?"

His sister answered him.

"You know she cannot, Jaime."

He stood up to straighten his clothing, and turned to his sister and grandfather. Meschianza was still on the floor, so he helped her up. He left the great room and entered the hall by the front door. His cloak was draped over a table. He picked it up and returned to the room. Meschianza was seated on a couch before the fire, with Amahl standing beside her. She looked up at Jaime, and seeing the cloak in his hand, she realized her brother must leave the castle. He was pale and haggard, and appeared older.

"Where will you go, Jaime?"

"To Mateo's family. Perhaps they will not hate me."

"I will come tomorrow. I will bring your things."

Jaime backed out of the room, his eyes fixed on his sister's face. He did not say anything else to his grandfather before he left. As Meschianza heard the great wooden door slam shut, her body tensed. Sitting on the couch, her back straight, her shoulders lifted with determination, the tearless Meschianza stared at the fire until late into the night. Amahl had followed his grandson to the door, trying to console him. She did not hear him as he stood in the shadow of the stairs, whispering prayers for his family.

8

Pisa was locked in her room. Señora Gomez reported directly to her mother upon their arrival. They spoke in her mother's parlor as Pisa hurried to her room to change her muddy clothes. She was barely dressed when her mother entered the room, her face white with rage.

"Is it true? You abandoned your duenna again? For that Jew?"

Pisa, terrified, could neither move nor speak. Her mother approached her and slapped her across the face before Pisa could reply. Pisa fell, trying to look up at her mother, but Esperanza had taken her by the arm and pulled her to her feet. Pisa cringed, crawling across the bed in an effort to escape her mother's blows.

"Have you been with him, let him touch you? I can see you with him. How dare you defy me! I will tell your father to lock you in a convent. No man will ever want you."

Esperanza slapped Pisa as she threatened her. Her long finger-nails scratched against her daughter's face as Pisa tried to flee. Esperanza grabbed Pisa by the hair and threw her to the floor.

"You will not leave this room. You will never leave this house. You are to send no messages to that Jewish pig. Do you hear me?"

She yanked Pisa's head up and looked into her face. Bruises and red welts were already rising on her daughter's cheeks, her left eye swollen. Defiantly, Pisa did not answer her mother. Esperanza released Pisa's hair and dropped her to the floor as she left her daughter's room.

Pisa tried to get up, but her entire body was ravaged with pain. She reached for her quilt and covered herself with it. She was cold, and her body was shaking uncontrollably. Her face was on fire, and there was blood in her mouth. It was too cold to cry. She pulled more blankets down to the floor and crawled into them. Her shift was torn, and she tried to cover herself, but the fabric was missing. She wrapped the blankets more tightly.

All her life, Pisa had never been able to please her mother. She had been twelve years old when she realized that her mother did not love her father. Esperanza was always ridiculing him. Andres never retaliated with words. He would remain silent.

Pisa knew at an early age that her mother's sole concern was her own status in Tarifa. Pisa and her duenna often accompanied Esperanza to Mass, and Pisa observed her mother as she charmed the people of the village, always playing the role of the great lady. Pisa did not understand why her mother feigned pride in her children and devotion to her father. In the privacy of their home, Pisa was also scorned.

Andres, absorbed in his work as a merchant, spent most of his time away from his family, unaware of Pisa's desperation. Her friends, Jaime and Meschianza, represented her only true happiness.

As the son and heir, Raul was allowed to travel unescorted, liberated from Esperanza's wrath. But Pisa never experienced freedom, except when she escaped her duenna.

The Davila household was usually in a state of emotional turmoil. Their few moments of peace were experienced when Esperanza was stricken with her headaches. Wine was her relief. When Esperanza was locked in her room with her maid, Pisa would creep around the silent house, occasionally startled by the ominous cries that escaped from her mother's bedchamber. As the tension in the house increased, Pisa hid in her room, her body trembling in anticipation of her mother's temper.

Pisa believed that she was the cause of her mother's misery. She craved her mother's approval and love, but she was met only with her mother's disdain. There was no one to protect her. She grew up a captive of her mother's histrionics.

It had been dark for many hours when Andres Davila unlocked Pisa's door. He bent down before his daughter and lifted her from the floor, gently carrying her to bed. When he saw her swollen face, he left the room and returned with a silver bowl of hot water and clean linen towels. He carefully wiped the blood from her mouth. When he saw her torn shift, he went to her wardrobe and picked out a nightgown.

"Pisa, go into your dressing room and change your clothes. I will wait here for you."

As she undressed, she noticed that her body was covered with bruises. Her legs were laden with welts, and her arms were black and blue. Her shame overwhelmed her as she put on the simple white gown. She returned to her bedroom and sat next to her father.

"Your mother is greatly disturbed."

"Yes, Father."

"Can you tell me what happened?"

"No, Father."

He hesitated, then resumed speaking.

"Is it true that you are in love with Jaime?"

"Yes, Father."

He sighed and placed his arm around his daughter's shoulder.

"You realize you cannot marry him. Your mother will not tolerate it."

She gazed up at her father, but he could not look at her battered face. He looked away, ashamed of his wife. He was more ashamed of himself, for he hadn't protected Pisa from Esperanza.

"He will convert. We have been to see the priest, and he is preparing Jaime for baptism."

"Pisa, you must realize that Jaime's father and mother will never permit this."

"He is telling them tonight. He will not change his mind. Jaime loves me, and I love him, too. We will be married by the priest as soon as the baptism takes place."

Stunned, Andres rose from the bed and went to the window. The starlight appeared crisp against the lucid, rain-washed sky. He sighed again, silently anticipating his wife's reaction to Jaime's conversion.

"Pisa, I must tell you something, and you must listen to me."

He turned to see that he had Pisa's full attention.

"There is talk of an expulsion. The talk grows, and I am beginning to believe it is true."

"What do you mean, Father?"

"The Jews are to be driven from Spain, and I believe it will happen soon."

"You mean like they were in Seville and Cordoba?"

"Yes, but this is even more serious. Eight years ago, many of them were forced to leave Andalusia. This time, they will be expelled from Spain."

"That cannot be. Does Jaime's father know? Jaime has not spoken of it."

"No. Señor Cozar-Velasquez is aware of the rumors, but he does not yet know of this announcement."

"Father, are you against it?"

"Of course I am, but you must understand, your mother is not."

"But Jaime will not be a Jew anymore."

"Pisa, the conversos will continue to be persecuted with the

Jews. Jaime will not escape the edict. His life may be in more danger if he converts. The burnings of the conversos in Cadiz have not stopped."

"He will be safe if we help him. You can help him. You know you can."

"Your mother, Pisa—"

"Father, please. You must help us."

She reached for her father and embraced him. He placed his arms around her and felt his resolve weakening.

"You really love Jaime, don't you."

"Yes, Father. I will never love another."

"He is a fine young man. If I had to choose a husband for you, I would have difficulty choosing one better than Jaime. He is of a fine family, and I would be proud to have him as my son-in-law, but, Pisa, your mother will never consent to this, even if Jaime converts."

"Father, we don't need her consent. We only need yours."

He was silent for a long time. Pisa was very hungry, and her stomach began growling. Andres went to the door and called for Pisa's maid. He told her to bring a tray of food, then returned to Pisa. The two sat silently as the maid entered and placed the tray on the table. She hurried from the room when she saw the bruises on Pisa's face.

They did not speak as Pisa ate. When she was finished, Andres addressed his daughter.

"I will help you."

Pisa hugged her father again.

"Thank you, Father. I knew you would not abandon me. I told Jaime you would help us. He is so earnest in his studies; he is so courageous. Even the priest can see his dedication to the catechism. You will see, he will not fail you."

"Yes, I know. We cannot tell your mother yet. I must speak to Jaime's parents, and to the priest. There is still so much to be done. In the meantime, you must obey your mother, Pisa. Do not make her angry. She wants me to send you to a convent far from here. I will refuse, but this will make her more resentful. I will try to help you with your mother as much as I can, but she is so determined. If you defy her, she will only try harder to interfere with your life."

"I will obey her."

"Good. Now go to bed. I will see Jaime's father tomorrow."

Pisa embraced her father. She climbed into her bed, and he covered her with a woolen blanket. He sat on the edge and kissed Pisa on her forehead. He had begun to leave the room when he asked her one final question:

"Pisa, your mother suspects that you have already . . . that you have . . . been . . . with Jaime. Is this true?"

He looked at Pisa as her eyes filled with tears. She tried to speak, but her voice was intercepted by sobs. He returned to the bed and took Pisa into his arms. She clung to him.

"I am sorry, Father. I am so sorry."

"All right, all right. Perhaps we must have this wedding sooner. I will speak to the priest tomorrow. In the meantime, you must pray for forgiveness, Pisa."

"Yes, Father."

He left the room, and Pisa, her rosary in her hands, began praying. After a moment, she crawled out of her bed and knelt on the cold floor. She was there through most of the night, repeating her Aves. Her maid found her the next morning asleep on the floor.

✤

9

✤

Meschianza was already dressed when the sun rose. She went into Jaime's bedchamber to gather his clothes. She packed them in the large leather bags Jaime had used when he left the university. The bags were now by the door of her duenna's room. Carefully, she opened the door of Señora Luna's room to awaken her. The woman sputtered and began to scream. Meschianza muffled Señora Luna's mouth with her hand and spoke in a whisper.

"You must wake up. We are leaving to visit the de la Vegas. Hurry, get dressed. I will help you."

Her eyes large, her mouth silenced, the duenna refused.

"If you call to my parents, or refuse to accompany me, I will go by myself. I will ride my mare along the beach to the seawall and then walk alone through the village to the de la Vegas."

Terrified for Meschianza's safety, the duenna agreed to go. She rose from her bed and began dressing, chastising Meschianza in harsh whispers.

"You shame your good parents. Why do you do this? Your mother has enough grief with your brother's foolish betrayal! Now you want them concerned for your safety!"

"Hush! I did not say you could talk, Señora Luna. Now hurry."

They left the castle before the cook woke up. The lane leading to the village's main road was shrouded by fog, but as they neared the end of it, the fog began to lift. The groom steered the horses through the gate to the Sephardic community as pale green shadows gave way to a crystalline light. Vendors were already setting up their stalls inside the walled village, and the bright oranges and lemons glistened in the morning glow of the waking community. Artisans began setting out their wares as Meschianza waved greetings to her friends. Her duenna had fallen back to sleep during the drive, and now Meschianza was irrepressible as she leaned out the carriage window.

Jaime and Mateo, who had been waiting, ran to meet Meschianza and removed the bags from the carriage. Jaime took them into the de la Vega house, leaving Meschianza with Mateo. She looked at him shyly. Mateo did not know anyone as beautiful as Meschianza; he could hardly believe his good fortune to be her betrothed. He had returned from the university two days ago, and had yet to call on her parents. After a distraught Jaime had appeared at his door the night before, the two young men had talked all night. Mateo had desperately tried to convince Jaime to abandon his plan to convert.

"I welcome you to my father's house, Donzella. Won't you please come in? My mother will be so happy to see you."

"Yes, but first I must wake my duenna."

Meschianza turned and reached her head and arms through the carriage, jerking on her duenna's arm to rouse the poor woman from her peaceful sleep. Meschianza then followed Mateo into his parents' home.

The three-story stone building was narrow, with only two small windows on the top floor. There wasn't a single window on the two lower floors. They had been removed, filled with mortar two generations earlier by Mateo's great-grandfather to protect the family from the many attacks by zealous priests as they led their unruly flocks into the Jewish quarter to disrupt their Sabbath observances.

Mateo led Meschianza to the inner courtyard garden and gathering place for the family. Flowers and shrubs were everywhere, and a tall date tree at the center of the patio extended three stories high. The tree reached for the blue sky and sunlight that radiated on Señora Luna as she closely followed her charge.

Mateo and Meschianza went to the other side of the room, where they could talk to Jaime out of the duenna's hearing.

"How is Pisa? I thought Raul would come here to see you this morning."

"He is not here, and I am beginning to be very concerned."

"Do you think she is all right?"

"I cannot know, Meschianza, but I will leave now and go to the church. I may be able to find her at the morning Mass."

Jaime kissed his sister, leaving to change his clothes.

"Your parents? How are they?"

A servant brought food for Mateo and Meschianza as they continued to talk. Her duenna, grateful for the repast, ignored the young couple as she helped herself to breakfast.

"Not well. Father has declared Jaime dead. Did he tell you?"

"Yes. What will they do now?"

"I don't know. Mother was in bed when I left this morning. Usually, she is up before the cook."

"And your father?"

"I did not see him."

She hung her head and shaded it with her hand.

"Are you all right? It must have been terrible for you last night with your parents."

"I am not supposed to be here."

"You have always had courage, Donzella."

"You are a good friend to us, Mateo, a good friend to my brother. I am so afraid for him, and for Pisa, too."

"I know. It was brave of you to bring him his clothes."

"There is so little I can do. What will become of them?"

"Señora Davila is probably flaying Pisa right now."

"That is not funny, Mateo!"

"Yes, I know, but I like to see you laugh. You are so serious this morning."

"I'm scared."

"Let them be scared. It's their decision to go against their families. We can only offer our friendship and our love. This is not a good decision for Jaime to make. He will place himself in grave danger if he converts. I am doing everything I can to convince him of this."

"I do not think any of us can change his mind."

"Come. Walk with me. The day is beautiful, and there's joy to be had."

They left the house and walked down the busy street. Jaime rode after them, and as he passed, he waved.

"I am off to see Pisa and Señor Davila, but first I will see the priest."

"You must be careful, Jaime," Meschianza yelled after him, but he did not hear her. He continued down the road until he and the horse disappeared into the crowd of people that quickly filled the street. The *feria* in the village of Tarifa always took place on Saturday, though the people of the walled community did not attend, as it was their Sabbath. Because their religion forbade the handling of money on the Sabbath, the market for the Jews was held on Thursday.

She and Mateo walked through the many stalls, the wares laid out to invite passersby. Women bustled along the street, scarves on their heads, as they carried their purchases in cloth sacks. The pounding of the blacksmith's hammer mingled with the smoke and heat of his fire. Shoemakers displayed their shoes and sandals. Meschianza and Mateo passed tanneries, shopkeepers, silver-smiths, bakers, and the kosher butcher shop. Señora Luna fol-lowed too closely behind them, absentmindedly bumping into Meschianza. Meschianza tried to be polite with her, following her mother's admonitions, but she finally turned to her duenna.

"Will you please stop stepping on me?" she hissed.

The duenna, taken aback, stopped walking and waited for Meschianza and Mateo to advance a few feet before she began her officious bustling behind her charge again. The two young people stopped at a stall that sold intricately woven bamboo cages with small yellow birds inside. One little bird began serenading Meschianza, who was so delighted that Mateo asked permission of the duenna to purchase the bird for his betrothed. After a short deliberation with her conscience, the duenna deemed it proper, and Mateo handed the cage to Meschianza. She talked to the bird the whole way back to Mateo's house.

They were walking past the synagogue when they witnessed a commotion. Four Inquisitor's guards stood along the tenement wall next to the temple. A vendor was imprisoned behind them as two Franciscan friars destroyed his stall. The vendor was a *shochet* who had spent the early hours before dawn ritually slaughtering lambs so that he could sell his kosher wares to the community.

Now carefully wrapped cuts of meat were being thrown into the street. A leg of the lamb landed with a dull thud at Señora Luna's feet. As she bent to pick it up, Mateo entered into the fray by taking another cut of meat from one of the mendicant monks. They struggled until a guard grabbed Mateo by the arm. Mateo tried to attack the soldier, but he was dragged to the wall next to the vendor. He began yelling at the friars.

"This is our community! You have no rights here! The King has guaranteed our safety in our own community. Get out!"

Other people then joined his objections until they were chanting, "Get out! Get out!"

The crowd closed in on the guards, backing them into the remains of the stall. Others picked up the now-soiled cuts of meat and threw them at the friars. Mateo pushed against the soldier in front of him and ducked under his arm while the guard watched the amassing crowd. Mateo tried to reach Meschianza.

Señora Luna sought to pull Meschianza away from the scene, but her charge resisted her efforts. Meschianza ran to Mateo, who was now on the ground, struggling with another guard. She began hitting the guard, and he turned to her and reached back to strike her. Mateo got up from the ground and shoved the guard into a group of young boys who were throwing rocks at the friars. He grabbed Meschianza's hand and pulled her from the scene. Her duenna followed, carrying the yellow canary cage, the bird flailing against the wooden grills, creating a flurry of yellow feathers that floated behind Señora Luna.

Soon the riot stopped, and the guards and friars fled. People hurled their wares and purchases at them as they passed. Oranges and tomatoes, eggs and cabbage heads pelted them. One of the guards, the one Mateo had shoved into the stone throwers, eyed Mateo with malice, conferring with the Franciscan monk behind him. The monk nodded as he continued to follow the guard out of the community.

The two young people stood in front of Meschianza's carriage as they bid each other good-bye.

"You have a cut above your eye, Mateo."

"It is nothing. My mother and father will regret not seeing you this morning. I know they are awake. My mother would love for you to stay for our morning meal."

"I cannot. I must return. My parents will be worried about me once they see that I am gone. You will come to see them? I will tell them you have returned from the university. My father will be pleased."

He helped her into the carriage and offered his hand to Señora Luna. As they rode off, Mateo stood in the crowd, watching her carriage pass through the gates. Mateo was the only motionless person in the bustling crowd at the *feria*.

✦

10

✢

When Jaime entered the church, he found Don Andres waiting for him, seated on a bench in the far corner. He motioned to Jaime. The young man hesitantly approached him.

"Sit down, Jaime. We must discuss your intentions to marry my daughter."

Jaime stepped over the rows and seated himself facing Pisa's father. Though he had known Señor Davila most of his life, and knew him to be kind and fair, he was still very nervous. What if he reacted as Jaime's parents had? Not knowing what to expect, he began defending their plans for marriage.

"Your Grace, I wish to marry your daughter. I love her very much, and she loves me—"

"Yes, I know, Jaime. I spoke to Pisa last night, and I came here this morning to speak to the priest. He tells me that you have nearly completed your preparations."

"Yes, Señor. I will be baptized soon."

"The priest and I have arranged for your baptism to take place after confessions on Saturday. Will you be ready?"

"Yes, your Grace."

"Good, good."

Andres rose from the bench and began pacing before Jaime. As he started to speak, Jaime interrupted him.

"Señor, where is Pisa?"

Andres stopped his pacing and faced Jaime.

"She is confined to her bedchamber."

"Is she all right?"

"Yes, but you cannot see her until the wedding. Her mother is very distraught, and will not allow her to leave the villa."

"But Señor—"

"Jaime, my wife is against this marriage. I am doing all I can to help you and Pisa, but I have not yet informed Señora Davila that Pisa will marry you."

Jaime slumped on the bench and continued to stare at Andres.

"Have you told your mother and father?"

"Yes."

"And?"

"I am dead to them now. I have hurt them deeply. My father and mother will not even look at me. I am dead, Señor."

"Yes, I understand. I'm sorry, Jaime. Do you think your father will see me? I would like to speak to him this afternoon."

"I don't know. My mother is distraught, and my father is very angry. It is my fault, but I cannot sacrifice my love for Pisa. I have loved her since we were children, and I will not live without her."

"Jaime, I am about to tell you something that you must not share with anyone. It is very dangerous for you to have this information, but I believe you must know."

"Whatever you tell me, I will respect with the greatest confidence."

Andres sat facing Jaime again. He placed his face close to the young man's ear and began whispering.

"There is to be an expulsion of all the Jews. It will be announced soon."

"From this region? When? How did you come by this information?"

"You must keep your voice down!" Andres whispered.

Contrite, Jaime looked at the floor.

"This expulsion is an evil thing, Jaime. It banishes all Jews from Spain."

Jaime looked up at Andres and began shaking his head in denial.

"My father and mother, Meschianza, all of us?"

"Listen to me, Jaime. I can help you and Pisa. As a converso, you can remain, but your parents and sister will be expected to leave."

"Oh no! They have no place to go. This is our home, our land. My family has been here for hundreds of years. Where will they go?"

"I am uncertain, Jaime. I have little information right now, but I am attempting to get more. Months ago, these were rumors, but now they are true. The Inquisition demands that the King expel all Jews, and they will appropriate all the Sephardic community's holdings. As I understand it, no gold or silver may be removed from Spain. Property will be confiscated. This is why it is urgent that I speak with your father."

"The estate . . . "

"Yes, your family's estate will be taken by the Inquisition."

"And the de Lucena property? It will be taken? The de Lucena estate is Meschianza's dowry."

"I know, Jaime, but there may be a way to save it."

"How?"

"If I can convince your father to relinquish all his property to you and Pisa, there is a possibility that we can save the estates. Especially as you will be a converso, and my son-in-law."

"He will not agree. I am dead to him now. He will not relinquish the properties to me."

"Your father is a reasonable man. He is my business partner, and he has made me very wealthy. I believe he will recognize the wisdom in this."

"Perhaps. I wish I could be present when you tell him of the expulsion. This will destroy him. I have already harmed him greatly."

"Your father is a very strong and devout man, Jaime. I think he may surprise you."

Jaime shook his head with doubt, but Andres took him by the shoulders and gently shook him.

"Jaime, you must help your father. You must do this for Pisa. She needs your strength, and so do I. We will proceed one day at a time, and you will see, all will be well. It is through you and Pisa that the Cozar-Velasquez name will survive in this country. This will be very important to your father. I will make him understand."

"Why are you helping us? Why do you not hate me, like your wife?"

"My wife is wrong. The Inquisition is wrong, and it is vicious. It is the machinations of men who do not know God. They dwell in the darkness of Satan and all his cohorts. We are powerless against their unholy efforts, but God will not desert us in the end. He will desert none of us, and this includes the good people of your parents' community. Do you agree with me, Jaime?"

"Yes, I do."

"Good. We must both be strong, for Pisa, and for your family. Are you with me?"

"Yes. I am your devoted servant. Without you, there would be no hope for us."

"Now you are to return to the de la Vegas. If I need you, I will go there. You are not to communicate with Pisa. You will only cause her harm. Your wedding will take place in four days, here in the church."

"Yes, Señor. I will now return to Mateo's. Will you tell Pisa that I love her?"

"I believe she knows, Jaime."

II

✥

Pisa's stomach was knotted with hunger. Her maid, Zulema, helped her dress, though she did not return with her breakfast tray. The villa was silent and ominous. Pisa could not hear the servants' voices. Even her tiny lap dog was absent. Pisa waited, her fear and tension building.

Suddenly, her bedroom door was pushed open. Her mother stood in the doorway, a stricken expression across her face. Her eyes were glazed from the wine. Esperanza walked over to Pisa's bed, her legs unsteady.

"How could you do this to me?" Sobbing, she launched into her tirade.

"You were my pride. My pride!"

Pisa did not move as her mother continued:

"I did not raise you to marry a Jew! I raised you to marry well, to bring prestige to this family. How dare you fail your father and me!"

Esperanza waited for Pisa to reply. Pisa sat up against the headboard of her bed and refused to answer her mother. She braced herself for the anticipated blows.

"Soon the entire village will know my shame. They will laugh at me. At me, the wife of Andres Davila! You did this, and no man will ever want you now. They will all scorn you. You are soiled, dirty, no better than the slut your father visits. Oh, he thinks I don't know, but I know. I know how men are. They are animals. And you . . . you are no better than your father. How could you let that . . . that pig use you like that? How could you let him touch you? I can see you with him, see you! You are a whore. You were never my daughter."

Esperanza left the room as ominously as she had appeared. Pisa ran to slam the bedroom door. She stood against it, fighting the tears that threatened to reemerge. She put her hand to her cheek and winced. Her face was swollen on one side, and her eyes burned. She did not want to cry anymore. She was exhausted. She returned to her bed, crawling under the covers, and fell asleep.

Late in the afternoon, Zulema entered the room with food. Pisa ate without tasting the meal. The maid waited with a sympathetic look in her eyes. She said nothing to Pisa, having been ordered by Esperanza not to speak to her.

Later, as night approached, Pisa longed for her father's return. She tried to stay awake, but her fatigue was a black, smothering garment that weighed her down into a paralytic sleep.

✠

12

✥

The castle was silent as the servant led Andres into the great room. In the past, the room had been illuminated with brilliant light from the draped windows. Books with gilt-edged pages had lain open on tables next to crystal vases filled with lilacs and roses. Today the drapes were drawn, and there wasn't a single flower in the room. The Cozar-Velasquez home was in mourning. As he looked about, Andres grieved for his friends.

Efraim entered the room, his hand outstretched, his face somber. Amahl followed his son-in-law and silently took a seat opposite Andres. Efraim took his friend's hand in both of his own.

"You honor my house and my family, Andres."

"Thank you, Efraim. I come on an unhappy errand."

"Then you have heard of our loss?"

"Yes. I have heard."

Efraim sat on the chair in front of the fireplace and motioned Andres to sit across from him.

"My family is in mourning. My son is dead. Tomorrow I will sit *shiva* for him, but today I must care for his mother. She is inconsolable."

"Efraim, I have come to ask you to reconsider your objections to the approaching marriage of our children."

Efraim shook his head.

"Please, my friend, listen to what I have to say? There are graver matters at hand, matters that we must discuss before it is too late. It distresses me greatly to tell you this."

Efraim waited as Amahl moved forward in his chair.

"There is to be an expulsion. There will be an announcement soon. I have come to warn you, and offer my assistance to you and your family."

Efraim looked as if he had been struck. His face became ashen. Concerned, Andres went to the sideboard and poured wine from a crystal decanter into a small goblet. He handed it to Efraim and waited as he drank it. Color returned to Efraim's face as Andres continued.

"All property owned by Jews will be confiscated."

"Are you certain of this, Andres? It is not just another foolish rumor?"

"This is not rumor. Several months ago, I believed it was only rumor, but I have received word this week that the edict will be announced soon. All the Jews of Spain will be expelled. You will not be allowed to take gold or silver with you. You will be allowed to carry only your personal belongings."

Efraim's face went slack. He fell to the side and propped himself against the couch with his hands. Andres reached out and placed his arms around Efraim's shoulders.

"I am here to offer my aid, my friend. I will do all I can to ease your pain. You must not despair. There are things we can do to cope with this tragedy."

"What? What can we possibly do? All of this is to be lost. Do you know our family has been here for four hundred years?"

He looked at Amahl, who was shocked by Andres's news. Amahl remained silent as Efraim continued.

"We have contributed so much to the King and Queen in their effort to drive out the Moors. Now that they've taken

Granada, it is done. And with our money. With our money, Andres! And we gave it gladly. Every year, more and more. How can the King sanction this?"

"I do not know. I only know the Inquisitors demand it. There will be persecutions, auto-da-fés. All of it will start again with a vengeance."

Efraim looked at Andres, terror on his face.

"How could I have been so complacent?"

He paused, his face pensive.

"Andres, my children . . . "

"Yes, Efraim, our children, Pisa and Jaime, Raul and Meschianza. There is a way to help the children and save your property."

"How? Tell me."

"Will you hear me out before you give me your answer?"

"Of course. I have always listened to you, Andres. You are my good friend."

"You must acknowledge the marriage between your son and my daughter. You must be present at their wedding, and at the baptism. You must give your public consent."

Efraim began to object, but Amahl stopped him.

"You promised to listen, Efraim."

Efraim was silent.

"I will purchase this estate and the de Lucena estate from you, and I will give you a fair price. The gold will be placed in safe-keeping for you with my associates in Lisbon. I trust them. I will give this estate to our children, Pisa and Jaime, as a wedding present. As a member of the Catholic faith, he will be allowed to own the estates. This land will be inherited by their children, and the Cozar-Velasquez family will survive here in Spain, but only if you publicly acknowledge your son's conversion. This must be done before the announcement of the expulsion."

Efraim looked at Andres, an incredulous expression on his face.

"I do not think it will work—"

Amahl stood up and interrupted his son-in-law.

"It will work, Efraim. I still own this property. If Andres buys it, he will not be buying it from a Jew. He will be buying it from me, and the Inquisition will recognize it as a legal transaction. There is no other way we can save the estate. If what Andres says is true, then Jewish property will lose its value. We must do this if we are to save our land."

"Yes, and we will succeed if we act quickly. I have arranged for Jaime to be baptized on Saturday afternoon. You all must attend."

Efraim sat and gazed out the window for several moments. Andres waited, sympathetic to Efraim's struggle. Sighing with resignation, Efraim looked up at his friend.

"I believe you are both correct. I will speak to Jaime's mother. Meschianza already supports her brother, so I will not have to convince her, but their mother, that is another question."

"You must make her understand!"

"Yes, yes. I will."

Amahl walked over to Andres and reached out his hand to him.

"My daughter will obey her husband. She will see the wisdom of our plan."

Andres took the old man's hand, realizing what he was willing to do for the sake of his family. He put his arm around Amahl's shoulders. Andres marveled at his inner strength as he felt the man's physical frailty.

"My Lord General, Efraim, the wedding is scheduled to take place in four days. We must have the transaction completed for the property transfer before then."

"I understand."

Efraim walked to the leaded windows. He looked at the meadow as it stretched to the sea below. He turned to examine the great room, then he looked at his friend. Andres walked to him, his hand outstretched. Efraim grabbed his hand, aware of the risks that his business partner was taking.

"I must see Jaime. I must ask him to forgive me. We love Pisa. She has always been a daughter to us. Often I forget she is your daughter, and I know I speak for Justina when I say this to you."

"I have already told Pisa that I will be proud to have Jaime as my son-in-law. I will not allow him to forget his heritage, nor will I allow our grandchildren to forget. I promise you this."

"Will you stay for lunch, my friend? I hear the servants preparing the table."

"Another time soon, I will be happy to stay. Now I must go to Jaime and send him to you. I will also attend to the transfer. There is much to do, Efraim, but when it is done, we will dine together and celebrate our friendship."

Efraim led Andres to the door and watched as he rode away. Amahl stood in the small courtyard before the castle entrance, then made his way to the bluff to perform his *salats*.

Efraim closed the door and went to find his wife. He approached the stairs and took a deep breath when he fell against them, suddenly weakened as he contemplated telling Justina of the coming expulsion. He remembered the predictions she had shared in the tunnel before they were married. He had reassured her that he would always protect her, but now he realized he couldn't protect anyone. Justina's premonitions would now be realized. Her demons must be rejoicing.

He leaned against the stairs, his agony complete. He began the climb to the upper floors.

✢

From the memoir of
Meschianza de Lucena Cozar-Velasquez
March 25, 1497
Lisbon

It is spring again in Lisbon. At home, I know the orange blossoms are blooming. The tiny petals are porcelain-white against the deep green leaves, and the trees are languorous with their heavy perfume. There is only the sound of the busy bees laboring. Soon the violets will bloom again, peeking from beneath the stones where they have slumbered all winter. Spring rains, clean and healing, will awaken the crocus, and my mother's rose petals will open to celebrate the sun.

Springtime in Tarifa is as lush and obscene as a forsaken woman who dresses in her finest garments after a winter of gray clothing. Cimmerian skies are banished, conquered by an ethereal light reflected from the water below the bluffs. Mother and I used to prepare for the *fiesta de pan cenceno*. We would remove all the *chomets* so that there would be no leavened bread during the eight days of the celebration. Ana and I did this today to prepare for the approaching Passover.

We celebrate the deliverance of our people from slavery in Egypt long ago, though today we are enslaved by our grief and loneliness. Passover celebrates the freedom for our people, yet we have not been released. Our homes, our land, our loved ones? Should I celebrate this?

Ana says I must not be bitter, but I carry a rage that is immensely burdensome, and I am as oppressed by it as by a relentless tyrant. I now understand the symbol of bitter herbs. If I surrender my own acerbity, what will be left? I would disappear.

I want to visit my parents' graves, but Raul doesn't think it is safe for Ana and me to walk through the streets of Lisbon. If my mother and father had died on our beloved estate in Tarifa, I could be their dutiful daughter and place flowers on their graves. They would be buried in our family's cemetery. My brother, Jaime, and his wife, Pisa, would accompany me to their graves, and together we would say the Kaddish, and my grandfather would sing a *siguiriya* that even God could hear. Everything would be done according to custom: Jaime would sit *shiva* for our mother and father, the mirrors would be covered, the community would share our grief. The community is not there anymore. We have been expelled from our homes, and our families are scattered. There will be no prayers whispered over my parents' graves, no songs sung, for the cantor has been silenced.

The bougainvillea, the poplars, the graceful oaks, and the crape myrtles will not stand guard over my parents, and there will be no one here to place a marker on their graves.

Raul says I must try not to grieve. I wrote to Jaime, but I do not know if he received my letter. He has not arrived. I want to write to him again, but Raul has admonished me, for I will endanger Jaime and Pisa. The Inquisitors monitor all communications to Spain. We are not supposed to return, or seek aid from anyone there. I know that if Jaime does not receive word from us soon, he will search for us in Lisbon. What if we are already gone when he arrives?

The morning of my parents' death, we heard the footsteps of

the mob as they entered our community. It was still dark, and their cursing shouts echoed off the buildings as they ran down our streets. Ana and I looked through the shuttered window from our upstairs bedroom. The horde filled the narrow lanes, knocking down anyone unfortunate enough to be in their way. This was the morning of our *feria*, and the vendors preparing their wares were all crushed. Those who tried to escape were pelted with stones and spit on. Windows were broken, and two houses were torched.

They broke down doors and entered our homes. I did not know that my father and mother had gone downstairs to check that the door was bolted. The mob broke through it anyway. I thought my father and mother were escaping to the roof, as my father had always instructed us. I would not have left without them otherwise. As Raul helped Ana and me through the trap door in the attic ceiling, he turned to assist my parents, but they were not behind us.

We heard them die. Ana and Raul struggled with me when I attempted to return to the house. My mother screamed, her cries repeating my father's name. These cries were followed by a deafening silence. We waited, Ana muffling her sobs, as they climbed the stairs. They tried to enter through the roof door while we prepared for our own deaths, but they could not break through the heavy iron hasp my father installed during the first month of our lives here.

Finally, they left. Raul would not let us follow him into the house. We waited, Ana and I clinging to each other in terror. Raul soon returned, his face streaked with tears. Sobbing, he told me that my mother and father were dead. I would not believe him. This time, he did not try to stop me as I hurried into the house and down the stairs.

He had covered their bodies, and as I reached for the bloody sheet that lay on my parents, Raul was behind me, staying my shaking hand. I believed that if I screamed long enough, I could obliterate the reality of the murder of my mother and father.

My father had always taught me that, as Jews, we are born into sorrow. If my grandfather was here with me now, could he teach me how to grasp this reality?

I believe I know what my grandfather would say to me. He would take me to the circular room where he kept all my grandmother's books. He would take out the bound manuscript of Jewish proverbs my grandmother loved so much, and begin reading:

The rose dies and leaves behind its sweet rose water, which is its finest value; does not man leave behind a wake that is lasting?

If what my grandfather taught me is true, that our souls return to those we love, then I know my mother and father, Justina and Efraim Cozar-Velasquez, are now walking through their olive groves in Tarifa. Mother is reaching through the leaves of a tree, seeking the first hard buds of the newborn olives. Father is searching the sky, anticipating the harvest. He looks at my mother with love in his eyes. I remember this . . . I remember.

13

※

Andres found Raul and Jaime at the seawall standing on the deck of Raul's nearly completed ship. They discussed Pisa's fate with her mother. Andres knew only that Pisa was locked in her room.

"Jaime, I have spoken to your father. You must go to him. He is expecting you."

"He wants to see me, Señor?"

"Yes, he wishes to see you immediately."

"What does he say?"

"I think it is better that you speak to your father yourself, Jaime. You and Pisa will be married this week, and there is much to do."

Raul turned to his father and started to speak, but Andres was not listening. He was watching Jaime as he mounted his horse and rode down the beach to his father's estate.

"He truly loves Pisa, doesn't he, Raul?"

"Yes, Father. They are devoted to each other. They have always been."

"And you? Are you devoted to them?"

"They are my friends. They are the only friends I've ever had, and I love them both. I would die for them."

"We will not have to die for them, Raul, but we will need to help them. There is much grief coming to this country."

"What do you mean?"

"There is going to be an expulsion of all the Jews in Spain very soon. You must not speak of this to anyone. I tell you only because they will need our help."

Raul looked at Andres with disbelief.

"How do you know this? Perhaps it is not true. I have heard talk of expulsion for months, but I don't believe it."

"It is true, Raul. This time it is not the scandalmongers who speak of it."

Stunned, and having no reason to doubt his father, Raul climbed down the wooden ladder to the sand. Andres followed him, concerned for his son's apparent desperation. He followed Raul as he paced along the edge of the water. His body was rigid with anger, his steps measured and determined.

"Raul, we cannot change what is about to happen in Spain—"

He turned on his father, his rage a white specter on his face.

"Damn Spain, and damn the Inquisition! They cannot do this!"

"Raul, they can and they will. It is already decided. Ferdinand and Isabella will expel the Jews. The edict will be announced soon, and there is nothing we can do but try to help our friends."

"How can we help them?"

"Arrangements are being made. I cannot protect them from the expulsion, but I can ensure their well-being after they leave Spain."

"After they leave? Where will they go? This is their home. What about Jaime and Pisa? Their marriage? What about Meschianza and her mother and father?"

"We must help them in every way we can, Raul."

"Are you not frightened for them? Who will protect them?" He whispered his question again. "Where will they go?"

"They will go to Portugal. I have trusted friends there. They will not be alone."

Raul was calmer as Andres told him about the plans for the family's survival. His anger had not abated, but as he listened to his father, his resolve grew stronger. After Andres left, Raul remained on the beach, pacing along the sand, his own plans slowly forming in his mind.

14

Jaime and Meschianza stood hesitantly in the entryway of the great room. Efraim and Justina were waiting for their children. Amahl sat close to the fire, relief evident on his face. Jaime paused in the doorway, uncertain of his next move, but Meschianza proceeded ahead and embraced her mother. She turned to her father, who stood in front of the fireplace.

"Father, Jaime is here as you requested."

She waited, turning toward her brother. Efraim nodded to his son, and Jaime came forward, standing before his father and mother. His head bowed, he spoke to Justina.

"Mother, forgive me, please? I did not intend to hurt you. I am so sorry."

He turned to his father.

"Father?"

Justina watched her husband, waiting for a signal of acceptance. When Efraim nodded his head, she embraced Jaime as Meschianza joined them, her arms holding her mother and brother. Efraim stood quietly and observed the family's reunion. Jaime broke away from his mother's arms and turned again to Efraim.

"Father, thank you for welcoming me back to our home. It is not my intention to hurt you."

"It is I who should ask forgiveness of you."

"No, Father. You did only what you had to do. I understand."

Efraim held his son, tears streaming down his cheeks as he looked at his wife and daughter.

"Come, come. We will sit and discuss our future."

He motioned them to the couch next to Amahl's chair, and with his son sitting beside him, Efraim began speaking.

"There are very grave and tragic events coming about. I have told your mother about Andres's visit, and his dreadful news. If what he says is true, and I have no reason to doubt his sources, our lives here in Spain, and the lives of this family are about to change. As I have told your mother, Andres has offered to purchase our land and to give it to you and Pisa as your wedding endowment. Your grandfather and I have agreed to this offer."

Jaime could not disguise his alarm.

"Father, what are you saying?"

"The Inquisitors will take our property, Jaime, but if we sell our estate to Andres, it will remain in our family through your children's inheritance. In this way, the family will continue here in Spain."

Bewildered, Meschianza questioned her father.

"What do you mean? Surely, we will not have to leave?"

"Meschianza, your mother and I have already begun preparations."

"But perhaps it is not true."

Meschianza's voice was shrill and desperate. She looked at her brother, who had walked over to his mother. He sat beside her and held her in his arms.

"Jaime, did you know this? Why didn't you tell me?"

He looked at his sister, feeling her sense of betrayal. He could think of nothing to say. Meschianza turned to her father.

"Father, there has been no announcement yet, has there?"

"No, but Andres feels the announcement will come soon."

"He could be wrong. Maybe he is wrong."

She went to her grandfather, and Amahl held her in his arms.

"Where will we go?" she whispered. "How can we leave Spain? This is our home. Father, say something!"

He looked at his wife and son, and then at his daughter.

"Plans have been made, Meschianza, and you must help your mother. Andres is making arrangements for us to go to Portugal. There will be gold for us there. We will begin a new life."

"No! I will not go. We cannot leave Spain! What about Grandfather? He is too old to travel. We cannot leave him!"

She turned to her brother, but he would not meet her gaze.

"Mother? Tell Father we will not go. This is our home!"

Justina fell against her son and began crying softly as Meschianza turned to her father.

"I will not go!"

Efraim reached for her again, but she ran from the great room and picked up her cloak from the table. As she opened the door, she turned to her father once again.

"I will not go!"

She left the castle and ran toward the bluffs. She remained there until Jaime found her.

She sobbed while Jaime held her in his arms. "I will not leave you and Pisa. I cannot leave Raul. I love him, Jaime. I know Father wants me to marry Mateo, but though he is good and kind, I cannot be happily married to him. Now I must leave Raul? What will I do?"

Breathless, she waited for her brother to answer.

"We will think of something. You must not be afraid."

"But what if there is nothing we can do?"

"You must not lose hope, Meschianza. I will not allow anything to happen to you. I will think of a plan."

"Do you think it is true? Do you think they will expel us?"

"I think that Señor Davila has reliable sources, but perhaps it will not come true."

He held her, both of them sitting on the bluff as the moon rose over the water below them. The starlight provided a glowing backdrop as Efraim and Justina left the castle to search for their children. They found them, Meschianza somewhat calmer now, and led them back to the warmth and security of the castle.

15

⁘

Andres Davila, accompanied by Jaime, rode slowly toward his home. On both sides of the *calle* leading to the door of the villa, the whitewashed, stone-walled tenements towered over them. As they passed beneath the *rejas*, the iron-grilled windows stared at the two men accusingly. Andres's silver-inlaid saddle made the only sound on the silent and foreboding lane. The creaking of the polished leather was rhythmic and competed with the steady clicking of the horse's hooves on the cobblestones.

Andres was exhausted. The night before, he had had to lock his bedchamber door against his wife's rantings. The pains he felt in his chest had settled into an innocuous ache during the day as he arranged his daughter's life. Now the ache had traveled to his arm. He tried to rub the numbness from his wrist, but his fingers tingled and burned.

They rode into the courtyard of the villa, hardly noticing the bougainvillea and tiny miniature orange trees. The trees had not bloomed until last spring. Pisa had helped him plant them while Raul was away at the university. This was the first opportunity he had had to spend time with his daughter. Raul had always been his constant companion as Andres attended to his business of ships and trading. During the summer when he and Pisa had planted the courtyard, Andres had come to understand his daughter's vulnerabilities. Now his sense of urgency came from his need to protect her from her mother.

He had always provided for Esperanza, leaving her to raise

their two children, as was the custom. He had educated their son, and was making wedding arrangements for Raul, according to Esperanza's wishes. Now she demanded that he place their only daughter in a convent. Tonight he had to tell Esperanza of his refusal.

As they entered the villa, Andres instructed Jaime to wait in the sitting room. He walked across the entry hall. The house was silent except for the echo of his riding boots as he climbed the marble steps to his wife's bedchamber. He knew he would find her there. She would be drugged with the elixirs the physician had prescribed for her.

She had taken them since Pisa was born. Esperanza had moved from their bedchamber into the room on the floor above, leaving him alone. Whenever he approached her, she walked away from him, finding refuge in her medications. She didn't want more children.

He felt despised and abandoned. He had solicited women on the streets of Tarifa until he met a widow who lived in Cadiz. She had ordered linens from him. When her requested parcel arrived, he had chosen to deliver the goods to her small house. It was not long before he bought a house for her in Tarifa. As he climbed the stairs to the upper floors of the villa, he realized how much he needed Maria Elena at this moment.

He knocked on the door of his wife's bedchamber. Her maid opened the door a few inches from which to peek, but he pushed past her and looked at his wife lying on the bed. Her dressing gown was wrinkled and bunched under her body. Her hair, unkempt and tangled, was spread on the pillow. Her eyes were glazed as she looked at her husband with her condemning resentment.

"Leave us, Maria."

The maid hurried from the room, and Andres slammed the door shut.

"I want you to get dressed, madam, and come downstairs to the parlor. We need to discuss our daughter's future."

"She is ruined. She has no future!"

Esperanza sat up on the bed, spitting the words at her husband.

"I will wait downstairs after I tell Pisa to join us."

He left the room and walked down the corridor to Pisa's bedchamber. He knocked and listened. There was no sound coming from the room, and she did not open the door. He tried the doorknob and found it locked.

"Pisa," he called to her. "Open the door for me."

He heard her rush to the door. She opened it and threw herself into his arms.

"Father, I am so glad you are here."

As he held her, he noticed the bruises on her arms. Some of them were turning from blue to green. New bruises, dark blue and ugly, competed with the red welts on her neck. He could barely contain his rage at Esperanza as he told Pisa to change from her nightgown and join him in the parlor.

His footsteps echoed determination as he walked down the stairs to the parlor. Esperanza, dressed now, swept grandly into the room and seated herself on a settee opposite him. She did not speak with her mouth, but her glaring, hateful eyes spat tirades. When Pisa joined them, Esperanza's rage was redirected toward her daughter. Pisa sat next to her father and avoided her mother's gaze. She did not look at Jaime. The silence was heavy as Andres began their conversation.

"I have made some decisions, and I wish to tell them to you both."

Esperanza, waiting for her husband to continue, stared at Jaime.

"In two days, Pisa will be married to Jaime. The marriage will take place in the cathedral."

Esperanza stood up and began to object.

"Sit down, Esperanza, and be quiet." Andres yelled for the first time during their marriage. Shocked into silence by his anger, Esperanza sat gasping for breath. She clasped her hands to her chest and stared at her husband.

Pisa turned to Jaime with tears in her eyes. She smiled at him, but Jaime stared at Esperanza, the wariness on his face competing with his amazement. He had seen the marks and scratches on Pisa's face. Now, seeing Esperanza in all her rage, he understood the source of the bruises.

"Jaime will be baptized by the priest on Saturday. He will embrace our faith, Esperanza, and we will never hear any of your denigrations of his parents' faith again. Is that understood?"

Esperanza's face reflected a bluish cast as she tried to breathe. Andres was frightened that she would have an apoplectic attack. He left the room and ordered one of the maids to fetch the physician who lived next door. When he returned to the room, Esperanza was on her feet. She was walking toward Jaime, and even though Andres tried to intercept her, she managed to reach Jaime first. Drawing back her hand, she slapped Jaime across the face. He did not respond when Pisa cried out, but placed his hand on his cheek as it reddened and swelled. Esperanza left the room with a smug, satisfied expression on her face. Andres turned to follow her, but she ran up the stairs and slammed her bedchamber door.

Her maid followed, tripping on one of the steps in her efforts to catch up to Esperanza.

When Andres returned to the parlor, Pisa was sitting next to Jaime, her hand on his cheek. As she began to cry, Jaime pulled her into his arms. Andres sat on the other side of his daughter and gently took her from Jaime's arms. He tried to calm her.

"Do not be afraid, Pisa. I'll remain here in the house with you until the wedding takes place. You will not be harmed by her anymore."

"Father, where will we go after the wedding? Where will we live?"

Jaime took Pisa's hand.

"We will live in Meschianza's villa on the de Lucena estate. She has offered it to us. You will be safe from your mother there, Pisa. I will protect you."

"Meschianza's villa?" Pisa looked at Jaime, and then at her father.

"Yes, the de Lucena estate was to be a part of her dowry. She wants us to live there while I build a villa for you near the castle."

"You did this for us, Father? I am so grateful to you, and I know Jaime is grateful, too. How can we thank you?"

"It is not necessary—"

Just then, Esperanza's maid ran into the room.

"Sir, sir, come quickly. Please. My lady . . . she has done something terrible!"

Andres followed the maid out of the room to Esperanza's bedchamber. Pisa and Jaime waited at the bottom of the stairs, afraid to follow. There was a knock on the door, and Pisa went to answer it. The physician who lived next door appeared, per Andres's earlier request. Pisa led him into the entry hall just as Maria appeared. The maid grabbed the physician by the hand and escorted him to Esperanza's room.

"Come quickly. My lady is ill. She is dying."

The doctor followed Maria, and after he examined the unconscious woman, he and Andres carried Esperanza down the stairs.

"Jaime, my wife is very ill. We are taking her next door to the physician's house. Please stay here with Pisa. Do not leave her alone!"

When Andres returned several hours later, he found the young couple asleep on the couch. He sat on a chair and watched them, his exhaustion slowly overtaking him. His wife was in a deep sleep at the clinic, but the physician had assured him that she would recover from her apparent suicide attempt.

Andres placed his head on the back of the chair and fell asleep.

✢

16

✢

Esperanza refused to stand with her husband as Jaime's godparent, so Andres was forced to stand alone beside the young man. He forbade his wife from entering Pisa's room, but still he stayed in the villa on the morning of Jaime's baptism. Pisa remained locked in her chamber, leaving only with her father and brother when they went to the church.

Efraim and Justina arrived, accompanied by Amahl, Meschianza, and Mateo. The young man had not stopped his campaign to sway Jaime from his decision to convert. Though he accompanied Meschianza's family to witness the baptism, he was still committed to bringing Jaime back to the Jewish community. He and Jaime were the same age and had celebrated their Bar Mitzvot together. They were diligent students of the rabbi, often debating situations in the Jewish life that needed resolution and religious guidance.

Mateo was being groomed by the rabbi to follow the path of their synagogue's elderly cantor. His voice, a clear tenor, expressed a special lyrical beauty as he performed the *hazzanut*, the liturgical melodies of the Sephardic community. Today he watched with undisguised distress as his future brother-in-law prepared to surrender his covenant.

Justina and Efraim stood stiffly beside Amahl as they waited for the priest to begin the ceremony. The priest instructed Jaime to kneel before the baptismal font. Andres, glancing at Efraim, accompanied Jaime and stood with him before the priest. Meschianza moved close to her mother and placed her arm around her waist. She looked at her father, at her grandfather, and then at Mateo. As Jaime knelt before the priest, Meschianza's face was rigid, her smile unwavering. She looked straight ahead, as did her parents. They appeared to be watching Jaime, but they actually were staring above his head, unable to observe the travesty taking place before them. Meschianza kept her arm around her mother as the priest intoned the words of the ceremony.

"I baptize thee in the name of the Father, the Son, and the Holy Ghost. And I christen thee, by the name you shall be known from this day forward, Antonio Velasquez."

As the priest sprinkled the holy water on Jaime's head, tears of happiness came to Pisa's eyes. With the holy oil, the priest made the sign of the cross on Jaime's forehead. Efraim continued to smile, a false expression of pride on his face. He did not look at his wife.

"Gloria! Gloria! Gloria in Excelsis Deo!"

Andres repeated the words, as did Raul and Pisa. The priest raised Jaime to his feet and presented him proudly to the small congregation. For the benefit of the priest, as instructed by Andres, Jaime walked over to his parents and embraced them, first his mother and then Efraim. He kissed his sister, who held him for a long moment. He then turned to his grandfather, who nodded at him. Mateo stood unmoving, his face stern. The priest observed Mateo as Jaime walked over to Raul and shook his hand. Jaime now stood before Andres and Pisa.

Andres reached out his hand, but before Jaime could take it, he was caught in a brisk hug by his new godfather. Pisa kissed him briefly on the lips. Her father turned to thank the priest, and placed a small bag of gold maravedis into the priest's hand. Andres then guided the group out of the church.

They arrived together at the Cozar-Velasquez castle just before nightfall. Raul was obligated to be with his mother. He found Esperanza waiting for him in the parlor.

Esperanza was agitated, and she paced the full length of the room as Raul sat, ill-at-ease, and listened to his mother.

"So is it done?"

"Yes, Mother."

"And the wedding?"

"Tomorrow. It will take place in the church after the evening Mass."

Raul cringed as his mother shot him a piercing glare. Since his childhood, he had felt incarcerated by his mother's presence. He was afraid of her, his terror equal only to his disdain for her. He was thankful that she favored Pisa with her attentions. He had escaped from her wrath when he left for the university. Now that he was living with her again, he found her grip to be just as para-lyzing as it had been throughout his childhood. Esperanza looked at him, suspicion clouding her face.

"Were his parents there?"

"Yes, Mother."

"And the sister?"

"Yes, she was there."

She began to release the pent-up frustrations that had boiled in her the entire day.

"Your sister has no shame, and your father—"

"Mother, Jaime is now one of us, now that he is baptized. His new name—"

"Be quiet! Do you think I believe in his devotion? He is a con-verso only so that he can continue defiling my daughter!"

Raul, his face reddening, rose to leave. As he opened his

mouth to object to her remarks, she approached him and pushed him back into the chair.

"Sit down. I am not finished with you."

He sat and looked at the floor, his resentment growing.

"Your father? Where is he?"

"I believe they all went to the Cozar-Velasquez estate."

"Why?"

"I don't know, Mother."

She resumed her pacing. It was cold in the room, and Raul wondered why the servants had not started a fire. Perhaps they were hiding at the back of the villa. Raul remembered how they had withdrawn in horrified silence during his childhood when his mother launched into one of her tirades.

"Mother, I must—"

"I said, be silent!" She stood in front of him, her body shaking with rage. She crossed the room and picked up a wine bottle from the small table by the door. She removed the glass stopper and drank its contents. She dropped the empty bottle on the table, and it rolled across and fell to the floor. Esperanza ignored the sound of the breaking glass. She held on to the edge of the table as her body settled. When she turned to her son, her eyes were transfixed on him.

"Raul, I will retire now."

"Mother, can I help you to your chamber?"

She waved him away as she weaved through the doorway. He followed her, as he had done many times before, and stood at the bottom of the stairs, watching her climb to the top. She did not stumble. Esperanza knew the way, and silently counted every step. Her clawlike fingers clutched the banister, sliding herself upward on the staircase. Her firm grip prevented her from falling backward. Long ago, she had realized that this feat—not falling—was the only thing on which she must concentrate when maneuvering the stairs to her bedroom. It was a point of honor to Esperanza, that she negotiate her retirement without anyone's help. As she reached the top step, she walked to her door without turning around.

"Good night, Raul."

"Yes, Mother," he responded.

He waited for the sound of her door closing. Esperanza never slammed it. Raul, filled with revulsion for his mother, rushed out of the villa.

17

✤

Andres stumbled as he and Pisa entered the great room with Jaime's family. Mateo turned to him and offered his hand, but Andres waved him away. Mateo glanced at Pisa, but she did not see her father stumble. He addressed Andres in a low voice.

"Are you all right, Señor?"

"Yes, Mateo. I think it is just fatigue."

Amahl also noticed how Andres tripped, concerned for him as he watched the two men. They followed Efraim into the dining room, where a table was set for them. Since it was Saturday evening, an *adifada* was at the center. Before yesterday's sunset, Justina had prepared the stew and placed it in the warm oven. She had stoked the fire so that it would burn slowly for twenty-four hours, and now she lifted the lid. At the center of the large pot, a mixture of ground lamb and veal, mixed with honey and cinnamon, onions and parsley, simmered amid fat kernels of rice. Eggs still in their shells mingled with juicy dates and slivers of garlic. Amahl experienced a sense of well-being as he remembered his own early childhood in his mother's kitchen. There was silence as they each took their seats. Efraim said the blessing, and Justina followed as she lifted the lid from the large black pot and held out her hand to Andres.

"May I fill your plate for you, Andres?"

He handed his plate to her, and she filled it from the steaming iron pot. She ladled another spoonful of vegetables onto the plate, and then graciously offered it to him. She repeated the gesture for each of her guests, and smiled at her husband as she handed him his plate.

"And so, tomorrow is the wedding of your daughter and our son, Andres."

She looked at Pisa's father and smiled. Andres nodded and replied.

"Yes, tomorrow is the wedding. This will be a joyous occasion for all of us as our families are united through the love of our children."

Efraim stood up and lifted his glass. He looked at each person at the table, then nodded to the general. Amahl stood up and smiled at his grandson.

"We will toast our children, Andres."

They all stood except Pisa and Jaime. Amahl looked at his grandson and began the salutation.

"Today we rejoice at the joining of our two families. Again, as in the past, with my marriage to my beloved wife, Bianca, love has overcome our differences. May the love of my grandson, Jaime, and of your daughter, Pisa, continue to endure throughout their life together. Bianca would bless your union, as do I."

Efraim then took his turn and offered a toast.

"To my daughter, Meschianza, and her betrothed, Mateo de la Vega, who will soon be married. I also bless these two unions of my children, for they designate continuance and new beginnings for our families. From this night on, our lives will change, but we move forward fearlessly as we know the comfort our shared love will bring us. I wish everlasting joy to these children."

After they finished the toast, Efraim led them back to the great room, where Andres warmed his hands in front of the fire. Lately, it seemed his hands and feet were always cold, as if it were the middle of winter. He went to his cloak and removed some documents from the inner pocket. He offered them to Amahl, who sat in a chair in front of the fire, motioning the man to sit opposite him.

"These are the documents showing the transfer of this property from you to me. The others concern the transfer of the estate to Pisa and Jaime. We need to sign the first documents now, and then I will sign these after the marriage ceremony. The gold we agreed on is now with my friend in Portugal. He holds it in safekeeping for your family."

Amahl opened the documents and studied them, reading the words slowly. Amahl handed the papers to Efraim. He looked at Justina, who was sitting on a couch, Meschianza and Pisa on either side of her. Her arms were around both young women. He looked at his grandson, and then at Mateo. He took the quill Andres offered him and dipped it into the small ink bottle on the table beside him. Amahl signed it and handed the deed to Andres. He nodded at Efraim as Andres signed his name. When Andres was finished, Amahl continued to stare at the document. Andres paused for a moment before he folded the deed and offered it to Efraim.

Amahl was grateful to Andres for his decision to help his family retain their land, but his relief was in tragic conflict with the realization that his daughter and granddaughter would be forced to leave him to survive.

Pisa rose from the couch and walked across the room to Amahl. She knelt down in front of him and looked into his eyes.

"General Cozar, I thank you for your gracious offer of the de Lucena villa as a home for Jaime and me. I will be honored to be his wife, and to be a member of your family."

"We are proud to welcome you into this family, Pisa. You have always been a granddaughter to me and a daughter to Jaime's parents."

Andres stood up and offered his hand to Efraim, who took it in his own. Jaime helped Pisa to her feet, while Meschianza and her mother joined the group before the fire. In the midst of their hugging, no one noticed Raul, who had just entered the room. As Raul watched them, his sadness for the family appeared like a shadow on his face.

18

✣

The wedding ceremony of Pisa and Jaime took place in the cool and impersonal evening light in front of the altar of the large, empty church. Darkness hovered over the small gathering, relieved only by the four candles that reflected off the *retalbo*. There were no flowers for Pisa, and her mother was absent. She wore a simple gown. Her veil was a silvery white mantilla.

Padre Cardenas motioned for all of them to gather before the altar. Andres placed his daughter's hand in Jaime's, and the priest began the ceremony. Efraim, Justina, and Amahl stood next to Meschianza and Raul as the priest joined the young couple in marriage. His voice floated to the ceiling of the church, softly echoing, disturbing the doves that nested in the stone corners of the roof. They flew high above the altar, witnesses to the joy of Pisa and Jaime. The newly wedded couple walked out of the church, their families behind them, and the doves flew out the door. They alighted on the cobblestones in the plaza, walking about in an awkward dance, as the carriage took the wedding party to the castle for the feast that awaited them.

Late that evening, the same carriage took Pisa and Jaime to their new home at the de Lucena estate. Andres and Amahl stood in the courtyard of the castle with Efraim and Justina as they waved their children away.

The announcement of the Alhambra Decree, ordering the Sephardic community from Spain, would not come for several weeks. As the three of them entered the great room, Andres knew

there was much to do, for they did not know how long they had
before activating their plans. After Meschianza and her mother
retired, Raul joined Efraim and Andres before the fire.

"Señor Cozar-Velasquez, I have a request to make of you."

"Yes, of course, Raul. I cannot think of any request you could
make of me that I would deny. Especially on the night of my son's
wedding."

Raul glanced at his father, then again addressed Efraim.

"I wish to accompany you and your family to Portugal. I offer
my protection, Señor."

"That is very generous of you, Raul, but I don't understand
why you would choose to leave your home for something that is
unknown, and probably very dangerous."

Raul looked again at Andres before he answered.

"I am in love with Meschianza, and I do not want to be separated from her. I wish to marry her."

Efraim turned to Andres and could see that he was just as surprised to hear this news. Puzzled, he queried Raul.

"Is it your intention that Meschianza also convert to the
Catholic faith?"

"No, Señor. She is devout, and I am not. I question the teachings of the Church, and I certainly question the justice of the
Inquisitors' imminent actions."

Andres was shocked by his son's words. He responded with
concern in his voice.

"Those are blasphemous words, Raul. I hope you have not
repeated them to anyone else. The Church would say that they are
the words of a heretic."

"Yes, I know, but it is what I believe. This is a heinous thing,
to rob a people of their home. They say it is done in the name of

God, but I don't believe God has anything to do with it."

Efraim, alarmed, interrupted Raul.

"You must be careful of what you say—"

But Raul continued.

"This expulsion will be done in the name of greed. Their reasoning is grotesque and their corruption knows no boundaries. I am ashamed to call myself a Spaniard."

Andres turned and looked out the window, trying to gather his thoughts, his energy. In the silence that followed, he spoke to his son.

"Raul, I have done everything to protect the Cozar-Velasquez family. Now I realize that your anger may expose them all to the dangers of the Inquisition. I advise you not to repeat these sentiments. They are treasonous, and you bring danger to all of us!"

"Father, forgive me. In the future I will be careful."

Efraim, concerned about Raul's declaration of love for Meschianza, urged the young man to sit down.

"Raul, you are aware, of course, that my daughter is betrothed? She is promised to another man."

"Yes, Señor, I know."

"Then you understand that you cannot marry her?"

"Yes, I understand this, but I can still offer her my protection. You will need my help in Portugal."

He turned to his father.

"Father, is that not true? He cannot go to the partners in Lisbon for the gold. He would be suspect, but I can go and speak for him."

"Yes, that is probably correct. Certainly, it would be safer for you, Efraim."

"And Father, we must not wait for the edict to be announced.

We must plan for them to leave Spain now, before the expulsion takes place. If we begin now, we can provide a way for them to take many of their belongings with them."

"I know you are right, but it will take me months to make arrangements. All my ships are at sea, and none of them will return until the end of summer."

"My ship is not at sea."

He turned to his son, startled at his offer.

"You would give your ship for our escape?" Efraim had been silent until now.

"Yes. It is ready, and I trust my crew. I will accompany you and your family to Lisbon. We can place your belongings on the ship if we carry them to the sea cliff through the tunnel. We can load everything from there using the longboats. The monks will have closed the harbor for inspection. But we will sail from the cove beneath the bluffs. It will work. They will inspect my ship before it leaves the harbor, and find no one on it but the crew. If I leave the port at sunset, it will be dark when the longboats are rowed to the opening of the tunnel. No one will know."

Efraim was still concerned for Raul's well-being.

"Don't you realize the amount of grief you will feel when my daughter marries Mateo? How will you live with that? Wouldn't it be better for you to remain here in Tarifa?"

"No, Señor. With all respect to you, please understand. I cannot stay here in safety while Meschianza leaves to face whatever is coming. I would rather bear the pain of her marriage to Mateo than tolerate my fears for her life and yours. Please let me accompany you?"

Efraim looked at Andres, and seeing his resignation, nodded his agreement to Raul.

"This family will be fortunate for your added protection, Raul. I thank you for your offer, and your sacrifice."

The three men spoke late into the night. By the time Andres and his son left the castle, their plans for the journey to Lisbon were complete.

19

⁜

Five weeks passed before Mateo's arrest. The Franciscan monks who had disrupted the *feria* reported Mateo's actions to the office of the Inquisitor of Cadiz. They sat on the hard wooden benches that lined the whitewashed stuccoed walls, watching the people who were hoping for word from imprisoned relatives. Some of them had been there for many days with their large, empty food baskets by their sides, exhaustion and apathy on their faces. One old woman who appeared to be in a daze hummed an unintelligible tune, her fingers playing along the fringe of her shawl.

When one of the black-robed inquisitors emerged from the large oak double doors, the crowd rushed to him, their entreaties a cacophony of pleading despair. The Franciscans returned daily after morning Mass, patiently awaiting their turns.

It was three weeks before the monks were ushered into the chief Inquisitor's office. They were allowed only enough time to utter the name of the suspected heretic. To their relief, they were not questioned about their source of information. Instead, the Inquisitor, without speaking a word to them, dismissed them summarily. As they exited the anteroom, the cold light of late morning chilled them. One of them stumbled as they hurried down the steps, the cobbles still slick with the early morning rain.

The downpour continued as they arrived in Tarifa. Their priests' habits were soaked as they crossed the plaza. They entered the church and fell to their knees before the altar in their damp robes. Padre Cardenas joined them, and together they thanked the generosity of their Creator for giving them the opportunity to bring another heretic to justice.

Padre Cardenas was grateful for his dedication to the Church and its members. He was aware that the fiancée of the young heretic was the sister of Don Andres's new son-in-law. Even this complex connection between Don Andres and the heretic could taint the reputation of the man. Andres Davila was one of the congregation's largest donors. His wife was a devout woman who attended morning Mass with diligence, appearing every Saturday afternoon to confess her sexual fantasies to the priest. Padre Cardenas listened to her confessions and gave her long and thorough penances. His concern for her soul was further demonstrated in his observance of her from the back of the church after the other penitents had left. Señora Davila recited her rosary before the statue of the Blessed Virgin until her son came to escort her home.

The priest, hidden in the dark corners of the back pews, would hurry to the church cellar to grab a bottle of sacramental wine. Taking the bottle with him, he would retire to his bedroom and console himself into the night with the blood of Christ.

✦

20

The Inquisitors entered the de la Vega villa amid the lightning and thunder of the early morning storm, waking Mateo's parents and dragging their son from his bed. They chained his hands and pulled him into the central patio, where he stood under guard, bewildered and terrified, as they searched the villa.

They took Mateo out of the villa and tied him facedown onto the back of a horse. His parents stood in the dark in front of the villa with their awakened neighbors, and watched as the iron chains binding their son's hands were tied under the horse. The horses galloped through the gates of the community as Mateo's terror and the relentless pounding against his body from the horse's motion caused him to lose consciousness.

When the soldiers reached their destination, the dark and horrifying regions of the Inquisitor's office beneath the building in Cadiz, Mateo's body was blue with cold. The first stages of hypothermia were taking effect. His circulation had slowed, and his heartbeat barely murmured. Mercifully, he was still unconscious as they beat him, their repeated blows falling onto his numb body and mind.

The following day, Mateo awoke to survey his surroundings with pain. There was a dim light entering his cell, though he could see the iridescent dampness of the stone walls that encased him. The room was tiny, and he could not lie down. For the first time in his life, he cursed his height.

He was overcome by the smell of urine from former prisoners.

He lifted his face from the puddle and tried to wipe his cheek, only to discover his hands were still chained. Painfully, he tried to sit up, but the effort left him faint. The cell turned on its side and began spinning. His head crashed to the floor, and Mateo lost consciousness again.

When he awoke a second time, two monks stood over him, holding scented handkerchiefs to their noses. A large man, dressed only in ragged pants, lifted Mateo by his hair and beat him unconscious. Mateo would not recant, insisting on his innocence. He was questioned about the riot in the *Aljama*, but he would not name the young woman who had accompanied him. He was accused of conspiring to entice Jaime Cozar-Velasquez back to the Jewish religion. The interrogation continued for several days, until the morning finally arrived when he was allowed to wake up without being beaten. His hunger was as strong as his unbearable pain, and thirst had become a constant, stupefying companion.

There was a bucket of dirty water, along with some dried, moldy pieces of bread served on a grimy, warped wooden plate. He tried to pick up the bucket to drink from it, but his left arm did not respond. He looked at it and found that he had a compound fracture above the elbow. A piece of bone protruded from the blackened flesh, and he had lost all feeling in his flesh and bone.

He began scooping the water with his other hand into his mouth. He reached for the bread and stuffed it into his mouth. Dragging the bucket, he crawled to one of the walls and sat against it. He waited, but no one came for many days. His arm festered and his mouth bled every time he ate the dry bread.

On March 31, in 1492, the secular arm of the church came for Mateo. The monks carried buckets of water that they tossed at him in an effort to rinse him of the stench and filth of the cell. They covered him with a long ragged shift of rough brown fabric. Soldiers had to drag him through the dank corridors of the prison cells, because he could no longer walk. His legs had been crushed the night before as they forced him to provide the names of his associates.

They took him to the upper floor, placing him in a large sunny room filled with spectators seated on tiers and balconies. They sat him on the floor in an outer room with other prisoners who were similarly muted by their misery. They looked away from one another, their common shame at once uniting and dividing them.

Andres Davila and Mateo's father sat high in one of the balconies of the courtroom. Their bribes to the monks in charge of admission to the available seats had secured their spaces above the milling throng below. Andres watched the spectacle taking place beneath them. People were passing food to one another and climbing over one another to obtain a better view of the proceedings. Fights often broke out, quelled instantly by the soldiers who lined the walls.

Andres and Juan de la Vega had attended the trials daily in Cadiz for three weeks, in hopes of seeing Mateo. Their efforts to obtain information about him were fruitless. They did not know if Mateo was still alive, but they came every morning, looking at the faces of the prisoners, praying that Mateo would be among them.

That morning, as Andres crossed the plaza on the way to the trials, he noticed a crowd gathering in one corner of the cobbled square next to the cathedral's entrance. He stood at the edges of the crowd in time to hear the reading of the last paragraphs of what was to be called the Alhambra Decree.

And we further order in this edict that all Jews and Jewesses of whatever age that reside in our domains and territories, that they leave with their sons and daughters, their servants and their relatives, large and small, of whatever age, by the end of July of this year, and that they dare not return to our lands, not so much as to take a step on them nor trespass upon them in any other manner whatsoever. Any Jew who does not comply with this edict and is to be found in our kingdoms and domains, or who returns to the kingdom in any manner, will incur punishment by death and confiscation of all their belongings.

Andres had not waited to hear the rest. In agony for his friends who were now his family, he had continued toward the trial hall. He was tired, his exhaustion reaching to the core of his emotional and physical being. His daughter, Pisa, had come to him upon discovering Mateo's arrest. She had begged him to seek information about his welfare for Meschianza's sake. Efraim and Justina were overcome with grief and terror for Mateo.

The strain on Andres was evident. As he reached his place at the trials, he had been short of breath. His physician's attempt to modify his activities had fallen on deaf ears. His two children, as well as Jaime, Meschianza, and Mateo, were his greatest concerns now.

The trial was about to begin. There was a rustling in the room as the spectators hastened to their seats. The Inquisitor and his assistants entered the room first. They were dressed in black robes, their faces hooded and sinister. Following them were the Franciscan monks, their brown robes swaying about them as they entered and took their seats.

Each prisoner was brought in singly and disposed of quickly. Each was condemned to the purification by fire. The execution would take place in Tarifa. When they brought Mateo out, they dragged him along the floor, and tied him to the chair. Andres did not recognize him, nor did his father. It was not until his name was read, as he was condemned to the fire, that the two men realized who he was.

His father began to rise and cry out, but Andres silenced his friend and pulled him down into the chair beside him. He held him around the shoulders as his cries were muffled against Andres's arm. He half carried Mateo's father out of the courtroom. They were outside the building before Juan de la Vega was able to regain control of himself.

They traveled through the night to Tarifa, and when they arrived, Andres escorted Mateo's father to his house and into the arms of his bewildered wife. As he rode away from the de la Vega villa, he heard the piercing cry of Mateo's mother, realizing that Señor de la Vega had just informed her of their son's death sentence.

Slowly, Andres rode to his daughter's villa on the de Lucena estate.

✣

21

Justina looked out of the carriage at an empty street. It was a devastating contrast to the crowd she and Meschianza had witnessed at the central plaza of Tarifa. A despairing silence hovered over the walled Sephardic community as they entered through the gates. The noise of the carriage echoed from the shuttered windows and locked doors of the tenements that lined the narrow lane. The groom stopped the carriage at the door of the de la Vega villa, and held out his hand to Justina and Meschianza. The two women were greeted at the door by a neighbor. She led them into the outer patio, where Graciela de la Vega sat surrounded by the women of the *aljama*. The room was crowded as servants tried to serve refreshments, but no one could eat. The fear and grief in the room were palpable as Justina and Meschianza approached Mateo's mother. She rose and embraced her son's betrothed. Her sobbing resumed as Justina took Graciela into her arms to comfort her.

The elderly cantor sat in a corner with a group of children. They stared at Meschianza, their eyes large with apprehension. Women were gathered in groups, rocking in unison as the cantor attempted to calm the children by teaching them an ancient prayer. His clear voice, strong and beautiful, often trembled and broke as he tried valiantly to hold the children's attention.

For these things I weep
Mine eyes swelleth with tears
Because He who comforts me . . . is far from me,

Even He that should refresh my soul,
My children are desolate,
Because the enemy hath prevailed,
Zion spreadeth forth her hands,
But there is none to comfort her.

Meschianza knew that the auto-da-fé was about to begin in the plaza before the church. Early that morning, her father had left with Jaime and Andres. They were accompanying Señor de la Vega to the plaza to make one last appeal for Mateo's life. She looked at the villa's entrance, and noticed that her duenna was not in the patio with her mother. Justina was talking in hushed tones to Graciela and did not notice Meschianza leave.

Meschianza hurried through the silent street, the emptiness crowding her grief for Mateo. She cared for him greatly, despite her love for Raul. Her acquiescence to her father and mother's wishes to marry Mateo was the result of an entire life of submission to her father's demands. The de la Vegas were close to Efraim and Justina, and it was a natural progression of this friendship to marry their two children. Now, with his imminent death, Meschianza could no longer wait for the return of her father and Señor Davila. She had to know what was happening in the plaza, despite the dangers. As she passed through the gates of the community, she was quickly swept into the crush of people scurrying through the streets toward the church.

As the crowd turned the corner of the building, Meschianza realized that they were at the edge of the plaza. She came up behind a great horde of citizens, all milling about with a sense of high expectancy. She began working her way through the crowd, pressing between them, unaware that Raul had caught sight of her.

Concerned that she would be crushed, he tried to move closer to Meschianza.

Raul spotted the tall wooden stakes at the center of the plaza before Meschianza did. He tried to pull her back before she saw them, but she had broken through the front of the crowd as he reached her. He watched with defeat as she stared at the brown stakes. He saw, as she did, the bundles of sticks beneath the large cedar logs piled at the base of each stake. Small platforms were built above the wood, only large enough for the feet of the penitent.

Meschianza was mesmerized by the horror before her. Her eyes filled with terror as she looked at Raul, though she did not recognize him. She turned back to the center of the plaza as the first sounds of the tumbrels were heard. The condemned were paraded into the plaza through a break in the crowd not far from where Meschianza and Raul were standing. For a moment, the six wagons appeared to move in slow motion as Meschianza looked at the people inside each tumbrel. They were tied to the sides of the small wagons, as many as ten in each conveyance. Some could not stand, and several were unconscious.

Meschianza stared with terror at the scene before her when Raul reached for her. In her grief, she was unaware of his hands on her shoulders. Raul spotted Mateo. As the wagon passed before them, Meschianza let out a small cry when she saw Mateo. She tried to run after the wagon, and as Raul restrained her, Mateo looked at them, their struggle catching his attention. He watched Meschianza, turning his head to see her as the wagon passed out of sight. He nodded at her feebly, and Meschianza cried out.

She tried to escape Raul's arms, but he held her. When he caught sight of the red patch on her right shoulder, he took off his cloak and threw it around her. With the crowd in a bloodthirsty frenzy, he was afraid of what they might do to her if they realized she was a Jew. Meschianza turned and looked up at Raul, her face desolate. Recognizing him, she clung to him.

"Raul, Raul. Thank God you are here. We must help him. Hurry, come with me. We must tell them he is innocent!"

"No, Meschianza. Come with me now."

Screaming Mateo's name, she broke away from him, but he followed her, pulling her back to the edge of the crowd. He held her as she struggled, and watched as Mateo was dragged with the others to the stakes. The crowd's approving roars drowned Meschianza's screams. He held her now, her face against him, her screams projecting loudly into his chest. She would stop to gasp for breath, and he would implore her to leave with him. She continued in her frenzy. He pressed her face against his shoulder as they tied Mateo to the stake.

She struggled and tore away from him in time to see the faggots thrown onto the piles of wood. The monks had painted the fronts of all the penitents' clothing with melted tar. As the flames burned their clothing, their screams could be heard above the roar of the spectators.

Meschianza, her voice hoarse and almost gone, opened her mouth for one final scream, but no sound came. As she watched the flames consume Mateo's body, she fainted. Lifting her, Raul pushed his way through the crowd and away from the plaza. He hurried to the seawall, her body light in his arms. Carefully, he made his way to the sand below. As he approached his horse, she struggled against him.

"Meschianza, I am going to put you down. Then I will help you onto my horse."

He stood her next to the horse and began to assist her onto the saddle.

"Raul, where are we going?"

"I am taking you home. Come. Put your foot here in the stirrup."

"No, we must go to the de la Vegas. My mother is there."

He lifted her onto the saddle and climbed on behind her. Smoke was beginning to drift over the beach toward the water. The smell of burning flesh nauseated Raul, and fearful that Meschianza would smell it, he wrapped her in his cloak.

When he reached the home of Mateo's parents, he called to the occupants. Efraim rushed out of the front door and took Meschianza in his arms. Raul dismounted and followed Efraim as he carried her into the villa. Meschianza had fainted again, so Efraim placed her on a couch. He stood as Justina took care of her, and turned to the young man. Efraim guided the trembling Raul into an adjoining room and waited as he composed himself. Raul began to speak.

"I have brought Meschianza from the plaza. I tried to get her to come away sooner, Señor, but she would not leave."

Raul took several deep breaths as Efraim waited, a great foreboding overtaking him. He listened with growing dread as Raul continued.

"Señor, Meschianza saw Mateo in the plaza."

"She witnessed the burning?"

"Yes, Señor."

Raul waited as Efraim fell into a chair. Exhaustion and despair plagued his face. He continued to speak to Raul.

"Her mother and I are grateful to you, Raul, for bringing our daughter to us. She was in grave danger there, but because of your bravery, she is safe here with us again."

"Yes, Señor. I must go now, and find my father, but, with your permission, I would like to come tomorrow and see Meschianza. She has suffered a great shock."

"Yes, yes, of course, Raul. Come tomorrow. I know she will welcome you."

Raul left the villa. He raced his horse to his father's warehouse. He entered to find his father in his office. Andres's head was on his desk, and at first Raul thought his father was sleeping. Without waking him, he sat in the chair across from Andres. The leather of the chair creaked, and Andres raised his head. His eyes were bloodshot as he gazed at his son.

"Where have you been, Raul? I have looked for you since early this morning."

"I was with Meschianza. I am sorry that you did not find me."

Andres looked at his son with affection, but Raul did not return his gaze.

"Mateo is dead."

"Yes, I know."

"Were you there?" Andres asked, surprised.

"Yes. I was there with Meschianza."

"She saw it?" Andres roared at his son.

"Yes. I—I tried to take her away from the plaza, but she would not come. She struggled, and I did not want to have attention drawn to her. I believe she is in danger."

"Why?"

"Because she is Mateo's betrothed. What if the Inquisitors believe she is also guilty? What if they believe she has tried to sway Jaime, as Mateo did?"

Raul continued, his voice urgent.

"We must help them leave Spain. It is not safe for them to

wait until August. If the Inquisitors suspect Meschianza, they will come for her."

"Yes, you are probably correct."

"There is no time to lose. My ship is ready, and I trust my crew. If the Inquisitors search for Meschianza, they will close the harbor for inspection of all ships. I will pick up the family at the tunnel, as we have arranged. No one will know."

"We cannot risk endangering Meschianza. We must go to Efraim now and tell him."

Andres left the room, his son hurrying after him.

22

✤

During the rest of the day, Meschianza was traumatized by what she had witnessed. She would see visions of Mateo, his body in flames. In its efforts to protect her, her mind would shut off, clouding her vision, leaving her imprisoned in an empty, white, and soundless place. She heard her mother's voice calling to her. Hours passed before she would wake up to her reality. Her mother forced wine between her lips. Because she had never tasted it before, the strong liquor her father favored jolted her from her withdrawal. Soon she was pushing the glass away as her mother bent over her.

"Meschianza, my darling, wake up. You have suffered a terrible shock."

She sat up and looked around. She was in her bedroom. Late afternoon light entered through the casement window, melting onto the oak-planked floor. A pale green haze filled the room, and dust motes sparkled to the floor. She shut her eyes and listened to her mother's entreaties.

"Meschianza, you must try not to grieve. You are making yourself ill."

Justina looked down at her hands clasped in her lap. She glanced out the window, an expression of grave concern on her face, and then returned her gaze to her daughter, who was now sitting up in the bed.

"I will send your maid to you. Ana will sit with you while I speak with your father. She will not leave you alone, so you sleep now, and when you awaken, I will be here with you, Meschianza."

Justina left the room, and Meschianza waited for Ana. Soon the door of her bedchamber opened, but Ana did not enter. Her grandfather slowly came into the room, his body bent forward by his old age. Amahl stood at the foot of Meschianza's bed. For a moment he did not speak while he gazed at his grand-daughter.

"Meschianza, your father told me what happened today. I am very sorry for Mateo. The sun is setting soon, and I would like you to come out to the bluff with me. We will pray for Mateo. Will you come, child?"

Meschianza left the bed and went to Amahl. He took her into his arms as she began to cry.

"It was so terrible, Grandfather. When I close my eyes, I see the fire."

"Yes, yes. You must come to the bluff with me now. We will talk to the angels."

He led her through the door, down the stairs to a table in the entry where Amahl kept his prayer rugs. He took two and put them under his arm. Carrying the rugs, he led Meschianza out of the castle and to the bluff. The sun was floating above the horizon as Amahl spread the two rugs on the ground before them.

"Meschianza, you sit here next to me, and I will sing the prayers for Mateo."

Meschianza helped her grandfather kneel on the rug next to hers, and seated herself alongside him. When she was a child, she had often joined her grandfather in his prayers, holding the *morisca*, his Moorish guitar, as he performed his *salat*. Today he had also brought the Koran that had once belonged to his father. Meschianza waited in respectful silence as Amahl turned the pages. He stopped, pleased to have found the passages he was seeking. He began to read, his voice trembling barely above a whisper.

As for the truth-concealers, their works are as a mirage in a spacious plain which the thirsty man supposes to be water, till when he comes to it, he finds nothing. There indeed he finds God, and he pays Him his account in full—and God is swift at accounting. Or their works are as a darkness upon a deep sea covered by a wave, above which is a wave, above which is a cloud— darknesses piled one above the other. When a truth-concealer holds out his hand, he can hardly see it. And to whomsoever God assigns no light, no light has he.

Amahl paused to look at his granddaughter, and silently acknowledged her tears. The sun was halfway behind the horizon, its rays shining golden on the calm sea before them, as Amahl continued praying for Mateo.

Upon the day when you see the faithful, men and women, their light running before them, and on their right hands. "Good news for you today! Gardens through which rivers flow, therein to dwell forever! This is indeed the mighty triumph." Upon the day when the hypocrites, men and women, shall say to those who had faith, "Wait for us, so that we may borrow your light!" It shall be said, "Return you back behind, and seek for a light!" And a wall shall be set up between them, having a door in the inward whereof is mercy, and against the outward whereof is chastisement. . . .

Upon that day faces shall be radiant, gazing upon their Lord, and upon that day faces shall be scowling, expecting a calamity to fall on them. . . .

As for those who have earned ugly deeds . . . abasement will cover them—and they will have no defender against God—as if their faces were covered with dark slices of night. Those are the inhabitants of the Fire, therein dwelling forever.

Meschianza moved next to Amahl, and he placed his arm around her shoulders, pulling her close.

The angels will intercede, the prophets will intercede, the faithful will intercede, and none will remain but the Most Merciful of the merciful. Then he will take a handful from the Fire and remove a people who never did any good whatsoever.

The old man and the young woman continued sitting on the ground as stars began to dance in the sky before them. For several moments they watched the celebration, until suddenly one of the stars fell like a bright signal in the heavens. Then Amahl began whispering to his grandchild.

"Soon you will leave Spain with your parents. You must survive, Meschianza. You must survive for all of us."

Meschianza threw her arms around her grandfather's neck.

"I don't want to leave you. I will miss you until we can return."

"When you come back, child, you will find me here on the bluff imploring God to protect you. I will pray for you every day. Promise me that you will do whatever is necessary to survive. Promise me you will tell your children about me, and this land. You must not forget the land."

"I will tell them. I will teach them everything you have taught me. I will sing the songs to them as they sleep."

"Good, good. They must know their heritage. It will make them proud, Meschianza. It will make them strong. When each of them knows who they are, then the stars will follow them, and when they return with you, the land will still be here. This madness cannot last. Allah will not allow it."

They were still sitting in the darkness, whispering to each other, when Ana found them.

23

✠

Raul was in the hold of his ship, a bill of lading in his hand, overseeing the loading of a consignment of furniture from his father's warehouse. As he checked off the last item, he heard heavy footsteps on the deck above. He had barely reached the top of the wooden ladder when he saw the sandaled foot and rough cloth of a monk descending above him. He moved quickly down the ladder to allow the monk to enter the hold. He was followed by six of the chief Inquisitor's liveried guards. They searched the hold for passengers as the indignant Raul followed them, asking what they were doing on his ship.

The monk, smug in his official duty, looked at Raul, carefully inspecting him.

"We are looking for a young woman whom we believe will attempt to leave Tarifa. She is a criminal, and she must be found. Have you any passengers on this ship?"

"Of course not. This is not a passenger ship. We have no quarters for paying guests."

"What is in these crates?"

"Furniture and household goods."

"Where are you taking them?"

"To Lisbon. We leave at high tide, which will come soon enough. Do you wish to go to Lisbon?"

The monk looked at Raul with disdain. He glanced at the soldiers, a slight smile on his face as he watched them pry open the crates and spill their contents onto the rough wooden floor. He calmly surveyed the goods, and then cast his gaze upon Raul. Turning, he spoke to the guards as he proceeded up the ladder.

"There is no one here. We will leave now."

The soldiers left the ship. Raul sat on the bottom rung of the ladder, his face covered with sweat. He waited to compose himself before he emerged from the hold, then called to the ship's captain.

"How is the tide? Are we ready to cast off?"

"Yes, Señor Davila. If we leave now, we will be able to clear the harbor."

"Cast off, then. We leave for Portugal now."

He entered the cabin and carefully stepped over the luggage that littered the floor. He had not said good-bye to his mother. Unlike his father and Meschianza's family, she was unaware that he had no intention of returning to Tarifa.

As the ship pulled anchor, Raul stood at the small circular window. The sea air was clean and crisp; he closed his eyes as it bathed his face. The ship rocked through the harbor, and Raul began to feel at peace for the first time since his return from the university.

It was already dark when the ship reached the coastline beneath the Cozar-Velasquez estate. The captain, according to Raul's instructions, ordered the anchor to be dropped from its mooring. The sound of the chain woke Raul. He put on his boots and hurried out the door. The longboats were prepared to be lowered, and Raul joined the seamen who were to row the heavy wooden boats to the shoreline. They climbed in, and as the boats were dropped into the water, a strong wind struck Raul in the face. He wrapped his cloak about himself, protecting his face from the sting of the spray that fountained into an arc of water as the vessel entered the cove at the base of the cliff.

Raul knew exactly where to direct the boat, and as he pointed for the sailors, he could see the opening of the tunnel. Light from a small lantern cast a tiny glow, providing a faint beacon for the rowers. The surf was choppy, the water churning its way into the mouth of the tunnel. One of the seamen threw out a rope, and Jaime emerged from the opening, handing the lantern to his father and catching the rope as it nearly passed him by. He pulled it in and tied it to one of the large boulders next to the tunnel. As the longboat came alongside, Raul reached out and took Jaime's proffered hand as he leaped to the boulder. The sailor followed him, another rope in his hand. He anchored the stern, securing the conveyance against the rocks. Three other longboats rocked in the surf, waiting their turn. Raul entered the tunnel to find Meschianza sitting inside. Ana was beside her holding a small candle, and the light glowed beneath Meschianza's stricken face. She looked at Raul with a blank expression. It appeared as if she did not recognize him, but Raul knew this was impossible. He approached her, but she looked away. He turned, searching for his father, and found him entering the mouth of the tunnel. Andres took his son aside and handed him a folded parchment.

"I am giving you this *suftaja*. It is the letter of credit that will help you to obtain Señor Cozar-Velasquez's gold when you arrive in Lisbon. If I give it to him, he will be arrested. The authorities will know that he has taken gold out of Spain. It would mean his certain death."

"Yes, Father. I will see to it."

"As soon as you obtain the gold from my associates, you must place it on your ship for safekeeping. Guard it well, and be careful, Raul."

Andres studied his son. He put his hand on the young man's cheek and then pulled him into his arms. Raul, surprised, put his arms around his father. He realized that Andres had not embraced him since he was a small boy.

He saw that there were tears in his father's eyes.

"Father—"

"My son, I charge you with this family's care and safety. I will wait for your return."

"Yes, Father. I will write to you and let you know where we are. I ask that you care for yourself. You must rest now."

"I am all right. I want to tell you that I know you love Meschianza. I give you my blessing, as I have given it to your sister. I pray for everyone's happiness now."

"I am grateful to you for saying this to me, Father. It will strengthen me in the days to come."

Raul placed the parchment into his pocket and turned to see Pisa carrying a bundle of clothing. She placed it at Meschianza's feet and then addressed her brother.

"She has not spoken for days since we have been preparing for the journey. I am so concerned, Raul. What will become of her?"

"What do you mean, she has not spoken?"

Pisa's sadness and exhaustion showed in her eyes as she answered her brother.

"She is silent, Raul, withdrawn. She has barely moved, remaining in her bed or sitting in a chair. We cannot get a response from her. She eats very little."

"She will be all right. It will take time, but Meschianza is resilient."

"No, Raul. I don't think she will be strong enough for what is to come."

Raul watched Meschianza, who, guided by her mother, was approaching the mouth of the tunnel. Justina looked at the choppy sea, and then at her husband, with fear and despair on her face. She had said her good-byes to her father and to the home where she had raised her children. Efraim had escorted her through the castle. Their linens and clothing were packed in large trunks brought to them by Andres from his warehouse. Justina and Efraim had never been to Portugal, and they had no idea what awaited them in Lisbon.

When Efraim told Justina about Andres and Raul's concern for Meschianza's safety, she immediately began to pack their belongings. Their concern was for their daughter's survival, which was more important than their own. Efraim had held Justina in his arms as she cried to him.

"I have always known that we would be cast from this paradise, Efraim."

"No, no. Justina, this is not the work of your dark angels. This is the doing of a different evil."

"All evil and ill-doing come from the same source, and as we leave our home, Efraim, we will carry our souls like a burden. Our grief will lead us, and I fear we will follow it to our deaths."

"Long ago, my darling, I promised to protect you from the destiny you feared. I have never broken that promise, and I never will. You must not be afraid."

Together, they had decided what to bring, and what to leave behind.

Carefully, they had inspected the books in the circular room, removing all that bore Gershom Soncino's printer's mark. During their marriage, they had amassed this collection, Andres bringing the books to them each time his merchant ships sailed to Italy.

The Soncino family, long descended from German rabbis, had settled in Italy in 1454. Their endeavors had expanded the printing of Jewish books throughout the Sephardic communities in Spain.

Justina and Efraim also chose books by two writers, Juan de Mena and Alfonso de Baena. De Baena, a converted Jew, had been a secretary to King John, Isabella's father. He had composed the first collection of courtly lyrics, called *Cancioneros*, in 1445. Efraim had given a copy to Justina on their wedding night, and it was important to him that Meschianza's children would have the beautiful books.

Early that morning, Justina had awakened to find Efraim gone from their bed. She arose and quickly dressed. The stone steps were still darkened by shadows as light played about the walls of the stairwell. Carefully, she felt her way down the steps and out through the front door, searching for her husband. She walked around the northern end of the building, the grass weighed down by the heavy mist, dampening her skirt. She continued walking through the meadow and into the olive groves, where she found Efraim standing beside one of the olive cisterns, the small wooden door open, a long-handled scoop in his hand.

She approached him, dragging her sodden skirt through the weeds that flowed endlessly between the rows of gnarled trees. Dawn was just breaking above the grove, and light dappled the silver leaves, casting more shadows on the tortured trunks of the ancient trees. She stood behind Efraim, watching him as he ladled several black, plump olives from the sea water. He turned to her, taking one of the olives from the ladle, and placed it in her mouth.

"The olives are ready, my love. I believe they are our best crop in years. Jaime will make a good profit."

Tears escaped Justina's closed eyes as the bitter, earthy taste of the olive filled her mouth. He studied her face lovingly, took another olive from the wooden ladle, and put it in his mouth.

"Come, we will check each cistern. We will taste our olives, Justina."

The two of them walked to the next cistern. This one, filled with rock salt, had produced a small, wrinkled black olive. Efraim brushed the salt particles from his fingers before he placed the olive in Justina's mouth. She smiled at him. He knew these tiny, pungent olives were her favorite. She took his hand and kissed it as he gathered her in his arms and comforted her.

"We will find another home, Justina. I promise you. And there will be olive groves."

Their arms around each other, they approached the cistern filled with spring water. Green olives, the size of grapes, bobbed and floated in the emerald liquid. Dressed in a lye solution for several weeks, they finished their curing in the sparkling water that was pumped up from the wells in the groves. Justina reached through the small wooden door and took a handful of the olives. Lifting them to her husband, water spilling from her hands onto her dress, she smiled as she offered them to Efraim.

"We will take these to Meschianza. She loves them so much."

Justina poured the olives into the pocket of her skirt, and with their arms around each other, they left the grove for the last time. The sun was as dull as pewter in the gray sky surrounding them. They walked through patches of fog along the path to the bluff. The silver sea below them was iridescent, casting reflections of cobalt-blue and silver-green on its calm surface. As they walked through the copse surrounding the ruins of the stables, the angels, in their grief, did not sing for Efraim and Justina.

They followed the path from the stables and entered the castle through the kitchen door. Placing the olives in a silver bowl, they ascended the stairs to awaken their daughter. They found her sitting in a chair by the window. Meschianza was staring blankly at the sky, her hands lying limply in her lap. Ana had combed her hair, braiding and piling it atop her head. She had woven tiny seed pearls into the wine-colored plaits, but Meschianza was indifferent to Ana's ministrations.

Efraim bent over his daughter, placing the silver bowl in her lap. He lifted her hands and held them as he talked to her.

"Meschianza, today we start a new life, and we leave all this grief behind us. Raul will bring the ship this evening, and we will begin a new adventure."

Meschianza looked at her father.

"Father, I know we must go, but it is so difficult. I am worried about grandfather."

"Jaime and Pisa are moving into the castle today. They will take good care of your grandfather. They will protect him. You must not worry about him."

As he led Justina from Meschianza's bedchamber, he spoke quietly to Ana, who was sorting through her mistress's clothing, which she had piled on the bed.

"Do not leave her today, Ana. Stay with her at all times."

"Yes, Señor. I will wait here until you come for us. I am almost finished packing. My own things are in that bag there by the door."

"Good. I will put it with the others. The day will pass quickly, and then we will go."

"Yes, Señor."

Ana returned to work, her eye on Meschianza, as Efraim and Justina left the room.

✢

24

❖

Efraim and Justina looked out at the dark, cresting waves. Behind them, Pisa was standing next to Meschianza, her arms around her friend. She was murmuring something in her ear, and as Efraim turned to hand their valises to Raul and his sailors, Justina took two small wooden boxes from her cloak and approached the two young women.

Opening the boxes for Meschianza and Pisa, she held them out as offerings.

"These are the pearls that my mother gave to me on my wedding day. See, Meschianza, I have had them divided into two necklaces. One of them is for you, and the other is for Pisa. My mother told me that I was to give the pearls only to my daughter, and that they must be handed down as a legacy from daughter to daughter. I have two daughters now, so I wanted to give the necklace to both of you. Promise me that you will never allow the pearls to leave the family, and that, someday, you will give the pearls to your daughters with these same instructions."

Shaken from her depression, Meschianza reached out and carefully lifted one of the necklaces. She placed it against her cheek and turned to Pisa.

"Here, let me put it around your neck, Meschianza."

Pisa placed the necklace on her friend and fastened the intricate silver clasp. The *platero* in the walled community had designed the clasps according to Justina's instructions. The Star of David was interwoven with olive leaves, and two tiny clasping hands, one holding the Star, the other embracing the opposite side, were finished with brushed silver. The Star was cleverly hidden within the tiny sparkling leaves.

"Meschianza, will you fasten my necklace for me?"

Pisa waited as Meschianza lifted the other necklace from its box and fastened it around her neck.

"See, now we are true sisters. When you return, Meschianza, I will be waiting here for you. We will have our daughters then, and we will stand together at their weddings. They will wear the pearls, and we will rejoice for them."

Meschianza, a look of wonder on her face, turned to her mother, her fingers on the pearls at her neck. Justina smiled her approval at the two young women, and then she embraced her daughter-in-law. Jaime walked up behind Meschianza. He turned her around and took her into his arms. She clung to him and would not let him go.

"I'll be waiting here for you with Pisa and our grandfather. We will take our children together and show them all the places we love. I will not take my children to hear the angels sing, Meschianza, until you come with me. They will wait for you, and when you come back, they will sing new songs for you. I promise you this."

Meschianza let him go as Pisa took her into her arms. Both women clung to each other. Jaime held his mother and father together.

"I will take care of the estate, Father. Everything will be here when you return. This madness cannot last."

"Yes, Jaime. I know you will care for our family here in Spain. I have the utmost confidence in you, and I am proud of you and Pisa."

Jaime turned to his mother.

"Mother, take care of Father and Meschianza. I will miss you. I will write to you often, and you will write to me and let me know that you are all safe."

Justina reached into the cloth bag she held in her hands. She took the heavy silver candelabra that had always graced the center of their Sabbath table and offered it to her son.

Jaime, startled, tried to return the treasure to his mother.

"You mustn't do this, Mother. This belongs to the family."

"No. Take it. It is for your children. It is so you will not forget us. Tell them, Jaime. Tell them about us, about our family. Tell them who we are."

Justina placed her hand on her son's cheek.

"You are my pride, Jaime, and your father's pride. Teach your children all that I have taught you."

"You will return to teach them, Mother."

"Promise me, my son."

"I promise you. I will not forget."

She held him again as Andres approached Efraim, his hand out to him. Efraim clasped his hand with both of his and looked at his friend.

"We must hurry, Efraim. The tide will not wait. Already it comes into the tunnel."

They turned to Meschianza and Amahl, who were in each other's arms. Andres went to them and gently took Meschianza by the shoulders. She would not let go of her grandfather. Andres looked back at Efraim, who came to his aid. Gently but firmly, they pulled them apart. Meschianza collapsed against her father as Raul rushed to lift her into his arms. He carried her to the edge of the boat and handed her to one of the seamen. He climbed into the boat, and the seaman lowered her into his arms. Ana waited as Efraim lifted Justina into the rocking boat, and then followed her.

They sat, the five of them, and looked back at Jaime. He was standing at the mouth of the tunnel, water sloshing above his ankles. Amahl, his face streaming with tears, stood beside him. He was oblivious to the water as he waved to his children.

The boat pulled away from the rocks, and Jaime fell to his knees, calling to his father. The wind picked up his voice and carried it high above the water. Andres pulled Jaime and Amahl away from the rising tide and into the tunnel.

Pisa was sitting on the ground, leaning against the stone wall. Jaime knelt before her, and she reached out and took him in her arms. His cries echoed off the tunnel's stone walls. Andres waited, his fatigue overwhelming, as Amahl stood inside the opening of the tunnel and watched the longboats disappear in the darkness.

"We must go back to the villa now. We cannot stay here. It is only a question of time before the soldiers arrive for Meschianza. They may already be on the way. Come, we will go and await word from Raul."

He helped them both to their feet, and with the small candle, he guided them back along the tunnel and up the stairs to the parlor, where a fire was still burning.

Andres sat in one of the chairs, leaned his head back, and closed his eyes. The pain in his chest was suddenly sharper, and his arm was numb. He moved his fingers, but they had no feeling in them. Pisa, seeing her father's face lose color, rushed to him.

"Father, are you all right?"

"I am only tired, Pisa. Do not worry about me."

"You will stay here with us tonight, Father. You must not ride into the village."

"Yes. I believe you are right."

Amahl approached with a glass of marc for Andres. As Andres reached out to take it, he clutched his chest. His face grimaced with pain, and as the agony rose to his neck and jaw, Andres lost consciousness. Pisa, terrified, knelt beside him and tried to rouse him. His face was the color of chalk, and he was breathing in short gasps. Suddenly, Andres stopped breathing. He slumped in the chair and nearly fell into Jaime's arms.

Pisa began pulling at her father's shirt. Jaime grabbed her hands and drew her away from the chair.

"Pisa. Pisa, listen to me. We must get him to the physician. I will wake the groom, and he will bring the wagon."

Jaime hurried out of the castle and soon returned. He brought blankets from closets upstairs and began to wrap them around Andres.

"Jaime, I think my father is dead."

"No, Pisa. He has only fainted."

He watched as Pisa laid her head in her father's lap.

"He is dead, Jaime. He is dead."

Amahl crossed the room to the young couple and stared at Andres's body. He raised his hands in despair, covered his eyes, and returned to the fire, where he sat in a chair.

"Pisa, help me get him to the wagon. We must hurry."

Amahl held the door open for Jaime and Pisa as they carried Andres to the wagon. He stood in the doorway as the young couple rode away with her father. Jaime drove the horses into Tarifa, arriving at the physician's door next to the Davila house. He banged on the door so loudly that Esperanza's maid opened the front door of the Davila house at the same moment the physician answered. He pulled the doctor to the wagon as the maid ran to rouse Esperanza. They carried Andres into the physician's house and placed him on a couch when Esperanza entered and ran to her husband.

"What is this? What have you done to him?"

She turned to Jaime as the physician began his examination of her husband. Jaime began to speak, but Pisa stepped forward and confronted her mother.

"It was Jaime who brought him here after he became ill."

Esperanza backed away from her daughter and went to the physician.

"Señora, your husband is dead. I am sorry."

Esperanza stared at the physician in disbelief. She walked to the couch and bent over Andres. Examining his face, she spoke to the doctor.

"Are you certain?"

"Yes, Señora."

She turned to Jaime and Pisa.

"You did this! Both of you. You killed your father!"

"No, Mother. We loved him. We would not harm him!"

"Señora Davila, he collapsed in our home. He was ill, so we brought him—"

"Be quiet. You are to blame for this—"

"Mother, don't say that."

Esperanza glared at her daughter, and then turned to the physician.

"I will send someone for his body."

Without looking at her husband again, she left the room and

returned to her villa. Pisa, stunned by her mother's outburst, went to her father and knelt beside him. She began praying, but soon her prayers turned to sobs. Jaime went to her, and taking her by the shoulders, lifted her to embrace her.

"Pisa, let me take you home now."

25

They waited for word from Pisa's mother, but it did not come for two days. Finally, a messenger arrived to tell them that the funeral for Pisa's father would take place the following morning. When they arrived at her mother's villa, they found Esperanza in a state of extreme agitation.

"Where is your brother?"

Pisa glanced at Jaime before she answered Esperanza. Raul had made them promise not to reveal to Esperanza that he was in Lisbon with Jaime's family.

"I don't know where Raul is."

Distrusting her daughter, Esperanza turned on Jaime with disdain.

"And you! Do you know where he is?"

"No, Señora. I have not seen him for many days."

"Nobody seems to know where my son is on the day of his father's funeral. I am certain he does not know his father is dead, or he would be here."

She left the room. Pisa and Jaime remained standing, but Maria approached them.

"I am so sorry about your father, Señora. I wish we knew where your brother is, but he has been gone for many days. There have been no messages to your mother, and his new ship is not in the harbor. She is very worried."

"I am certain my mother will hear from him soon, Maria."

They all sat down when Esperanza returned to the room, her face veiled.

"Come, we will leave for the church. It is time for your father's Mass. After the burial, we will return here for the reading of his will."

She left the villa and was already in the carriage when her daughter and son-in-law joined her. She would not look at Jaime as they rode to the church.

The solicitor for Pisa's father accompanied them to the villa after the funeral. Esperanza and Pisa sat in the parlor as he took out the papers containing Andres Davila's last will and testament. When Pisa tried to bring Jaime into the parlor, Esperanza objected.

"This involves our family only, Pisa. It is none of his business."

"But Mother, Jaime is my husband. He is a part of our family."

"Now that your father is dead, Pisa, I will say who is in this family, and who is not."

Esperanza sat in her chair, her body tense as she leaned toward the solicitor. Her husband had vast holdings in the shipping trade. His warehouses were built along the docks, and the upper floors hosted the offices of the many accountants he employed to keep records of his wealth. She waited impatiently for the solicitor to begin. As he straightened out the papers, he glanced at Pisa. He read Andres's will, and continued to look at the young woman as her shock slowly grew, for Andres Davila had left his entire estate, including the villa, to his daughter. When the attorney concluded his reading, he waited in the cold silence of the room.

Esperanza began to rise from her chair, but, suddenly weakened by her shock, fell back into it and turned to her daughter. As the realization came to her that she was penniless, her rage quickly changed to fear. She addressed the solicitor, her voice weak.

"There must be a mistake."

"No, Señora Davila, there is no mistake."

"Give me those papers."

He handed them to Esperanza and looked cautiously at Pisa. She was still sitting in her chair, staring at her surroundings.

"When did he make this will? It is a new one. This is not the will he always had. Before, he left everything to me, as is proper. I am his wife!"

"He made this will several days ago. He was quite specific as to his wishes. He wanted everything to go to his daughter."

"I do not believe you. He was ill, of course—he did not know what he was doing. He would not have left me penniless, Señor!"

The solicitor looked at Esperanza, but he did not reply. Finally, he addressed Pisa.

"Señora Cozar-Velasquez, if you will ask your husband to come to my office tomorrow, there are papers for him to sign."

Pisa, her face still pale, stood to address the solicitor.

"Señor Vargas, my husband will come to your office tomorrow morning."

"I will take my leave now. My condolences again for the loss of your father. He was a good man, and a friend to me. I will miss him."

Pisa escorted him from the room. Esperanza waited for Pisa to return, but when she did not, Esperanza went to the entrance of the villa to find that both Jaime and Pisa had left. In shock, she stood for a moment in the open doorway of the villa, then returned to the parlor and sat on a couch, her fears growing. She was still there when the cook called her to dinner.

⁜

26

⁜

Esperanza waited several days for word from her son. She knew he would share her outrage when he learned of his father's will. In growing desperation, she went to the docks and to the accounting offices of Andres's shipping company, but no one knew where Raul was. All she could discover was that he had set sail the previous week for Portugal.

When she returned to the villa, Pisa's carriage was waiting at the front door. Esperanza entered the villa, but she did not see her daughter. The maid directed her upstairs to Pisa's bedroom, and when Esperanza entered, Pisa was directing two workmen as they prepared to carry a trunk to the carriage.

"What are you doing here, Pisa?"

"I have come for the rest of my things, Mother. I will be taking them to my home."

Esperanza looked around the room at the disorder. The bed was dismantled, and chests of drawers were emptied of their clothing. Linens were folded into an open trunk, and Pisa was directing her maid to place the draperies from the windows onto the linens. She turned to the bed and picked up a dress, but Esperanza tried to take the dress from her.

"Stop this. I told you when you married the Jew that you would take nothing from my house."

She turned to the frightened maid, who stopped folding the blue curtains Pisa had handed her. As Esperanza tried to take the curtains, Pisa stopped her mother's hand.

"This is no longer your house."

"What are you saying? Of course this is my house!"

"No, Mother. It is my house now, and Jaime's."

"Get out! Get out of this house!"

Pisa approached her mother. Her determined expression frightened Esperanza, who stepped back and fell into a chair. Pisa stood over her, coolly surveying Esperanza.

"I have arranged through Father's solicitor to sell this villa. You will have to leave, Mother."

"You cannot sell it. Your father built this house for me before you were born. It is my house."

"No, Mother. Father left it to me. It is a part of his property, not yours. Your name was never on the papers."

"That is not true. He cannot give it to you."

Her voice was weakened by her shock.

"The house is now in my husband's name. You must leave. The new owners will be moving in as soon as the sale is completed."

"The new owners? What do you mean? Who are they?"

"Señor Contreras and his family."

"The accountant? Your father's accountant. He will be living here in my house?"

"He is no longer the accountant, Mother. My husband has chosen him as the new manager of Father's shipping company. He asked him to take the position yesterday."

"But what will Raul say? He has always planned to manage the business. It is what your father would have wanted."

"Raul does not own the business. Jaime and I do."

Slowly, the full realization of all that had happened since Andres's death occurred to Esperanza. She looked at Pisa and began to plead with her.

"Do not make me leave my home, Pisa. Where will I go? I have no money."

"Go to the church, Mother. Go to the priests. You have much in common with their murderous intentions."

"How can you say that to me? I am your mother!"

Pisa, with her hands on the armrests of her mother's chair, placed her face directly in front of Esperanza's.

"When were you ever a mother to me? Do you know that when I was a little girl, I believed you wanted to kill me? I was afraid of you."

"Pisa, you mustn't talk to me like this."

Esperanza began crying, but Pisa was relentless.

"I tried to please you. I would have done anything to make you happy, but nothing I did was good enough. I knew you hated me and Raul."

"That is not true. I loved—"

"You don't know the meaning of the word. From you I learned only terror. And Raul, what did you teach him, Mother?"

Before Esperanza could answer, Pisa continued and answered for her.

"Look at him. Look at my brother! He does not care about you. Have you had word from him? Of course you haven't. Has it ever occurred to you that he is gone for good, Mother?"

Esperanza tried to get up from the chair, but Pisa pushed her back into it.

"You are asking me to leave my home, Pisa. How can you do this? I have no place to go."

Pisa, moving away from the chair, ignored her mother's pleas. She went to the bed and picked up a small leather valise.

"Pisa, are you going?" Esperanza was standing by the bed, trying to grab Pisa's arm, but she dodged her mother's grasp and walked to the door.

"Tomorrow a carriage will arrive to take away the furniture I want to keep. The rest has been sold to Señor Contreras."

"Pisa, what are you doing? Please don't go yet. We must talk."

Pisa stopped at the door and looked at her mother.

"We have nothing to discuss. I will not see you again, Mother. Do not come to our home. Do not ever come to my husband's home. Do you understand, Mother?"

She walked through the door and down the stairs to the entrance of the villa. Esperanza stood at the top of the stairs shouting at Pisa.

"You cannot do this to me! I will speak to your brother. He will not let you do this. This is my house! My house, Pisa!"

Pisa opened the door to the villa and looked at her mother with contempt.

"Pisa, come back here, now! I order you to come back here!"

Pisa walked through the door and climbed into her carriage. She could still hear her mother's screams as the carriage went down the street. It passed the docks, and Pisa could feel the fresh ocean breeze on her face. Sighing with relief, she smiled as the driver flicked the reins over the horses and directed them toward home.

✤

EPILOGUE

From the memoir of
Meschianza de Lucena Cozar-Velasquez
August 26, 1497
Lisbon

Tomorrow we shall sail from Lisbon. Raul has not advised me of our destination, but I trust his decision, and I know that Ana and I will be safe with him. For many days he has gone to the docks to help the crew load the provisions for our journey. My parents' possessions are safely hidden in the hold of the ship. I am grateful for my mother's books and for all the things she chose to save for me, but it is the torn remnants of her dreams that I will cherish for my children. I will place the dreams in their hearts so that my mother's vision will not fade. Once we lived in a garden, but now we are cast out. Losing everything we had has brought to me a wisdom I never desired.

Raul has hired six soldiers to travel with us. He expects there will be dangers, but I am not afraid. My fears have been drowned in grief. The rage will be left here in Portugal. I will bury it in the hills, and in this Portuguese sky whose light mocks us with its brilliance.

When we arrive at our destination, we will appear as man and wife, without the benefit of marriage. This is my decision, for I cannot consent to a marriage in the Church that stole my brother from me and took my parents' lives. I have wondered, what is the greater sin? To live with Raul and bear his children without the blessings of my faith, or to marry him and maintain a façade for the benefit of our children?

I will not abandon my beliefs, and I will teach our children in secret. Last night, Ana and I burned all our clothes and destroyed the red badges we were forced to wear. My children must be born free of the stigma imposed by a culture that has stolen so much from us. My children will survive.

Last night, a cool breeze entered the room where Ana and I sleep, and brushed against my face. I know my grandfather is dead. I was awakened by the general's presence as he sat at the end of my bed bathed in a brilliant aura. He smiled at me, and I was not afraid. Then, reaching out to me with his hand, he caressed my cheek, and I was a child again, standing with him at the ruins of the old stables. He told me about the day the stables burned and how my grandmother died in the flames. He carried a book of poetry, printed in Arabic, the language he spoke when he was a child. As he read to me, he commanded the elements.

. . . *Wind, make the branches dance in remembrance of the day when you blew into the embrace of my beloved.*
Look at these trees, all of them joyful like a gathering of the blessed—

As I lay against my pillow, the vision of my grandfather slowly disappeared as I felt his spirit enter my heart. I will take him with me to our new life, and I will sing his prayers to my children. We will not be afraid, for I know now that we are all wayfarers, and that when our journeys end, we rise above our being. In the transcendence there are no mortal barriers; there is only love and the joy of reunion. It is the only promise kept.

My grandfather taught me this.

GLOSSARY

Al-Andalus—area of southern Spain named by the Moors.

Alhambra Decree—edict of expulsion declared by King Ferdinand and Queen Isabella of Spain, stating the terms whereby the Jews were expelled from Spain.

aljama—an assembly or community of Jews.

Andalusia—Spanish name for Al-Andalus.

anusim—Marranos looked on with scorn by the Jewish community.

baile—dance.

Cancioneros—the first collection of courtly lyrics compiled by Alfonso de Baena, a converted Jew, for King John II in 1445.

cante jondo—deep song of Spain; the wild, tremulous laments of love, sadness and loss, sometimes of religious passion, that arose spontaneously from the mixture of African-Moorish-Hebrew cultures of southern Spain.

chomets—leavened bread.

Cortes—Spanish parliament.

feria—market, or fair.

fiesta de pan cenceno—Festival of Unleavened Bread (Passover).

flamenco—Andalusian music, also called *cante jondo*.

halakhic—religious law, or that part of traditional Jewish oral law that deals with rules for living, both legal and ethical.

hostal—inn, hostelry, refuge.

kiddush ha-Shem—a principle by which, in times of persecution, every Jewish man, woman, or child was expected to accept death rather than abandon his or her religious faith.

maja—a person "all dressed up"; a sporty or flashy person.

Marranos—Spanish Jews converted to Christianity as a result of the anti-Jewish riots that broke out in Seville in 1391.

mayorazgo—custom of inheritance of Spain whereby the oldest son inherits.

morisca—a Moorish guitar, usually pear-shaped.

mudejar—a Moslem Moor living in Christian territory.

Morisco—a converted Moor.

Pesach (Passover)—a festival of the Jewish year celebrated in the spring for eight days, commemorating the Exodus from Egypt.

platero—silversmith.

reja—grille, grating of ironwork.

retalbo—altarpiece, carved work usually in back of the altar in a Catholic church.

saeta—arrow (of song) in the *cante flamenco.*

sajjada—"a place of much prostration," or prayer carpet used by members of the Moslem religion in the performance of the *salat.*

salat—a form of Islamic prayer.

shiva—the first seven days of mourning; the mourners may not sit on any chair or sofa of normal height. Usually, the mourner sits on a stool and does not bathe or shower, or wear footgear that contains leather.

shochet—ritual slaughterer, who slaughters clean animals properly so they are kosher.

suftaja—a letter of credit.

tayammum—in the Moslem religion, a simple form of ablution made with clean sand or a stone.

vihuela—a lute brought into Spain by the Arabs.

QUOTED LITERATURE

"Open the door to me,
Open it, face like a flower . . . "

> One of the earliest poems in the Spanish language, dating from the tenth century, originally written in Hebrew characters, and composed by Jewish poets. Comparable to the Mexican *corrido* of today.

". . . How could the traveler not be delighted
that love is the nearest house to the Lord?"

> The Persian poet Rashid Al-Din Maybudi, from the *Kashf al-asrar* (*The Unveiling of the Mysteries*), c. 1126

"The rose dies and leaves behind its sweet rose water . . . "

> From "Counsels to the King," composed by Sem Tob (or Santob), rabbi of Carrion de los Condes, Palencia. Sem Tob is ordinarily referred to as a gnomic or aphoristic poet, but he is also one of the first real lyric voices to cry out in Castilian.

"For these things I weep
Mine eyes swelleth with tears . . . "

> Lamentations

"As for the truth-concealers, their works are as a mirage in a spacious plain . . . "

> Koran (24:39–40)

"Upon the day when you see the faithful, men and women, their light running before them . . . "

Koran (57:12–13)

"Upon that day faces shall be radiant, gazing upon their Lord, and upon that day faces shall be . . . "

Koran (75:22–23)

"As for those who have earned ugly deeds . . . abasement will cover them . . . "

Koran (10:27)

"The angels will intercede, the prophets will intercede, the faithful will intercede, and none will remain . . . "

The Prophet

". . . Wind, make the branches dance in remembrance of the day when you blew into the embrace of my beloved."

The great Persian poet and sage, Rumi (d. 1274)